"You could kiss me..."

Wes cleared his throat again, taking a careful step away. "I cannot kiss you." Look at him, being all firm and decisive. Not a stumble of words.

"Why not?"

"Because." His steps away weren't careful anymore because the panic was building. Talking to Cara, working with her, might not make him have all those old feelings. But the thought of kissing her did.

He couldn't do it.

"You're heartbroken and in love with someone else? Although, really, you could still kiss me. I hear I'm good for that kind of—"

"No, Cara. No. I can't."

She smiled.

"You can't kiss me. So, technically speaking, I could kiss *you*..."

Dear Reader,

There are some books that come together fairly easily, perfectly on time, with everything happening just on schedule. And then there are books where everything seems to go wrong. Or if not wrong, hard. Hi, this is that book.

It's a book that started with a completely different hero. It's a book that was in a different line with a different word count for a while. It's a book that was canceled very briefly when the previous line was. Through the course of editing and line-changing, I've been tasked with adding ten thousand words, then twenty thousand words. Months apart. It's been a *challenge*.

But the thing is, no matter how many stumbles and roadblocks a book has set before it, it's still about two people navigating a tricky world to love. And finding a way for Cara and Wes to overcome their pasts and find each other was one I would go back to time and time again. An opportunity to go back to the Millertown Farmers' Market and the Pruitt sisters isn't *that* much of a challenge—I love this world. I love these characters.

And I hope you'll love them, too! (And if you've read *All I Have*, don't worry, Dell still appears shirtless even in a book that isn't his).

Happy reading!

Nicole Helm
www.NicoleHelm.wordpress.com

NICOLE HELM

All I Am

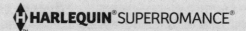

Recycling programs
for this product may
not exist in your area.

ISBN-13: 978-0-373-60945-1

All I Am

Copyright © 2016 by Nicole Helm

Printed in U.S.A.

Nicole Helm grew up with her nose in a book and the dream of one day becoming a writer. Luckily, after a few failed career choices, she gets to follow that dream—writing down-to-earth contemporary romance. From farmers to cowboys, Midwest to *the* West, Nicole writes stories about people finding themselves and finding love in the process. She lives in Missouri with her husband and two sons and dreams of someday owning a barn.

Books by Nicole Helm

HARLEQUIN SUPERROMANCE

A Farmers' Market Story

All I Have

Too Close to Resist
Too Friendly to Date
Falling for the New Guy

HARLEQUIN E

All I Have

Other titles by this author available in ebook format.

To everyone on Twitter who responded to
"wounded-veteran-dog-treat-making-bearded-
virgin hero" with a resounding YES.
Hopefully Wes lives up to the billing.

CHAPTER ONE

IF CARA EVER got engaged, the first thing she'd want to do would be get naked, not sell broccoli.

Her older sister did not seem to have that inclination.

Mia handed a bag of broccoli to an elderly gentleman, then once again admired her new ring.

Cara wrinkled her nose. "Ugh. Are you going to stare at that thing all day?"

"Hey, an hour ago you were jumping up and down and screeching." Mia wiggled her fingers some more, the grin never leaving her face.

"Sorry. An hour is the limit for engagement-ring gazing while us poor single women sit around and feel our ovaries dry up and fall off."

"Ovaries don't fall off," Anna chimed in, adding more curlicues to the sign she was painting for the new Pruitt Morning Sun Farms booth to hang over the table of produce offerings.

Cara scowled at her younger sister. "It's an expression." Being in the middle of these two was always a constant battle of reason versus... whatever she was.

"A dumb expression."

"You're a dumb expression," Cara grumbled. She didn't know why too-early Saturday morning after too-early Saturday morning, season after season, she agreed to help Mia with her farmer's market stand. Cara didn't get anything out of it except crap from her sisters and dirt on her clothes.

Now that Mia and Dell, her new fiancé, had merged their farms, which specialized in locally grown fruits and vegetables, Mia definitely had enough help. Cara was an unneeded volunteer.

Still, for the fourth year in a row, here Cara was. Tired and cranky—though, okay, maybe she enjoyed her sisters' company a little bit. It had been fun to help Mia while she came into her own, taking over the parts of the family farm suitable for produce and then building a business.

Cara had been a part of that. Sure, she wasn't a farmer, didn't want to be a farmer, but it was nice to be involved. To feel useful.

Then the Naked Farmer had come along and swept Mia away, and now they sold their goods as one entity.

"Can you three not talk about ovaries while I'm around?" Dell asked in between customers.

"Hey, you're outnumbered," Cara returned. "Get used to it. Where's Charlie, anyway?"

"Flat tire. Told him not to come. I think four people can handle one farm stand." Dell turned to a new customer, who laughed at the word *Taken* painted across Dell's chest. It was cold enough they let him keep his shirt on, but it remained unbuttoned.

"The Naked Farmer's taken? What a pity." The middle-aged woman sighed. A lot of his female customers would be disappointed he was off the market. Shirtlessness and flirtation had been his go-to business practice last season.

"Very much so." Dell winked back at Mia, who grinned, all lovesick and gross.

Man, Mia had all the luck. Not that Cara wanted to be *engaged*, but having a hot guy drooling over her would be nice. Usually she knew how to get that kind of attention, but lately the New Benton dating scene had been…bleh.

"Okay. Sign's finished." Anna packed up her supplies. "I've gotta go meet Jen and Zack at the library. See you at Moonrise at one?"

"I'll be there."

Anna said her goodbyes, and Mia studied the new sign.

"Oh, my God."

"What?" Cara asked in unison with Dell. She hated to admit it, but she missed the days when it was just her and Mia. This was less work, but Mia was a little preoccupied with her *fiancé*.

"PMS."

"No more lady-parts talk, please."

"No, look." Mia pointed at the sign. "Pruitt Morning Sun Farms is PMS."

Cara couldn't swallow down a laugh at the way Anna had made the *P*, *M* and *S* of Pruitt Morning Sun big, blue and swirly.

"This is a disaster."

"Aw, it's all right, sugar. We'll call it Morning Sun."

Mia glared at Dell. "I am not giving up Pruitt. Maybe we can put it at the end." Mia sighed, staring down at the sign again. "Morning Sun Pruitt Farms sounds terrible." Mia was obviously distraught. Cara opened her mouth to say something reassuring, but Dell wrapped his arm around his fiancée and gave her a squeeze.

"Have Anna make the *F* really big. No one will think anything of PMSF—or don't have the first letters stand out." He kissed the top of her head, and she leaned into him.

Cara didn't understand the clutching feeling that made her look away. It couldn't be jealousy, because the thought of a relationship made her break out in hives. It couldn't be dislike, because she liked Dell just fine, and she especially liked Dell for Mia.

But something about it—them—made her chest tight.

"You guys going to make out? If so, I'm going to get myself some breakfast."

"Yeah." Dell dug in his pocket and pulled some crumpled money out. "Here, take this five. My treat if you make yourself scarce."

She snatched the bill from Dell's hand. "Hard to sell broccoli with your tongues down each other's throats." Apparently neither of them cared. Figured.

Cara skirted the front table. They'd done pretty well with the broccoli, and even the greens were going okay, but the chard was all but untouched and—what did she care? What sold and what they grew was *so* not her problem. Cara certainly wasn't going to start worrying about it now.

She walked toward King's Bread and glanced around the market. The first day of the season was usually pretty slow, but because of the warmish temperatures and increased advertising this year, there were groups of people squeezing through the rows of tables.

She meandered through one row of booths. This wasn't her scene—she'd much prefer shopping at the new outlet mall in Millertown, even if it *was* out of her price range—but there was something fun about tables of honey, jam, vegetables and all manner of homemade, home-picked, home-baked things.

The sound of a dog's incessant barking stopped her in her tracks. A little white blob of fur stood at her feet, unleashed.

"Shoo, little doggy." Apparently, the shooing motion she made was asking for a fight. The dog lunged at her. As she tried to sidestep it, she tripped and fell square on her butt.

The ball of fur latched on to her pant leg, growling and biting. Cara wasn't sure whether to laugh or to kick the little booger, but then its jaw clamped down on her ankle. It had bitten her! Probably not hard enough to break the skin, but some strange dog seriously had bitten her.

"Ow, you little jerk!" She didn't want to actually kick this tiny thing, but she did nudge it a little with her foot.

"Pipsqueak! Pipsqueak! Come here, right now!" The dog finally responded to its screeching owner and hopped into the middle-aged woman's arms. "Oh, are you all right, sweetheart?"

Cara scowled at the woman. "Yeah, I'm peachy after getting bit by your little terror."

The woman wrinkled her nose and clutched the demon dog to her chest. "I was talking to Pipsqueak. I don't know what you did to provoke him."

"Provoke him?" Cara started to push herself up, but someone stepped in.

"They're supposed to be leashed," a low, gravelly voice said.

Cara looked up at the man who'd intruded in

the conversation, but all she saw were shadows against the bright sun.

"Pipsqueak has never hurt anyone in his life. He doesn't need to be leashed. It's inhumane. This woman must have done something to set him off."

"It needs to be leashed. It's the law," the deep voice rumbled.

"Why, I never! If this is the way you treat a customer—"

Cara looked up from her spot on the ground and was surprised to find she recognized the man's face. Wes Stone. She didn't know him personally, only knew *of* him. He'd been at least five years older than her in school, but New Benton had made a big deal out of it when he went off to Afghanistan.

The town had made an even bigger deal when he came back severely injured after working with some bomb sniffing dogs or something. He didn't look all that injured to her, but between all the hair and the flannel it was hard to tell anything. Except he was tall. And kinda scary as he scowled.

It took Cara a few seconds to realize that he'd held out his hand to her to help her up—that he was angry with this woman on her behalf.

Cara gathered her wits enough to take his hand and let him pull her up. She tried to remember what kind of injuries he'd suffered. Was it okay for him to be doing this? Of course, that'd been something like three or four years ago. Maybe he was all healed.

"You've lost a customer, mister." The woman stalked off, kissing the evil little minion in her arms as she went.

"Your loss," Wes muttered. His gaze didn't meet Cara's, and his question was mumbled. "You okay?"

She nodded. His dark blond hair was wavy and longish, his beard a touch on the side of grizzled rather than the trendily well-kept look. He was like a modern mountain man, one with piercing blue eyes.

Wait. Had she really just thought *piercing* in relation to eyes?

"It bite you?"

She looked down at her ankle and lifted the cuff of her jeans to inspect the skin. "Tried. Didn't break the skin. I'll live."

"People." He stalked back to his booth.

She looked up at the sign. Organic Dog Treats. No description of what that meant. No colors. No pictures. Just black letters on a white background. His table was just as sparse. Buckets of treats with black-and-white labels saying what they were and how much they cost.

An interesting contrast to most of the other

vendors with their colors and logos and fancy spreads.

"Well, thanks for yelling at her for me, Wes," she offered, giving his table a little pat. "Sorry if I cost you a customer."

He stopped and looked at her quizzically. "Do I know you?"

"Um, no. I mean, you might know *of* me. I grew up in New Benton, too."

He grunted. Well. All the rumors about him seemed to be true. Came back from the army, bought a hermit cabin in the woods, shut everyone out.

Except his legion of dogs. Sitting at his feet. Unfazed by Pipsqueak's earlier "attack." They swished their tails, three of the four napping. The other one panted happily in the sun.

Weird. Weird guy. Weird booth. Weird day.

She gave Wes a little wave and headed for the King's Bread booth. When she glanced back at him, he was staring after her.

Very weird day.

WES WATCHED CARA GO. She was a colorful blur of light. Pink cowboy boots, vivid green shirt, bright pink lipstick.

He hadn't recognized her at first, but eventually he'd placed the face with the name. New Benton had been home for so much of his life; it was impossible not to know the other whole-life residents, no matter how much he shut himself away.

Cara had been a few years younger than him, if he remembered right. Her family had a dairy farm, and someone she was related to had a stand here. Sister, maybe?

He shook his head. Trying to keep all the small-town bloodlines straight was asking for a headache, and he'd already given himself enough of one loading and unloading the truck and setting up the booth this morning.

It irritated him that after four years of recovery, his body still didn't do what he wanted it to when he wanted it to. Maybe if it was just one thing. The hand or the hip. But it had to be both.

Lucky to be alive, remember?

He'd never been very good at counting his blessings or his luck. Receiving dream-crushing injuries, no matter how non-life-threatening, hadn't exactly given him an optimistic outlook.

Cara glanced back at him, and he looked down at his money box, not quite sure why. So he was looking at her. So what?

He reorganized his buckets, focusing on this—on order and control. Like life in the army had, running his own business allowed him a sense of order and rules. Dealing with people, outside of selling them dog treats, had never been his strong suit, but even when he didn't love his job, he knew what he needed to do. How he needed to do it.

A customer came up, smiling and chatty about how cute his dogs were. Direct sales were his least favorite part, but they were a necessity, so he forced himself to smile and talk about his product.

Since he cared about his product, that wasn't hard to do. Just like the army. Tell people what they want to hear, and they bought his stuff and walked away. Long as no one knew who he was and asked how he was doing.

It was his first year at a market so close to home. He'd thought Millertown was far enough away, but Cara's appearance reminded him it wasn't. Maybe he should've stuck to the markets around downtown St. Louis, but that would be silly. If he really wanted to go without people, he could focus on the internet side of sales.

But there was something about coming to markets he liked. It wasn't human interaction, because he hated that, but it was a reminder he existed. He'd survived.

He shook his head in a lame attempt to clear it. Why dwell on this? He should be paying attention to what kinds of treats were selling, so he could make more of those next week. Compare today's popular sellers to his best sellers elsewhere. Be a businessman. Because, aside from his animals, that was all he had.

All he wanted.

The day went on without more New Bentonian run-ins. And no more yappy dogs with incompetent owners attacking people, either. Wes considered that a success.

At noon he started packing up, trying to ignore the pins-and-needles feeling in his arm. His hip ached. His head pounded, although he couldn't blame that one on his injuries. He'd had migraines since he could remember. A lovely result of the anxiety he'd pretty much been born with.

Phantom nudged his knee, his black-and-brown snout demanding attention. Wes sighed. Phantom was his trained therapy dog, retired military, too, with his own minor injuries. A limp and a missing chunk of tail.

He was the one being in the world who knew what Wes needed. Wes took the break Phantom demanded and scratched the German shepherd's nose and ears. Then, because his dogs were the jealous sort, he repeated the process with the other three.

When he went back to packing up, some of the headache had eased, and the tingling in his arm had stopped. It was the whole point of a therapy dog. He'd had Phantom for three years, and the fact the dog could do so much with so little still amazed him every time.

"All right, guys. In you go."

At the command and the open truck door, his crew hopped into the back. Phantom took his usual spot in the passenger seat. Wes climbed into the driver's seat and began to pull out of his space when he noticed a bright splotch of green standing behind a truck, waving.

The truck with a sticker that read Pruitt Morning Sun Farms on the side pulled away, and Cara stood there watching it go. She looked sad.

Not his problem, but seemingly of its own accord, his foot tapped the brake as he drove next to her. "You okay?" What the hell was wrong with him? He was not the check-on-near-strangers type.

Okay, checking on strangers was exactly the type of thing he'd do. Which was why he isolated himself on a few wooded acres. So he didn't feel the need to help and come up short. So he didn't feel the need to engage, then get laughed at.

She shaded her eyes with her hands, looking up at him. "Yeah, I'm okay. I don't think I've got rabies now or anything."

He almost, *almost*, smiled at that, which was kind of weird.

She hopped up onto the step of his truck, sticking her face way too close to his for comfort. He backed away and felt like a coward. But a safe coward.

Some stranger sticking her head into the window of his truck was not normal. Most people were too uncomfortable around him to do that.

"Hey, can I ask you a question?" she asked.

He braced himself for the inevitable. *How do you manage? You are so brave!* His good hand clenched into a fist.

"What are their names?"

"Huh?"

"Their names?" She pointed at Phantom, then to the back where the other three dogs had arranged themselves.

"You want to know my dogs' names?"

"Yeah, what did you think I was going to ask you?"

He wasn't going to answer that. Partially because it made him look like a tool, and partially because he didn't want to talk about it. "Phantom, Flash, Toby and Sweetness—which was the name she came with, not the one I gave her, by the way."

Cara chuckled at that. "You must be good with training them. I've been thinking about getting a dog since Mia moved out. Where do you get yours?"

"Wherever. Strays mostly. Except Phantom."

"Where'd you get Phantom?"

He tapped a finger to his watch. "Sorry, busy day. Gotta get going."

Her eyebrows scrunched together, but he looked away, focusing on the road in front of him.

Out of the corner of his eye he saw her hop back down onto the ground. With a little wave, she stepped away from his truck. He tapped the accelerator.

But he couldn't stop himself from glancing in the rearview mirror, and he wasn't sure what that meant.

Best not to let it mean anything, but he had a feeling a pretty woman in a bright green shirt was going to be on his mind a lot more than he wanted her to be.

CHAPTER TWO

CARA STARED OPENMOUTHED at Mia, trying to formulate some response beyond *are you crazy*. "Are you crazy?"

"It's not crazy! It's an amazing idea and opportunity."

"No." That was a gut reaction. In reality, Cara should be jumping up and down saying *yes, yes, yes,* but everything about this made her stomach sink.

She wasn't a professional baker. Making pies for one of Mia's clients' restaurants was way, way, way beyond her skill level, or at least her experience level.

"Cara. You make amazing pies, and Sam wants to add more desserts to his menu." Mia stood on the porch of their parents' house, hands at her hips, a determined look on her face. "It's a match made in heaven. You always make filling with local ingredients in your fruit pies, and that's exactly what he's looking for."

If it was a match made in heaven, why did she

feel nauseated? "He doesn't want to hire some chick with no experience."

"You have experience."

"Not restaurant experience. I have baked pies for fun or the random family member's wedding or event and occasionally for my sister's farmers' market stand. Not the same."

"Just talk to Sam. He's experimenting. Nothing is permanent or guaranteed. Think of it as a trial. He doesn't have to hire you, but him considering you is not as crazy as you're making it out to be."

Trying to impress him to get the job seemed even worse than just trying to get the job, because she'd have to deal with everyone's disappointment if she screwed it up. No, thank you. She'd learned a long time ago not to take risks like that. "Look, thanks for thinking of me and all, but I love my job at the salon." *Love* was maybe a bit of an exaggeration, but she liked it well enough.

She didn't need her sister's pity, and she didn't need to be fixed. When it came to dreams like going to culinary school or opening her own business, Cara choked. Botched her application, failed accounting at community college.

She was not cut out for "more."

"Sam's only entertaining the possibility because you supply, like, half his food." Cara did her best to pretend this whole thing didn't matter.

"It's not like that."

Ugh. Why did Mia have to be so stubborn? So determined to help her find a passion. Cara was happy the way she was. She didn't have to bring her work home with her, had set hours and got to have fun. She was in her mid-twenties. She was *supposed* to be having fun, not finding a fulfilling career or a husband like everyone around her seemed to be.

Since that thought caused the same pinching feeling as watching Dell swoop in to comfort Mia at the market Saturday had, she pushed it away. "Making pies is a hobby."

"It's your religion, Cara Pruitt. Saying any different would be like spitting on Grandma's grave." Mia wagged a finger at her.

Her stomach rolled. Mia had a point there. A mean point, but true nonetheless. If Grandma were alive to hear Cara call pie making a hobby, she'd get smacked on the butt with a wooden spoon.

She rubbed a finger over the tiny bluebird behind her ear. The tattoo was her own little safety net, like Grandma perched right there, ready to say something encouraging.

Sadly, Grandma's voice had been gone for six years now, and some of the initial reassurances the bluebird brought had faded. Sad and scared were two of Cara's least favorite feelings, and she avoided them at all costs. Which meant avoiding taking risks like this.

"Just stop big-sistering me, okay? I can take care of my own life."

"I'm not trying to take care of your life. I'm offering you an opportunity. Do not say no to help. I already have one of those in my life."

Mia glanced to the bottom of the hill where Dell was talking to some guy who wanted to buy vegetables or something. This whole melding of farms, added to Mia now living with Dell on Wainwright property, meant she almost never saw her sister alone.

"I was in your life first," Cara muttered, feeling petulant. Because petulant sounded better than lonely.

"Cara."

"Look, whatever. I'll go meet with Sam if that's what you want, but I don't think I'm right for the job."

Mia crossed her arms over her chest and mustered her best big-sister glare, which was pretty pathetic. "Give me one reason why not."

"Other than not being qualified?"

"Yes, other than that."

"That's freaking enough!"

Mia's glare morphed into something worse. Pity. Hurt. Geez, it was ridiculous. She was the one used to helping Mia out. Getting her to ditch the outdated hairdo and clunky glasses, supporting her at the market while Mia worked on overcoming her social awkwardness.

Now Mia had done all that and was getting married, and Cara had been officially relegated to one-and-only Pruitt screwup status. Mia was the favorite, Anna a close second, and Cara was the daughter who hadn't gone to college aside from a few failed classes, had slept around, had a tattoo.

Mom probably prayed for Cara's eternal soul morning, noon and night.

This day was blowing hard. "Whatever. I'll go. Can we stop talking about it?"

"I'm only trying to help. Don't you want to—"

She walked away. If she had to hear someone in her family say "do something more" one more time, she might be inclined to throw a punch. Unlike Anna, Mia wouldn't fight back. She'd look hurt and make Cara feel like a jerk.

Because that's what you are.

Ugh. Ugh. Ugh. She stomped down the hill, leaving Mia behind on the porch. Where was she even going? She couldn't leave; she'd already promised Mom she'd eat dinner with the family.

She'd have to pass Dell and the guy he was talking to in order to get to her quiet spot by the creek, but so be it. If they were talking business or farming, Dell wouldn't give her a second glance. He and Mia had that insanity in common.

She tried to cut behind them, but a bark distracted her. She glanced at the truck parked next to Mia's vegetable barn. She recognized that truck and the four dogs in the back.

Wes. In all his flannelly, bearded glory. What the heck was he doing here? Well, it wouldn't be hard to find out. "Wes?"

He turned, eyes wide. "Cara."

"Wait, you know my name?" She didn't recall giving it to him, and he definitely hadn't asked.

"You two know each other?"

Cara gave Dell a brief glance before continuing her examination of Wes's face. She wondered what he'd look like with a haircut and a shave. She had a sneaking suspicion he might be kind of hot. Luckily, Mountain Man was not her type. "Wes helped me out Saturday when that stupid hair ball attacked me."

"Oh. Huh. Well, Wes, unless you have any more questions, you can email us the quantities, and we can bring it to the market when they're ready."

"Yeah, sure."

Dell gave her a quizzical look, but she ignored him. "You bring your menagerie everywhere?" she asked Wes.

"Pretty much." He had his hands shoved deep into the pockets of his jeans. He didn't look at her. His eyes were locked on his dogs.

"Well, I guess I'll leave you two to chat." Dell gave her another *what the hell*? look.

She shrugged. She wasn't sure what the hell, either. But Dell left them alone, walking back up the hill to Mia.

"You make dog treats. What are you doing buying stuff here?"

"Sweet potatoes," he said, as if that explained everything.

"Sweet potatoes?"

"Organic sweet potatoes. And peas. And carrots. Ingredients. For the dog treats."

"Dogs like peas and carrots?"

"In my treats they do."

"Huh." She cocked her head and studied him at point-blank range. Rumor had it he was not very nice. Considering the way he'd treated Pipsqueak's owner on Saturday, she'd figured that rumor was true.

But she wasn't intimidated. His stiff stance, hard jaw and grizzly appearance just made her wonder what had made him that way. Well, besides war. She inwardly rolled her eyes at herself. War was probably enough.

But how exactly did a guy go from soldier to organic dog treat maker? It probably wasn't any of her business, but curiosity was a hard thing for her to ignore, even if she knew her questions would be really, really, really not welcome.

"I should get going." He headed toward his truck. Cara followed, and the German shepherd—Phantom, if she remembered right—put his paws on the side of the truck bed and panted at her.

"Aw. Aren't you cute?" Cara held out her hand, letting the dog sniff her before patting his head. He gingerly licked her fingers, much to her delight. "He likes me."

"He likes everybody," Wes said gruffly.

"Aw, cute little baby." She trailed her palm over his head, then scratched the soft fur behind his ears. "Aren't you the sweetest?"

He gave her a tentative lick on the chin. When she looked at Wes, he was staring at her. Intently.

WATCHING PHANTOM LICK Cara was weird. Like thinking-about-being-the-one-doing-the-licking weird.

So not normal.

Which seemed about right. He hadn't been normal possibly ever. His brief foray into romantic relationships in high school had ended in disaster. So he steered clear of women who made him feel anything. At least then he didn't have to be a laughingstock.

And, in all honesty, aside from his market days, he steered clear of all people. Not just women. Everyone.

Needing to get out of here and fast, Wes opened

the back of the truck to get the dogs into the cab. "Move it, guys."

Phantom, Flash and Toby obeyed and hopped off the bed, then into the truck cab. Sweetness, the little jerk, jumped on Cara's legs, pawing and yipping happily until Cara slid into a sitting position on the ground. Then Sweetness curled up right on her lap.

Toby and Flash jumped out of the truck and sniffed around Cara suspiciously. Only Phantom continued to obey the order, though he looked on from the passenger side window. If dogs had complex human emotions, Wes was pretty sure Phantom's would be wistful. Or longing. Or something.

Yeah, his head definitely wasn't screwed on right. "Get off her, you morons. In the truck."

"Aw, they're sweet. Our dog died a few years ago, and Dad hasn't had the heart to replace her. I miss her."

He liked the way she smiled at the dogs, the way she let Sweetness on her lap without hesitation even though the dog was getting dusty paw prints all over her skintight jeans. And she was right—the dogs did like her. Of course, they weren't exactly picky.

"All right, kiddos, do as your daddy says."

"Um, no. I am not their daddy. They are dogs. I am a man."

Cara grinned up at him. "Thanks for the animal kingdom lesson. I figured a guy who took his dogs everywhere with him would think of himself as a daddy."

"No."

This time Cara laughed, a low, sultry sound that made him think about making her laugh more often.

A joke in itself. He didn't know how to make anyone laugh, let alone a pretty woman. Just looking at her legs folded across each other made his hip ache.

She stood up, and Sweetness whined after her. "Aw, she loves me."

"In you go." Wes gave her collar a gentle tug until Sweetness jumped into the back with the others.

He turned to face Cara. "She likes women better than men. Except for me. Usually." Looking down at her bright red mouth and blue-green eyes, he felt a stirring in his gut that had not been there in a very long time.

Attraction. Interest. And, weirdly, it didn't come followed by panic.

Didn't matter. Not allowed. So he turned and climbed up into his truck, Sweetness yipping in his ear, trying to get close to the open window and Cara.

Cara hopped up on the stair. Again. "You're

trying to convince me I need a puppy, aren't you, little girl?" She leaned in his window. Again. Second time in a week this strange woman was poking into his personal space.

She reached for the dog, letting Sweetness lick her hand. Which put her breasts about two inches from his face. Uhh.

When she pulled back, she seemed to realize how weird that had been.

She chuckled. "Sorry about that."

"It's…fine," he managed to croak. Which seemed like the polite thing to say at first, but now it seemed…weighted.

Cara grinned, making a considering sound in her throat.

"Well, see you around." *And get the hell off my truck.* Which he managed not to say only by grinding his teeth together.

"See you Saturday," she said, finally hopping off the stair.

"Huh?"

"The market. I help Mia out every week."

"Right." God, he was an idiot.

She waved, and he pulled away from the Pruitt farm. The drive to his cabin was long, winding and slow. Away from New Benton, away from farmland, toward the river and the woods and his refuge.

It was a decent-size cabin in the middle of a

forest. Definitely an escape from well-meaning people and their parade of casseroles and intrusive questions when he'd first gotten back on his feet. Then the cabin had become his life, his sanctuary. And, okay, maybe it still was. Maybe it always would be.

He'd never be normal, and he'd never be a veterinarian. Those were irrefutable facts.

He got out of the truck and let the dogs out to yip and prance around with Franco and Monster, the two dogs who hadn't been trained well enough yet to go everywhere with him. The land around the cabin was his animals' domain. Six dogs, three cats and one sheep with a limp.

He hadn't been able to do the vet thing, what with the nerve damage in his arm and hand, making performing surgery, exams and just getting through vet school requirements impossible, but that hadn't meant he'd lost his love of down-and-out animals.

He let the dogs run around outside, Monster and Franco attached to their runner, then trudged into his cabin. It had everything he needed. A big kitchen for the dog treat making, a room expressly for packaging, an office for the business side of things.

Though the office looked more like the aftermath of a frenzied police search. He headed to his computer. It was nearly six. The video call with Mom was his least favorite part of the week. Hearing about how great Palm Springs was. How amazing her new family was, how successful her little chain of all-natural grocery stores was. She thought she was proving she'd gotten her life together, that she was a mother he could be proud of now.

She couldn't accept he'd always been proud of her, and the money she had now didn't magically change, well, anything.

Phantom rested his snout on Wes's knee, having not stayed outside with the rest of the—as Cara had put it—menagerie.

That almost made him want to smile.

The pinging sounded. Deep breath. Accept the video call. On the computer Mom had bought as a gift, in the cabin she'd bought as a homecoming present, surrounded by the debris of a business Mom helped fund.

He'd gone to Afghanistan because they couldn't afford any of the colleges with decent vet programs. Community college had been an option, but the GI bill had seemed a better one at the time. Better than piles of debt that had seemed insurmountable to a kid who'd grown up in poverty.

Then a bomb had exploded and ended any vet dreams or the possibility of staying in the structure and comfort of knowing how to act in the army. And no amount of *things* Mom offered him or forced on him was going to change that.

"Baby!" Mom's smile filled the screen, and he worked on matching it.

"Hey, Mom."

Her smile dimmed. "You're doing okay?"

It was the closest she ever got to mentioning his injuries. Four years later and she was still more uncomfortable discussing them than he was, which was really saying something.

"Sure. Found a new vegetable supplier a little closer to home."

Her smile returned to full wattage. Talk about business. That she could do. That *they* could do, and did do, for twenty minutes before she started talking about her husband, her stepkids.

She paused, biting her lip, a sure sign of nerves. The same way she'd bitten her lip when he'd been a kid, and they hadn't been able to afford anything. Not new shoes. Not school lunches. Not the colleges he wanted, even with government assistance.

"Maybe you could come visit." It was the first time she'd suggested it in a long while. Maybe ever. He got invited to go on vacations with the new family, but he always declined. Usually because he wasn't up to skiing or being shoved onto a cruise ship.

He'd never been invited to the actual house.

"There are a lot of steps and things to maneuver, but we can make it more—"

"I don't know when I'd be able to get away, Mom. High market season for the next few months, you know."

"Oh, right." She bit her lip, and he refused, absolutely refused, to read anything into her expression.

He wasn't handicapped, which made him a lot luckier than many of his fellow soldiers. If she wanted to treat him like he was, he'd keep far, far away.

"I miss you, baby."

"Yeah. Miss you, too. Gotta go, though. Talk next week."

She forced a smile and a sad little wave as she said bye, and he clicked off the connection.

Phantom's nose pushed into his chest, and Wes gave in to the urge to rest his head on top of the dog's.

CHAPTER THREE

CARA SHIVERED UNDER her bulky sweatshirt, breath huffing out in clouds as she yawned. "It's so freaking cold." It always took a few weeks to get into the more bearable mornings, and while she *could* stay home, what with the abundant help Pruitt Morning Sun now had, she was not about to get pushed out of being a part of it.

Why she felt that way was something she didn't want to analyze.

Mia smiled. Dell rolled his eyes. Charlie, Dell's brother, sipped his coffee. "Yes. It is. Why are all four of us here?" Charlie asked.

Cara looked away. Sorry, Charlie, but she wasn't about to let the Wainwright brothers push her out. Maybe she wasn't part of the farm, but she'd been a part of Mia's booth from the beginning. That wasn't going to change.

She hoped. She had to leave in about half an hour for the stupid interview Mia had set her up with. For making pies. At a real-life restaurant.

The cold dug deeper, and that little voice inside her head that was always right about things whispered, *you're going to screw it up.*

"You come of your own accord," Dell said to his brother. "Feel free not to. Less bitching I have to listen to."

Charlie sighed heavily, but he didn't say anything else. He sat on the truck bed, sipping his fancy coffee.

Cara stared at her knees, trying to focus on the cold and will the ominous feelings away. So what if she did mess up the interview? It was a dumb part-time job. One she'd have to quit her salon job over, and then she'd have to find another part-time job that would give her Fridays, Saturdays and Sundays off.

This was ridiculous. How had she let Mia talk her into this? How could Mia conveniently forget that if there was pressure involved, Cara was going to fold? And fold hard. If she dreamed it, she could *not* do it.

A little bolt of fur shot in front of her, followed by a few yips, then paws on her shins. Sweetness panted up at her expectantly, tail wagging on overdrive.

"Geez, when did you become the anti-dog whisperer?" Dell asked. "Are dogs going to attack you every market day?"

Cara bent down to pet Wes's littlest dog, a shaggy piece of fur that gave no hint at breed.

"She's not attacking me. Hi, Sweetness. And you are, aren't you? A bundle of sweetness."

A shadow stepped over the sun, and it didn't take a fortune-teller to know that when she looked up at the looming figure, she'd come face-to-face with beard and eyes. "Sorry about her. Apparently she's got a thing for you."

And what does her owner have for me? In another situation, like at the bar with her friends as an audience, she probably would have said it. "I don't mind." She gave Sweetness a scratch before standing up and moving away from the table where Mia and Dell were dealing with customers. "She escaped you to find me. I'm flattered."

"You must smell like bacon," Wes replied, following her and Sweetness to a cluster of trees outside the main row of tables.

"Or I'm irresistible."

He made a strange kind of grunting sound. "Come on, dog." His voice was low and grumbly as he patted his thigh to grab Sweetness's attention.

It certainly caught Cara's attention. It was a very nice, powerful-looking, denim-clad thigh. *Get a grip.* He might be hot, and that might usually be all it took for her to flirt with a guy, but she didn't think she should get involved with someone rumored to be a hermit after being injured in the military.

She wasn't the nurturing, empathetic, *there-there* type. She was the suck-it-up-and-let's-have-fun type. James had made it abundantly clear when he'd broken up with her that he was leaving because she wasn't at all comforting or helpful when he'd been dealing with his friend's suicide.

And he'd been right. So, Mr. Wes Stone and his gruff bluster and fluster was way off-limits.

Cara gave Sweetness a little nudge. "Go on with your grumpy daddy." But Sweetness whined, pushing against Cara's legs as Wes scowled at her.

"You can borrow her," he said in that gravelly voice.

"Borrow her?"

"Yeah. You said you were thinking about getting a dog. I have a couple of them I loan out. People wanting to see if their dog's compatible with other animals, seeing if they can work a dog into their schedule, you know, before committing. It *is* a commitment."

"Tell me again why you don't call yourself their daddy."

He narrowed his eyes, but there was humor in the look. "Not a daddy. Owner. Master."

It was probably her imagination that when he said *master* it sounded kind of dirty. And hot.

Nope. For once in her life she was going to make the right decision when it came to a guy and just not go there. "So, I could really borrow her? For how long?"

"I usually do a week. Lets people see how all aspects of their schedule would be affected and if they'll get used to any hiccups. It's not perfect, but it helps."

Sweetness yipped. "I don't have any dog supplies or—"

"I have a loaner kit. Food, treats, leash, you know."

"You really do this a lot?"

"I don't usually offer strange women my dogs for fun, no." He shoved his hands into his pockets. "I have to get back to my booth. You interested or what? You can take her after the market. I might have a kit in my truck."

"Yeah." Be nice to have a little company in her empty apartment, even if it didn't speak. "Um, I have this interview thing in a bit. Could I pick her up from you this afternoon?"

"From me?"

"We can meet at a centralized, public location if you're afraid I might peel off your skin and eat it."

"Skin…peeling?"

She wouldn't have pegged him as a guy with a great sense of humor, but there was a flash of one there. Maybe he wasn't all gloom and doom? "I promise to keep it to a minimum."

He snorted. "All right." Then he fidgeted. "Um." He pulled a wallet out of his pocket, then a little business card out of the wallet. All black and white. Organic Dog Treats. Wes Stone. Website and phone number. "Call me when you're ready to come, and I'll give you directions."

Do not make a dirty joke. Do not make a dirty joke. "Yeah, okay." And then because she couldn't work it out, asked, "You seriously do this just because?"

"I seriously do."

"You're not trying to hit on me or something?" Because she couldn't remember a time a guy had been nice just to be nice. To her, anyway. Her reputation in New Benton didn't exactly lend itself to a lot of nice from the male population.

He frowned. "If I was trying to h-hit on you, I would not do it by lending you an annoying little yap dog with a terrible name."

"Really? You don't know much about women, do you?"

She could have sworn that underneath the grizzly beard he was blushing.

It wouldn't be the first time she'd made a guy blush.

"Well, anyway, I should be done by twelve-thirty." She waved the card. "I'll give you a call. I could definitely use a furry friend after this dumb interview." All the good feelings Sweetness had produced faltered in the face of pre-interview nerves. So, she worked up her widest grin. "And I do mean the dog, though if that falls through, you'd be a good backup."

"Ha. Ha." Definitely blushing. He turned and stalked back to his booth, and this time Sweetness listened and followed him.

Cara looked down at his card. Okay, maybe flirting with him was inevitable, but she would keep in mind he was probably in a fragile mental state and she had no business being a part of that.

At least she would *try* to keep that in mind.

WES THREW THE rope bone as hard as he could with his left hand. It veered into a cluster of trees, and he cursed. The pins and needles in his right arm were doing their dance, and he wanted to cut his own arm off to end the annoyance.

His left hand and arm had gotten more usable with practice, but it had yet to give him the controlled response his dominant hand had before.

He was going to have to go to the doctor again, and that made him want to pound his fists in fury. When would this be over?

The headache throbbed behind his left eye. His arm bothering him caused stress, and that caused a migraine. A fun circle he didn't know how to escape, even after four years of being stateside.

When he heard the car in the distance, he knew

it would be Cara, since he'd given her directions about forty-five minutes ago. He rarely let people come out here, but she'd sounded odd on the phone and his arm was bothering him, so driving out to her didn't sound appealing.

Now the woman he had no business fantasizing about was going to be at his house. To pick up Sweetness for a loan week. Not to enact any fantasies. Lame fantasies, at that, considering how little experience he had in that particular arena.

His frustration simmered, his headache drummed. He'd get Sweetness loaded up with Cara, then he'd do some work. The methodical process of making dog treats, even when his arm sucked, was soothing. Possible. Not frustrating.

He'd learned in the army that having a precise way of doing things eased his anxiety and stress. Which helped him deal with people and life.

Cara stepped out of an old beige Toyota Camry. She wore black pants and high heels and a silky-looking green top under a black sweater.

Had he really offered a loaner dog to someone he'd met twice?

Yes, because she's hot, and you're very, very dumb.

Well, and Sweetness liked her. Which wasn't all that unusual. Sweetness preferred women, though she'd gotten used to him after a family had left her with him because she hadn't taken to their new baby.

"Hey," Cara greeted him, picking across the yard on her high heels, getting stuck once or twice in the thawing, moist mud of his yard.

"Hey."

Sweetness leaped off the porch, yapping the whole way to Cara. Before he could get half the stop command out of his mouth, Sweetness's front paws were muddying up Cara's pants.

He crossed to where Cara had knelt, right in the mud. "I'm sorry. She's usually better at obeying." He refused to see that as some kind of omen.

"It's okay." She held up her arms, showing off some patches of white dust and yellowish crusty stuff across the elbows and forearms of her black sweater. "I'm already a bit dirty."

"I thought you had an interview?"

"Pie-baking interview."

"That's a thing?"

"Well, it was supposed to be a thing. Turned into a fiery ball of super fail instead." She buried her nose in Sweetness's fur. Phantom approached and rested his head on Cara's shoulder.

Aw, crap.

Cara sniffled, but her head remained buried in Sweetness's fur even as one arm curled around Phantom's neck.

He had half a mind to tell her he was having his

own meltdown, and he didn't need hers to add to it, but this moment seemed so incongruous. He'd only spoken to her twice, but it had been obvious Cara was generally fun and happy, and the few times he'd heard her name bandied about town, those were the words used to describe her. Now she was crying all over his dogs. Hell if he knew what to do about it.

She cleared her throat, slowly released the two dogs and wiped her face with her sleeves before she turned to him. "Sorry about that," she mumbled. "Bad day."

"He's a therapy dog."

She swiped at her nose, watery bluish green eyes meeting his. "Huh?"

He shifted uncomfortably. "I just mean, don't feel bad for crying. Phantom is a therapy dog. That's why he came over. Trained to offer comfort. Sometimes it makes you cry."

She cocked her head, that kind of concentrated study he hated almost as much as the avoided glances. The avoided glances were *I don't want to deal with whatever is wrong with you.* The cocked-head study was *it doesn't* look *like something is wrong with you. Are you mental?*

"So, you need comfort?" she asked.

He swallowed down the "none of your damn business" and turned on a heel instead. "Let me get Sweetness's stuff."

Inside the kitchen, he hefted the plastic bin of food and treats and other dog paraphernalia. When he turned to walk back outside, Cara was stepping over the threshold.

Of his house. Someone else was in his house. A human being.

Phantom had followed her, resting his head against her thigh when she stopped. Traitor. Sweetness danced at her feet once she saw the plastic bin. The dog knew what was coming.

He wished he had some inkling, because he didn't know what to do about Cara being in his house, even if it was only a few steps into the kitchen.

"This is a great place," she said, looking around with avid interest. He looked, too. He liked it, of course, but he wasn't sure what was that great about it.

"Is this where you make your stuff?" She pointed to his equipment and setup tables. Yes, he tended to spend more time in his kitchen making dog treats than food for himself. That was probably not normal. His hand went numb, which, while welcome over the pins and needles, was not convenient when he was holding something. His headache picked up again, and he struggled to use his good hip to balance the small bin.

Small. Light. Shouldn't be a struggle.

"You okay?"

"Yeah." He gripped tighter with his good hand, but the bin was sliding, and his hip wasn't moving quite the way it needed to in order to balance the container. So it upended and fell.

He bent down to retrieve the scattered crap, doing his best not to shove her hands out of the way when she tried to help.

"Sure you're okay?"

"I've got it under control."

"Right. Yeah." She stopped helping and pushed into a standing position. He didn't look up; he knew too well the kind of expression he would see. Curiosity or discomfort or both.

She didn't make a big deal about it, but once he'd refilled the bin with Sweetness's things, she bent over and picked it up before he could.

He tried to come up with words to get her to leave immediately, but when he stood, she was already walking farther into his house.

Carrying the plastic bin as if it were nothing.

Dark feelings twisted in his stomach. Bitterness. Jealousy. Anger. Fear. Worst of all, fear that he'd never be okay.

She needed to go.

Cara let out a low whistle, angling her head into his office. "What *happened* in there?"

The rest of the house was, well, a mess. His organizational skills were lacking at best. His tidying skills were also problematic, except in the kitchen. If he had a process, a structure, an outcome, like he did with making the dog food or he'd had in the army, he could be very clean and meticulous. But a space all to himself to keep things put away? He struggled.

Cara didn't pause, didn't hesitate. She stepped right into the fray. As if she'd been invited. As if she were welcome.

He scowled and shoved his hands into his pockets to stop the urge to yank her away from his stuff. "Do you always barge into homes and places of business uninvited like this?"

She chuckled, and he thought she didn't look quite so beat down, like she had earlier. She was smiling and laughing, and this was the Cara he expected from town gossip and what little he knew about her. A smile. A joke.

"All those manners and things never really stuck with me, sorry."

He grunted. It wasn't so much about manners as… What? Normalcy. "I'm looking for an assistant to help with filing and organizing and stuff. I haven't had any luck yet." Why was he telling her that? What did he care if she thought he was a slob?

"Yeah? Why not?"

"People are annoying."

Again, she laughed. She dropped the bin of dog supplies onto a cluttered chair. She walked through his office, touching his desk of teetering piles as though this was normal.

Usually he dropped the loaner dogs off at the person's house, and this was precisely why. Probably also why he hadn't hired any of the three people he'd worked up to interviewing.

He didn't like sharing. He didn't like someone trying to look underneath everything. But Cara already was.

For the first time since his return to civilian life, he didn't know how to stop it.

CHAPTER FOUR

WHAT ARE YOU DOING? Cara hardly noticed her brain asking that question. It asked her that about ten times a day. On a good day.

This wasn't really a good day.

So, perhaps that answered her question. She was poking through Wes's things, Wes's life, because it sure beat dissecting her own.

She'd gone into the interview expecting to talk. Sam had asked her to bake an impromptu pie. Somehow she'd added too much salt to the piecrust. The edges had come out burnt. She'd self-destructed.

Typical Cara.

Even when she expected failure, there was always some sliver of hope she could turn things around this time. Not flunk the test or freeze in an interview. Find some way to make someone proud.

Mia would not be proud that she'd screwed up, even less proud that she'd given Sam the impression she didn't care. That it was all a joke. But what else were you supposed to do when every time you tried to do something "more," it blew up in your face?

Maybe Wes had the right idea. Hermit cabin in the woods. Surround yourself with animals who couldn't express their hope or disappointment in your abilities. No one could intimidate her with their expectation.

Wes didn't intimidate her, and she was good at organizing someone else's business. The idea took root easily enough. "Do you think I'm annoying?"

"You're pawing through my stuff, so you're not exactly not annoying."

She laughed at his gruff honesty. "But too annoying to be your assistant?"

His eyes widened, and she couldn't hide a smile. Surprising people always gave her a thrill. "I have references," she added. "I'm the receptionist at a salon in Millertown. I organize the appointments, answer emails, phone, all that." She looked around his mess of an office. "I could have this worked out in a couple weeks, tops."

"I'm only looking for someone to work part-time."

So, in theory, she could ask Sam for a second chance. She could possibly redeem herself in his, and in Mia's, eyes. She could take the reins of this little disaster of her own making and turn it around.

Though her instincts recoiled at the idea, she was starting to outgrow the stage of life where she could be funny, careless Cara. Pretty soon she'd be irresponsible, deadbeat Cara.

Her whole stomach roiled at the idea of asking for a second chance, the even bigger pressure. But she looked around Wes's cluttered, isolated house. The guy needed some help, and it was as if this opportunity was being dropped in her lap.

Could she really ignore it? "I actually might only need part-time if I can work something out."

"I don't think that'd be a good idea."

"Why not?"

"I'm not a people person. I don't like to talk or be friends. I get angry easily, and I'm rarely nice."

"You have no idea how much I like not nice." When he gave her a quizzical glare, she shrugged. "Seriously. Niceness carries with it a certain level of..." She couldn't believe she was about to be so honest with the guy, but if she couldn't be honest with the dog-whispering super hermit, who could she be honest with?

"Expectation. I prefer it when people are mean. No pressure to live up to anything. I'd take a good screaming fit over disappointment." Okay, she could probably stop talking any minute. "Anyway, believe it or not, you don't scare me in the slightest." Maybe a slight exaggeration. Something about the guy made her...she couldn't quite put her finger on it. Restless, maybe, but surely that was just her life and not Wes.

"I…" His eyes moved around the room as if taking in the enormity of the mess, then his gaze returned to her. She didn't think she imagined the perusal, though it was quick.

"On second thought, maybe it'd be a great idea."

"Really?" She wasn't sure if his sudden turn-about was normal or not, but she did thrive on spontaneity.

"Yeah, but I want the references before we agree on anything. And no negotiating wages or hours. I pick those."

"No problem."

"And there are rules." He crossed his arms over his chest, scowling. Somehow the dude with the long beard and unkempt hair was cute when he got all gruff.

"Rules? Like what? I'm not always super great at following rules." She never *meant* to break them, exactly; it just always turned out that way.

"I…I'm not sure what they are yet, but you'll have to follow them."

"Aye, aye, captain."

"I'm not a captain."

"Would you prefer *sir*?" She didn't mean to make that *sir* come out all sultry and suggestive. The words had a mind of their own. A dirty mind, at that.

"I j-just… Call me Wes. My name is Wes, a-and that's what you should call me."

Cara cocked her head. He was a strange guy. One minute he was standoffish, but the minute she did anything remotely flirtatious he got stuttery. Nervous. The two things didn't jibe. She found herself a little too curious as to why.

Maybe this wasn't such a good idea if she was going to be tempted to flirt with him. There was one line she'd yet to cross in the dating department, and that was the boss/employee line.

Of course, her bosses had always been women before, making it rather easy.

"It makes business sense to hire someone better with people than I am. If you actually think you can tackle this and follow my rules, maybe it could work. Maybe. I could fire you any time I wanted. *If* I hire you."

"Okay, well, do you have a pen and paper? I can write my references down for you. You can call everyone and get back to me with your *rules*, and we'll go from there." She looked around the stacks of paper, mail and God knew what else. "Or maybe you have a phone or laptop I could type it into, so you don't lose it."

He grumbled, then flipped open a laptop on his desk.

Cara cleared the chair off and settled herself in. Which, she knew very well, meant he would have to reach over her to type in his password. She told herself she didn't do it on purpose.

He grunted, then reached for the keyboard. On the back of his right hand there were a few small scars. Obviously something was wrong with his arm or he wouldn't have dropped Sweetness's bin, but she hadn't noticed the white marks before.

"It's a scar."

Busted. "I know."

"Rule number one. Don't stare at my scars. Rule number two, don't ask about them."

Well, poop. Now she was *really* curious. "Not a problem. Your scars. Your business." Maybe she could look it up. Surely the local paper had done a story on him when he came back.

He pulled up an empty document, and she typed in her references, reminding herself multiple times not to stare at his scars. Not to wonder about this strange man with his strange energy.

This so wasn't going to be easy, and challenges weren't her strong suit, but it wasn't as if failing here would be a big deal. All in all, what did she have to lose?

Not a whole lot.

EVERYTHING ABOUT HIRING Cara screamed *bad idea.* Bad, tempting idea.

No, the bad idea would be keeping her in that space of his life that would allow this little crush or whatever it was…to linger. Grow. *Want.*

Sure, if she worked with him she'd be around more than if he just ran into her at the market all season, but hiring her made her off-limits. Wes was very good at following the limits he set for himself. Following rules. *That* was where he thrived.

As much as he could thrive with a faulty body.

Besides, he'd never had any trouble repelling a woman before. Occasionally, they thought the blushing and stuttering was cute. At first. That never lasted past the whole kissing meltdown part.

So, it was better to have her around. Remind himself what happened around women. Not kid himself into thinking he'd grown out of his hang-ups.

She typed fast, one point in her favor. Long fingers whirring over the keyboard, her nails a flash of purple.

"There we go."

She pushed her hair behind her ear, a little glimpse of blue catching his attention. A tattoo behind her ear. A bird? It was hard to tell with strands of her light brown hair covering parts of it.

He wasn't sure why he was trying to tell. It

was colorful like the rest of her. What more did he need to know? But it was like a beacon. He couldn't look away—

"It's a bluebird."

"Huh?"

She turned in the chair to meet his gaze. "My tattoo you're staring at. It's a bluebird."

"Oh, um." Could he be any more of an idiot? Stuttering and um-ing all over the place.

She grinned. "For what it's worth, *I* don't have any rules. So, you can look at it. You can even ask about it if you want."

"I was trying to figure out what it was. You've told me now. A bluebird. Okay."

"All right. Anything else you want to ask me?"

"Anything else?"

"You know, what I consider my biggest weakness, what's one word that best describes me, my hobbies. How I feel about interoffice dating."

She smiled at him. A flirty smile. While he could recognize when someone was flirting with him, it always put him on edge and he never knew how to respond.

That kind of jokey flirting might be innocent, but in his experience, it was the kind used to ridicule him if he ever responded positively.

So he crossed his arms over his chest, standing at attention minus the salute. "No."

"Right. Well. Suit yourself." She gave a little

wave and turned to go. It was only because he saw the loaner dog kit that he even remembered why she'd come in the first place.

"Cara?"

"Yeah?"

"Aren't you forgetting something?"

She furrowed her brow, patting her pockets.

"Sweetness."

"Oh, right." She slapped a palm to her forehead comically. "She's what I came for. Not to hound you into giving me a job."

She seemed almost embarrassed. Of course, she didn't stutter, and she didn't stop smiling. "Guess I got distracted," she said easily, sauntering over to pick up the loaner kit.

Yeah, she might get embarrassed, *maybe*, but she certainly wasn't a basket case like him and the every-other-day reminder would do him a world of good.

CARA DUG THROUGH the loaner kit on her passenger side floorboard, pulling out a leash and attaching it to Sweetness's collar.

"Home, sweet home, Sweet," she said to the white ball of fur as she maneuvered them out of the car. "Well, temporary home." She walked the dog along the patch of grass next to her apartment building until Sweetness did her business.

Even with the dog in tow, loneliness washed

over her. She hated living alone. It gave her too much time to think, live in her own head, come up short.

Boo.

But Mia had moved out and none of her friends could up and move in. Cara's only other choice was moving home with Mom and Dad, and with Anna headed off to college in the fall, Cara would rather be alone for years.

"Come on, girl." She climbed the stairs to her front door and balanced the bin against it as she worked to get the key into the finicky, ancient lock. It made her think about Wes dropping the bin earlier.

He didn't limp or look as though he had injuries that continued to be painful, but he had scars and had dropped something light. So, he *was* injured, and it was probably permanent.

And she was the jerk crying over a failed pie interview. Ugh.

Once inside, she knelt down and unclipped Sweetness's leash. "You're probably hungry and thirsty, aren't you, girl?" She gathered the bin and went to the kitchen to fill up the dog bowls.

Man, Wes had thought of everything. She didn't know how anyone could be that organized in some things and so disorganized in others.

She flipped the tap on and began filling the first bowl with water. Above the sink she had all

Grandma's pie tins displayed. Some days it was a comfort to have pieces of Grandma right there in plain sight.

On not-so-great days, it reminded her of the hole in her life since Grandma passed away.

She ran her finger over the edge of the starburst pie tin. Regret and failure lumped together in her stomach. "Sorry I suck so bad, Grandma."

She cringed. She didn't need a ghost to knock her over the head to know Grandma would not approve of Cara being so down on herself.

Whereas her sisters and parents beat around the bush of her failures, pretending she could overcome it, Grandma had refused to see it. Had given Cara a lot of crap anytime she dared pity herself.

Something about that reminded Cara of Wes.

"I have a bad feeling about your daddy," she told the dog curled up on her couch. "He's going to cause me trouble." Which was something she normally thrived on, but something about Wes...

The gruffness, the scars, the blushing and stuttering. The way he hadn't pitied her or made the crying worse when she'd first arrived. Just explained Phantom was a therapy dog.

For him. The last thing she needed was to get wrapped up in a guy who needed therapy. She was barely holding on herself.

She put the now-full bowls on the tile by the

door, then settled on the couch. Sweetness sniffed the bowls, then hopped up next to her.

She felt broody. About everything. And, well, brooding was not her norm. Usually she went out to drink or laugh away any brooding, but today she was tired. Tired because she'd gotten up so dang early for the market, tired because she'd imploded at her interview and tired because everyone seemed to be a couple. Mia, her friends.

She hadn't been on more than two dates with the same guy since Kevin. Oh, that one still burned a little bit. She had no qualms about casual relationships or even casual sex, but she had some serious qualms about being the girl a guy used to get back at his girlfriend.

Now fiancée.

Grr.

Sweetness crawled into her lap, and Cara scratched behind her ears. "Are you going to be my therapy dog, girl?" Sweetness licked her chin, and she couldn't deny the fact that she might need it.

CHAPTER FIVE

"Knock, knock!"

Wes tensed. Okay, he'd already been tense. He'd carried that tension around all morning, knowing Cara was going to show up today and invade.

He'd tended to the animals, worked out, showered and eaten breakfast, knowing that she would be all up in his space not just today, but three days a week, every week, for as long as she wanted or as long as he could stand it.

Her references had been mostly glowing. Cara was good at customer service. She was organized and dependable as long as she wasn't tasked with too stressful of a project.

Those were the things he needed, and he didn't have stressful projects because he refused to let stress into his business. The fact she interacted so well with his dogs helped. *That, and you'd like to see her naked.*

He snorted at his own inner monologue. *Not gonna happen, buddy.*

So, two weeks and a few phone calls after

she'd offered herself up for the job, here she was. His assistant.

Without a response from him, Cara appeared in his office with Sweetness on a leash. A sparkly purple leash. Definitely not the one he'd packed in the loaner kit.

Then he saw the scarf.

"What the hell is that?" he demanded, pointing at the offensive swath of fabric.

Cara blinked and looked down at Sweetness. The scarf bandana thing around Sweetness's neck was also purple, with pink-and-green flowers on it.

"Isn't it cute?"

"No. It's ridiculous. She's a dog."

"She loves it. Don't you, girl?" Cara crouched, scratching Sweetness behind the ears. And, yeah, Sweetness seemed to like that, but he wasn't sold on the scarf thing.

She popped back up to her feet. She was wearing skintight jeans and some oversize purple sweater thing that had big holes in it, but she seemed to be wearing a black tank top under it, so the holes didn't show off anything important.

Seriously, there had been moments in time when he thought this would be a good idea?

"Thanks for letting me keep her the extra week."

"Look, you can keep her. Period."

Cara wrinkled her nose. "You can't just give me your dog."

"You bought her sparkly shit, and she clearly likes you better than me. Besides, you can bring her with you on workdays. It's not like I don't have enough dogs to keep me company, and she's only mine because someone knew I didn't turn away strays."

"Wes."

He already didn't like the way she said his name. It gave him feelings he'd rather not diagnose at the moment. It was one of the great things about the army. Everyone said *Stone* or his rank in the same harsh bark. No emotion to discern in that environment. Just do your job right and no one gave you a hard time for being poor or shy or anxious or helpful or nice, either.

They needed to get on that professional, detached playing field. He gave orders. She followed them. The end. "Are you ready to work?"

"Oh! I almost forgot." She shoved some papers out of the way and put her bag down on the spot she'd cleared. Carefully, she pulled out a big plastic container.

"I made you a pie." She unclipped the clasps on the lid. "It's kind of my version of a personality test."

"Pie as personality test?"

She nodded, her lips a brightly painted pink

smile. She lifted the lid with a flourish. "I give you octo-pie."

Wes stared at the bizarre-looking pie. It was indeed an octo-pie in that the top of the piecrust had been fashioned to look like an octopus. A big lump of pie dough made up the body, while strips made up the eight legs. It even had eyes and a mouth cut into the crust. The pie filling looked like cherry and made his mouth water.

It was ridiculous and hilarious. He actually found himself laughing. Which somehow only made Cara grin wider.

"You pass," she said happily. "You *do* have a personality under all that gruff I'm-so-tough beardy flannel."

Any humor faded. He didn't particularly want her to see him having a personality. This would be so much easier if he could be the silent soldier and she could…go about her business organizing him. His papers. Not him. "I wouldn't go that far."

"I would." Sweetness hopped up on the desk chair and began sniffing around the pie, so Cara put the lid back on. "Are you sure about me keeping her?"

"I don't say things I don't mean."

"You have no idea how much I like that about you." She said it kind of under her breath, but he caught it and was all too pleased by it.

"So, where do we start?" she asked, all sunny good cheer while Sweetness panted happily up at her despite her taking away the pie.

Yeah, the damn dog definitely belonged with Cara.

"Wherever you want. I have work to do in the kitchen. Find a way to organize all this in a way that works for you and that you can explain to a mess like me, answer the phones, and we're set."

Cara looked wide-eyed around the room. "That's it?"

"You have carte blanche. And I have carte blanche to tell you it sucks."

Instead of frowning or arguing like he would have expected, she grinned. "This might be the best job I ever had."

"I wouldn't say that yet," he grumbled. "I'll be in the kitchen if you have any questions." And he would stay in the kitchen, because being around her was bad news. Being pleased by anything she said was a terrible recipe for a replay of his teenage life, and nope, he wasn't going to do that again.

He left her in his office, Sweetness not even looking his way. Which was fine. At least Phantom...

He glanced back to where the dog hovered in between the doorway of the office and the hallway to the kitchen. "Another traitor," Wes muttered, trying not to feel too bent out of shape about it.

If he were a dog, he'd be panting in Cara's lap, too.

Irritated with himself for, well, everything, he took a deep breath and went about setting up for work. He had things to do. Things that did not involve his new assistant.

Besides, there was always the chance she'd make a mistake and he could fire her. *Because, of course, you have the balls for that.*

He had been isolated for too long. Talking to the dogs was one thing. Talking to himself this much? He still remembered his fourth-grade teacher, Ms. Purdue, telling him that talking to himself was a sign of insanity.

She might not be that far off.

He gathered his ingredients, flipping on the radio to drown out some of his inner monologue. All he wanted to think about was the correct ratio of sweet potatoes to whole wheat flour.

He lost himself in the routine, even managing to forget Cara was in the next room most of the time. He had the batter made and the molds filled before she interrupted the peace he'd found by entering the kitchen.

"Hey, um…" Her nervous energy filled the room. Obviously she'd run across something she had a question about, something that made her uncomfortable. His shoulders that had finally relaxed tensed.

"Um, someone from Dr. Pedelmann's office called to see if they could reschedule your appointment tomorrow."

Well. Yeah, he could see why that'd make her uncomfortable. And damn him for not having a personal phone line so he could handle these things without the chance of her...getting wind of it. Too late now. "Super."

"They asked if the sixth at two-thirty would work."

"Okay."

She didn't move. He didn't bother to look at her, but he could still hear her breathing, didn't hear any footsteps retreating.

"You're not, like, dying, are you?"

The question shocked an almost laugh out of him. "No, not dying." Any lingering desire to laugh died. "Just malfunctioning."

She stood there, hovering. Not asking any more questions but not leaving, either.

"Look." He glared at the molds filled with batter. As much as he loved what he did, it so often struck him as ridiculous. Making dog treats so idiot people like Pipsqueak's owner could pretend their dogs were children. All because he was too damaged to do what he really wanted to do.

But there were good customers, too. Non-ridiculous people who wanted to feed their dogs decent food. Which was the whole reason he'd even thought of this business when all other options had been destroyed.

Cara was still watching him. He could feel her gaze. Like a weight. Like a noose. "I have nerve damage in my arm. A pin in my hip. The nerve damage isn't progressing the way it should, hence the doctor's appointment. I'm not dying, and I'm not certifiable." Not totally, anyway.

"Okay. Can I help somehow?"

"No. Just reschedule the appointment for whenever."

"Okay." Another pause. "Okay," she said once more, and then, finally, her footsteps retreated.

He took a deep breath, looked out the window at the trees that surrounded his cabin. Help. A foreign concept. One he didn't know what to do with except push away.

But the offer lingered there, accompanied by a sharp pang of something he'd tried to eradicate from his life. Longing. Loneliness. He wasn't such an idiot that he thought he'd ever be right in the head enough to have a romantic relationship, but maybe they could have a friendly working one.

That wasn't...totally out of the realm of possibility, was it? He'd been friends, so to speak, with some of the guys in his regiment. The guys in the dog squad especially.

Cara might be a woman, but she was an off-limits woman, which meant he didn't have to get all nervous and uncomfortable at the prospect of anything more. There wasn't the chance for any-thing more. She was like a fellow soldier, work-ing toward the same goal.

And if she had breasts, a brain-cell-killing smile and always smelled like flowers of some kind, well, he'd find a way to ignore that.

CARA LOOKED DOWN at the desk and sighed. The enormity of stuff Wes surrounded himself with, half of it junk mail and old receipts that couldn't possibly be needed, made it feel as if she'd gotten nowhere despite working for almost three hours straight. Well, aside from the little break to tell Wes about his doctor's appointment and shove her foot in her mouth.

There was progress to be found on the desk; she just couldn't see it. And that made her feel stupid. Which wasn't exactly new these days. She needed something to gel.

Asking Wes if he was dying wasn't gelling. Nor was getting one hundred percent turned down on her offer to help. But, hey, at least she got to keep Sweetness.

Cara's stomach rumbled, and she chewed her

lip. She'd been hungry for an hour. Couldn't stop thinking about the pie she'd placed back in her bag. She'd need a knife, fork and plate to indulge, and she had brought it for Wes, so she probably shouldn't eat it.

Though him eating the whole pie didn't seem totally necessary.

When Wes stepped back into the office, he gave her a quizzical look. Probably because she was standing there staring at nothing. Doing nothing.

"I—I was trying to, um, I was going to take my lunch break. If that's okay. I—"

He grunted, cutting her off. *I suck, suck, suck.*

"You have three choices," he said. "You can eat whatever in here and take off at four. You can go get lunch somewhere in town, which seems like a total waste of time, and you'd have to work till five. Or you can come with me."

"What happens if I come with you?" Why, oh, why had her brain suddenly made everything dirty? So not okay to think about that right now.

"We take the dogs for a walk. We eat sandwiches out by the creek. We *don't* chitchat. And you can take off at four thirty, because it usually only takes me about a half hour."

"What exactly is your definition of chitchat?" A girl with any ounce of self-preservation would take the first option. She was not that girl.

"Pick a door, Cara."

He so rarely said her name or addressed her in any way. It was strangely nice when he did. "Door three, please."

Again, he grunted, offering nothing else as he walked back to the kitchen. For the first time she noticed it. Not quite a limp, but a stiffness. That right leg didn't move quite as easily as the rest of him.

Or had she noticed because she now knew he had a pin in his hip? Ouch, that sounded bad. Plus nerve damage that wasn't getting better. Poor guy.

When she stepped into the kitchen, he was standing in front of the small slice of counter that seemed reserved for people food. "Peanut butter or turkey?"

"Um." It took her brain a few seconds to work out he was asking about sandwiches. "I brought my own lunch." A sad little packet of tuna and some crackers. "But if you're offering, I'll take a turkey sandwich instead."

Another grunted nonanswer, and she didn't know what to do with herself. She didn't think offering to make her own sandwich would go over well.

"I've got Coke in the fridge if you want to grab two."

She did as he asked, then stood by the door

feeling like an idiot with two Coke cans freezing her hands.

Each sandwich went into a baggie. Grabbing a coat off a hook by the door, he shrugged it on, then took the cans from her. He slid one into each pocket, along with a baggie of dog treats. "You wanna carry the sandwiches?"

"Sure. Um, if you bring forks, we can eat pie, too."

He nodded, pulling open a drawer and taking out two forks. She grabbed her bag, dropped the sandwiches in, then followed him outside.

She'd expected some first day awkwardness—and gotten it with the doctor thing—but walking around and eating with your boss, who happened to be kind of hot and intriguing, felt really weird.

He walked around the cabin to what appeared to be a small barn in the back. Probably a quarter of the size of the ones on her dad's property, but the color and shape was all barn.

"I make sure all the animals have water and food. Make the petting rounds."

Cara looked behind them, where Sweetness, Phantom and the other two dogs pranced. "You have *more* animals?"

"A few cats. Two more dogs. A sheep."

"A sheep?"

He shrugged, tramping over to the barn and

pulling the door open. "He needed a good home. I had a barn."

"No partridge in a pear tree?"

"I like animals."

"Because they aren't annoying like people?"

"I've always liked animals. I never had any growing up."

"Never?"

"I tried a few times, but we always lived in no-animals-allowed places, so I always got in trouble. One time I got us kicked out, so I gave that up. I was going to…"

"You were going to what?"

He was frowning now, and not just his normal scowly resting face. This was full-on pissed off.

"Doesn't matter." He stomped into the barn. A few yips rang out, and a cat made figure eights between his legs.

"Why do you keep these guys in here?"

"The cats chose it. The dogs aren't trained enough yet. They run off if I give them free rein outside, but this gives them some space and we work on boundaries in the evening. Shrimp doesn't get around too good these days, so it's safest for him to stay in a pen, although he occasionally escapes."

"Shrimp?"

"Sheep with a limp. Sheep plus limp. Shrimp."

"Wes!"

"What? It's descriptive." His mouth quirked up. Not quite a smile, but because it was Wes she would count it as a smile.

"Come on." He went about filling dishes with fresh water and adding food to different bowls. It was obviously his routine, and it seemed to relax him. Except for the few times he'd look up, seem to remember she was there and get all tense and frowny again.

Cara had to wonder why he'd invited her at all if she made him so uncomfortable. But she didn't question it out loud, because she didn't want to eat lunch alone. Strange company was better than no company.

She followed him around, and eventually they left the barn. He brought one of the barn dogs with them, so the number of animals trailing after them was now five. He didn't look at her once as they hiked through the woods, eventually reaching a creek.

It was beautiful and reminded her so much of home, she wanted to splash in the water like she had when she'd been eight. Only it was barely fifty degrees, and walking through the sliver of leaf-filled water between two muddy banks would be ill advised in her flimsy canvas shoes.

"Buttercups! Oh, my favorite." Shiny yellow petals sprouted next to a big, flat rock Wes stopped at. Spring had always been her favorite season. Spring had meant freedom as a kid. Everyone busy with the farm and the weather finally okay enough she could go out without Mom blowing a worry gasket.

Fresh air and freedom. It made her believe in new beginnings, far more than any January resolution did. So, maybe she needed to seek a little rebirth and new growth of her own.

Grow up. Leave Cara the screwup behind.

Not possible.

She ignored the jerk of a voice in her head and plucked the delicate flowers out of the ground, arranging a few in her hair. A little visual reminder that flowers could grow from nothing but dirt and water and a little sunlight. "How do I look?"

He'd situated himself on the rock, and Cara had a little inward sigh over his pretty eyes before he looked down. Blushing. Definitely blushing. He might have acted as if he didn't care for her occasional flirting, but obviously he didn't think she was repulsive.

Maybe he was shy about stuff like that. For some reason, the thought of gruff and grumpy Wes being shy made her feel all warm and squishy.

Which was not okay. At all. He was her boss, and aside from this and a few emergency shifts at the salon, she had no income. Because she hadn't sucked up the courage to approach Sam again about the pies.

Well, buttercups as her witness, she would.

She settled herself next to Wes. And, yeah, maybe she didn't have to sit so close, but she was feeling bold now. She handed him his sandwich; he handed her a Coke.

"This place is perfect."

He cracked open his soda. "Yeah, I like it."

"You do this every day?" With Phantom, Sweetness and the three other dogs sitting or lying around the base of the rock, it obviously wasn't something new.

He made one of his grunt-yes noises as he bit into his sandwich.

"So, why organic dog treats?"

He lifted those broad, yummy shoulders—*bad, Cara*—but she pointed at him before he finished the motion. "No shrugging. You have to answer."

"I said no chitchat."

"It's not chitchat. It's an interrogation."

He glared. Glowered. All frustrated irritation. She couldn't stop herself from imagining him making that kind of look naked. If she did something sassy. And she would need to be punished.

Okay, if she were the blushing type, she'd be blushing.

"I was going to be a vet," he grumbled, attacking his sandwich as if it had done something wrong. "But, you know, you need a steady hand."

She had to try hard to not let the pity show on her face. It didn't take a psychologist to figure Wes was not the kind of guy who would deal well with pity. Oh, but her heart did hurt for him. He obviously loved animals, and getting hurt had ended his chance to be a vet.

Geez, this guy was a sob story. Usually those made her run in the opposite direction. Hurt feelings and tough emotions were *not* her forte, but Wes made everything that usually freaked her out seem irresistible.

Well, you better do some resisting, Cara Pruitt.

"So, anyway, my mom had opened an organic grocery store in California and done pretty well, and it gave me the idea for organic pet food stuff. Did some research. Set up a business. Blah, blah, blah."

"That's pretty amazing. Starting your own business. I watched Mia do it, and she had a farm to start with. It's really impressive you put together a whole business you can sustain yourself and a bunch of animals with."

He stared into the creek. "It's okay."

"Right. Well, I'm impressed. I can't even make myself go after a job I want, let alone start my own business."

"What's your excuse?"

She gave him a rueful smile. "Cave under pressure. Useless with expectation." She nudged a few pebbles with her foot. "I'm working on it."

"I would freaking hope so."

There was an undercurrent in the way he mumbled it. Kind of mean. The meanest she'd ever heard him sound. Even meaner than when he'd yelled at that lady at the market. "Huh?"

"Sorry, no patience for that bullshit." He stood, shoving his empty baggie and soda can in his pocket. He held a hand out for her trash, but she didn't give it to him.

"What bullshit?"

"Not going after something you want because you're afraid." He made a "give me it" motion with his hand, which, for some reason, made her clutch the trash even tighter.

"I'm not afraid. That's how I'm wired. Or whatever. I can't handle it. I've tried."

"You know what I have to say to that?"

"Something really nice and comforting?"

"Try harder." With that, he let out a sharp whistle that had the dogs jumping to their feet and scrambling after his already retreating back.

Cara stared after him until he was a few feet away. Sweetness stood at the top of the hill, whining at her. Only then did she move.

Oh, hell, no, that had not just happened. He had not barked "try harder" at her as if she was some soldier. She might be his employee, but she took orders from no one.

And he was about to find that out.

CHAPTER SIX

WES HAD WARNED HER. That was his one and only defense. Before he'd offered her the job, he'd warned her he sucked with people. So, you know, she could not be surprised that he'd been a total jerk.

Sure.

He stalked back to the barn, headache inching its way up the base of his skull. A ball of tension, dull for now. He forced Monster back inside, even though the dog whined. Usually he let both dogs out on their runner in the afternoon, but right now he needed to get inside the cabin.

Inside and away from the woman stomping toward him looking as if she was going to beat him up.

He'd probably let her. He didn't know where all that stuff had come from. It certainly wasn't his place to tell her she was wrong and ridiculous, even if she was. So much for trying to be pleasantly friendly to coworkers. He couldn't even get that right.

"You have no right to say that stuff."

He shrugged. "True enough."

She opened her mouth, and her eyebrows drew together. She huffed out a breath. "I—you—oh, I could punch you."

"I'd apologize, but…" He was an idiot. *Apologize* and *but* did not go in the same sentence. He knew that, but, well, he didn't feel like apologizing. She was fully functional and apparently had the opportunity to do something she loved, and she had caved?

She was gorgeous, funny, personable and, from all accounts, had a decent family life. What excuse did she have for not going after her dreams?

"But what?" she demanded, hands fisted on hips, muddy shoes tapping on the soggy grass.

"Would you be so angry if I wasn't right on the money?"

Her mouth dropped open, her foot stilling and hands dropping to her sides. She looked frozen. Like a statue or one of those mannequins that only came to life when someone wasn't looking.

"You—"

"Look, I warned you about how I am with people. So, you know, if that's a problem, feel free to quit."

Again there was a long pause before she reacted in any way. Which spoke volumes about how together she was. That she could pause and think before acting.

"I can't quit."

"Yes, you can. In fact—"

"This is all I have right now. As much as I think you're being kind of a, well, something I can't say to the man I want to not fire me. I'd rather be here than back at the farm supply store."

"What about that hair place?"

"They already replaced me. I can fill in, but that's only in emergencies. Even this job doesn't cover all my expenses. It's supposed to be my motivation to ask Sam for another chance at the pie thing. So you can't take it away. I won't let you."

Maybe that was why he didn't understand her self-deprecating, fold-under-pressure speech. He'd yet to see her fold under anything. She stood her ground. She swept in where she had no business being. She'd somehow convinced him to give her his dog.

She was a hurricane, and hurricanes didn't fold.

"Then let's go inside and work. And not talk. This, this right here is why I don't do the chit-chat thing."

She muttered a curse under her breath, and he was pretty sure it was directed at him. He couldn't hold it against her.

He walked toward the house, and she followed. This was some kind of truce. It was better than where they'd been when she'd put flowers in her hair and asked him how she looked.

Beautiful. Breathtaking. Words a guy like him didn't think, let alone say aloud. But Cara defied his norm. The talking about not having animals when he was a kid, and commenting on her life and choices. That wasn't something he did with anyone else. He'd been *trying* to be normal, but it had spiraled out of his control.

Thank God she defied his norm in annoying ways, too. As long as she could push his buttons, he was safe. *Don't worry, Wes, your virginity is very, very safe.*

But instead of heading inside, she stepped in front of him. He had no choice but to look at her. No choice but to be sucked into Hurricane Cara.

"I bombed the job interview. The pie-baking one. The one that would be *perfect.* Explain that. How I did that. Me, who has been making pies forever. I could do it in my sleep. I put in too much salt. I burnt the edges. He was standing there *staring* at me, and everything went wrong when it never has before." She poked him in the chest. "Explain that."

"Bake the pies beforehand." The way her tense expression morphed into shock was evidence enough that this had never occurred to her.

"Before…"

"If it's the pressure that gets to you, bake it in a no-pressure zone. Then take it to him. If he's the suspicious sort, have your sister watch you or video you or something."

"But what if I get the job? I can't video everything."

"Tell him you'd rather use your own kitchen. It's not like you're going to sit in his restaurant making pies to order. It takes too long, doesn't it? You'll want to make dough in batches, make the filling in batches, right? Like a diner."

"How did you...? That never even... Why didn't he...? Why didn't *I*...?"

Here was the choice. One he usually didn't struggle with, but Cara's vulnerability under all the strength she didn't seem to think she had made it hard to be the close-the-door-in-her-face kind of guy he would prefer to be. "I've spent a lot of time learning to avoid my anxiety triggers. You have an obstacle, you find a way to circumnavigate it. Defuse it."

"Wes." She said his name with wonder. As if he was helping or something, and that made him uncomfortable enough to bring the harsh side of him back out.

"What you don't do is wimp out, then whine about it."

Yeah, that snapped any sweet appreciation off her face as easily as a slap might have.

She crossed her arms over her chest. Which

tugged the top of her tank top down a little. A strip of neon pink lace poked out from beneath it.

Stop looking.

"But if it is anxiety, which I'm not all that certain it is, I can't make it go away."

"Do you think I'm telling you that?" He pointed at Phantom, who was sitting uneasily off to the side. Assessing. "Dude with a therapy dog. I had military-required therapy and psychoanalysis. I'm saying you find a way to deal. It's called coping. It's healthy and whatever."

"No offense, Wes, but you don't strike me as the most mentally healthy guy." She closed her eyes, and her mouth twisted in a pained expression. "Please, ignore me."

"I keep trying."

Her mouth quirked up. "I guess I'm not very good at fading into the background. But, um, I shouldn't have said that."

"I'm not mentally healthy." He was bitter, angry, frustrated. Then there was his physical health. "In fact, I'm a mess. Which—it is what it is. But you should know that. Accept it. You want to keep this job as your motivation, you're going to have to understand this is me."

She cocked her head, studying him in a way that made him want to squirm. Only calling on his military training kept him from doing it. He was tempted to stand at attention.

"You don't scare me, you know."

"I thought you folded under pressure."

"Pressure. Expectation." She frowned. "Hope. That's when I fold, when I know I *should* be better. Fear? Well, I'm not afraid of people who can't hurt me."

"I could fire you."

"You could, but for as much of a mess as you are, I don't think you're cruel."

She had his number. "No."

"Then, I'll get back to it." With that, she turned on a heel and waltzed into the house. *His* house, and yet again, he didn't know what to do about it.

CARA GLANCED AT the clock. 4:28 p.m. Two more minutes, then she was out of this loony bin. Of course, she was coming back on Wednesday. And Thursday. Week after week.

Unless she started looking for work elsewhere, which was probably what she should do. Every time she thought of Wes saying, "Try harder," she wanted to punch him. Right in the nerve damage.

But then she thought about the way he called himself a mess and she wanted to… She didn't know. Something warm and fuzzy and foreign. Because usually when it came to messes, Cara steered way clear. She was not the clean-up-a-mess girl. She maybe could help if someone needed something easy, like Mia had. But not deep-seated-issue messes. She was a hey-wanna-slap-on-some-lipstick-and-drown-your-sorrows type.

Why the heckity heck was Wes different? Just because she had the hots for him? That was sad, even for her. She'd overlooked a guy's flaws before, but they were usually flaws like he never paid for dinner or didn't have a job.

Not, like, therapy dogs and war injuries. That was heavy stuff. Stuff to run away from so she didn't make a situation worse, like she had during her brief relationship with James. And yet, given the chance with Wes, she hadn't run. Nor had she made light of the situation.

She'd stood up to him.

Huh.

Two thuds interrupted her obsessing, and when she looked to the office entrance, Wes was standing there. His arms were crossed, and his sleeves were rolled up to his elbows. For the first time, she could see that the scars on his hand went up the length of his forearm and disappeared beyond the sleeve.

She wasn't supposed to look, but it was hard. She was curious. She wondered what he'd gone through, if it still hurt, if she could help.

"You can leave now."

She wanted to laugh at how ridiculous he sounded. He'd hired her, but he didn't want her

here. Sometimes he acted as if he liked her—
he'd given her a *dog*—and other times he acted
as if she was gum on the bottom of his shoe. *Try
harder.*

She should quit. That was the bottom line. She
needed to quit and beg Miranda for her job at the
salon back. Or find a whole different job. Somewhere in Millertown.

But then Sweetness yipped happily at her feet,
and the desire to quit receded. He'd given her a
dog. *His* dog. He wasn't all bad. Just, well, like
he said, a mess.

Maybe if she learned how to deal with someone else's much harder mess, she'd figure out how
to deal with her own.

"I'll be back bright and early Wednesday morning." She lifted her chin, daring him to argue.

He gave her the slightest of nods, and she got
the distinct impression he was purposefully not
saying anything.

That was fine and dandy. They didn't need
to talk. They didn't even need to be friends. He
could be gruff, silent boss man, and she would
be A-plus administrative assistant lady.

She gathered up her things and clipped Sweetness's leash onto her collar, but when she walked
over to him so she could leave, he didn't move out
of the doorway. He blocked it, arms still crossed,
all frowny and…

Hot. *The word you are looking for is* hot. She had no idea how, but his mountain man flannel and hair had become something of an obsession.

"I'm sorry," he said, his voice so low and grumbly she barely made out the words.

It was possibly the most sincere apology she'd ever gotten. He was uncomfortable, and his enunciating could use some work, but that was what made it so genuine.

It wasn't BS. It was very real. Very honest. She didn't know what to do about that, except be honest back.

"You weren't wrong, even if you were kind of jerky about it."

"Yeah, well. I'm sorry for the jerky part."

Sweetness tugged on the leash, obviously ready to get outside, but Cara wasn't ready for it because she was still a little off-kilter from the apology. Instead of holding on tight and tugging back, she bumped right into Wes.

A hard wall of muscle. Yowza.

He gripped her elbow with his unscarred hand. "She needs some work on her obeying."

I would gladly obey. Talking about a dog. Not her. Right. Cara swallowed. "Well, I should get her outside, huh?"

He maneuvered her via the arm he held, so they switched places. He was now in his office, and she was in the door frame.

"Right. Well. See you Wednesday."

He nodded, giving no indication he felt any of the same crazy attraction electricity she got every time he was all whatever that was.

She should be glad he didn't feel it, but she remembered the way he'd blushed when she asked him how she looked with the buttercups in her hair. He wasn't immune, and she wanted to know why he insisted on pretending he was.

Except he was her boss and, of his own admission, not mentally healthy.

"Did you need something else?"

"Nope. I'm good," she said brightly. Too brightly, but oh, well. He was always too grumpy, and she could be too cheerful. Maybe they'd balance each other out.

Hardy-har-har.

CHAPTER SEVEN

WES HAD ALWAYS liked spring. The time between the chill of winter and the oppressive heat of summer. Growing up, there had been far too many extreme seasons where the use of heat was rationed and the use of air-conditioning did not happen. Period.

Spring had always been a relief. Warmth and sun and the promise of comfort for at least a few weeks. The promise of a new, fresh start that never really delivered, and yet he found himself hopeful, year after year.

The spring morning of the market swirled around him, almost promoting a good mood. The Millertown Farmers' Market wasn't as big as the one he sold at on Fridays, but the crowd was decent. A lot of them walked dogs. Which meant eventually they'd arrive at his booth.

Sometimes the prices scared people off, but mostly people couldn't resist buying at least one treat for their furry companion.

He'd never be known as an outgoing, charming salesman. But he managed, because it wasn't small talk or flirting or navigating difficult emotions. It was explaining how he made his treats, what benefit the ingredients offered and possibly complimenting a dog or two.

All things that came naturally to him, when so little did. It damn near made him cheerful.

Until a bright and cheery voice interrupted all the peace and quiet of people asking about the necessity of organic dog treats.

"'Morning, Wes."

He tried to muster up some kind of armor for facing her outside the prescribed boundaries of work and his house. This was the market. It was still work, even if Cara wasn't technically working for him at this very second.

"'Morning," he offered, not at all pleasantly. He couldn't help it. She had a short-sleeved shirt on, baring those long, slender arms and the occasional freckle. And she never had the decency to wear a shirt with one of those collars that went all the way up to the neck. No, always a deep V, an expanse of smooth white skin with a little beauty mark on her collarbone.

He wanted to touch her. He wanted his palms on her skin, and he knew that it couldn't happen. He'd self-destruct even if it would. He couldn't do it, and he knew he couldn't do it, so fantasizing about it was becoming torture.

Except that he might die of lust, and he'd *never*

felt that way before. Not with anyone. So, he mainly just scowled and ordered her around, because that was his default. His armor.

"What's Sweetness's favorite?" she asked, poking around one of the buckets of treats.

"I...I don't know. She'll eat anything," he grumbled, trying like he tried every Monday, Wednesday and Thursday to ignore the way the colorful polish on her fingers was mesmerizing. He wrenched his gaze away from her fingers amidst his dog treats and looked around. "Where is she?"

"Aww. Missing your baby?"

She had a way of smiling that made him want to smile back. It warred with his determination to keep his expression void of emotion so no one dared pry or ask him about anything.

Cara remained completely unbothered. She kept...poking at him. Not that she harassed him at work or incessantly asked questions or hovered. She was simply relentless cheerfulness with an offbeat sense of humor that continued to catch him off guard. Worse, he didn't feel uncomfortable around her, half the time. The other half the time, his brain got away from him and thought about sex.

Not conducive to a professional work environment, that half.

But he still wanted to smile the other half the

time. So he crossed his arms over his chest and scowled. "No."

"If you say so," she said in a way that was teasing, and yet he didn't feel *teased*, he felt in on the joke. How did she do that? He wanted it to stop.

He wanted it to go on forever.

He was sick in the head.

"Let's try one of the sweet potatoes. You made that with Mia and Dell's sweet potatoes, right?" She smiled up at him, the sun glinting off the shades of red in her brown hair, the dark pink color of her shirt offsetting the bright blue-green of her eyes.

Maybe the nerve damage had spread to his brain. "Yeah. Take whatever you want." When she started digging cash out of her pocket, he waved her off. "Just…take whatever. You don't have to pay me."

She cocked her head.

"Employee discount."

"Discount isn't the same as free."

"I'd be giving them to the dog anyway if she was mine." He shoved a bag at her so she could collect her treats.

She took it but studied the plain brown paper.

"You should name the treats."

"Huh?"

"Instead of the labels of what's in them, you should give them names. Sweet Pup-tato or Carrotalls. Have a label on your bags." She shook the little paper bag he'd handed her. "Have a saying on them, like 'have a tail-wagging good time.' You know, cutesy dog stuff."

Hc shook his head, scowling. It wasn't anything his mother hadn't gently suggested, but he wasn't the frilly sort, and neither were his treats. Adding all that…window dressing was wholly unnecessary, and he was tired of people suggesting it to him. Damn tired of Cara suggesting all manner of things, not always with words. But with looks and…

No. No cutesy dog stuff. "That's ridiculous."

Some of the cheer on her face vanished, and she looked toward her sister's booth across the way. "Fine. Don't use it. Just a suggestion. Anyway, I'll pay—"

"Cara!"

A younger woman leading Sweetness on a leash marched toward Cara, looking less than pleased.

"I draw the line at cleaning up your dog's crap," the girl said, shoving the leash at Cara.

"You clean up manure all the time. How is this different?" Cara glanced at Wes out of the corner of her eye. "Anna, this is Wes, my…boss. Wes, this is Anna, my little sister."

"Ooh," the girl said, and Wes couldn't even begin to understand why.

"Why are you oohing, you weirdo?" Cara gave her a shove, then turned a smile on him, almost all of her cheer so easily returned. "Ignore her. She's eighteen. And stupid."

"*I'm* stupid," Anna said with a snort. "Glass houses and stones, Cara."

There was a flash of something in Cara's expression. Brief but recognizable because he'd felt that kind of pang a lot growing up. The way an offhanded comment could hit the soft underbelly without anyone noticing.

Belatedly, he realized it was the same look on her face from a second ago when he'd told her the treat name idea was ridiculous.

Hell.

"Where is it?" Cara was asking her sister, taking Sweetness's leash and looping it around her wrist.

"Over by PMS."

Cara rolled her eyes. "Give her my sweet potato treat, will you, Wes?" Cara said, being dragged away by Sweetness.

Wes turned his attention to Cara's sister. Younger, obviously. Cara had said eighteen, so not the one who had a booth here. Eighteen. Yeah, he'd never much cared for anyone of an age ending in teen.

He plopped a few treats into a bag and then handed it to the teenager who was studying him.

He knew he shouldn't say anything, but somehow the words formed anyway. "She's not stupid," he grumbled.

Anna looked at him as if he'd just gotten on all fours and barked like a dog. "Oookay," she replied, backing away.

Somehow making him feel like the idiot when *she'd* been the one to dismiss *her* sister in a few words without even realizing it.

Yeah, he was not the idiot. In this scenario. Which was inevitably going to lead to him being the idiot in a different one, he had no doubt.

CARA DRESSED FOR her usual Saturday night out while Sweetness pranced at her heels. She shimmied into skinny jeans, clasped her pushiest-up of push-up bras, and gave herself a liberal swipe of bright red lipstick and dark black eyeliner.

She didn't know why each time this ritual, that had once been her favorite part of the week, felt… worse. More oppressive. Empty.

She didn't want to give the thing with Kevin any more weight, but she couldn't deny that part of it was her friends simply expected her to sit next to him and his fiancée and act as if he hadn't once used her as payback against said fiancée.

None of her best friends had thought she needed to make a big deal out of it. Only Mia had ever shown her any sympathy, and now that it was almost a year later, all of them thought she should be over it. So, he'd used her for sex and revenge. It wasn't as if Cara hadn't ever initiated a one-night stand before.

She stared at herself in the mirror. They were right, of course. There weren't too many guys she'd ever said no to. Why would Kevin have been any different?

Oh, the part where he promised *they were broken up and said he could really imagine starting something* real *with you.*

She stomped away from the mirror. She needed to get over it. Over. It. She was twenty-five. One guy didn't need to define her love life for the next twenty years. She needed to get a grip, like all her friends said. They'd known her forever. How could they be wrong?

"You're going to be a good girl for me, aren't you?" she cooed at Sweetness. In the downward spiral of a day, starting with Wes calling her idea ridiculous and Anna mortifying her and this... stupid melancholy following her around, Sweetness was a bright spot of warmth and comfort.

Hell, the animal could chew up everything in her apartment while she was gone, and she would *still* be the bright spot.

"I'll be back by ten thirty." Her friends would call her all manner of names for bowing out at ten, and really there was no reason to. No waking up early, no salon work in the afternoon.

Nothing.

Why did she feel like *crying*? She never cried. She never...moped. She was not this woman currently inhabiting her body, and it was irritating. It was all Mia's fault. Making her take the stupid interview with Sam, which had somehow led her into Wes's creepy isolated lair.

She blew out a breath, making sure Sweetness's dishes were full before she left. Truth be told, she *liked* Wes's cabin. She liked the quiet and the space to organize his little business. She liked the trees and the solitude and the little creek they ate lunch at.

She liked *him*, and he thought she was ridiculous. Well, her friends might not approve of her grudge against Kevin, but they didn't judge her. They didn't try to make her do more.

She was going to be the absolute life of the party. She was going to have the best Saturday night she'd had all year. One way or another.

An hour and three drinks later, she was pleasantly light-headed, her mouth hurt from smiling so much, and if she was having to remind herself every ten minutes or so she was having *fun, damn it*, well...that was just the way it was.

If only Kevin would stop moving his stupid chair closer, and if only Mackenzie wasn't so enamored with her new boyfriend, making sure he was perfectly comfortable and entertained at *all* times, Cara might be able to stop having to remind herself.

"Who wants another one?" C.J. asked, pushing away from the table.

Cara shook her head, immediately earning her boos. "You guys have to keep up with me," she said, holding her glass up and tinkling the ice. "I'm setting the pace here."

Truth be told, she'd love another drink. She'd love to keep going until she blacked out, but she didn't trust the way Kevin was looking at her or the absence of his *fiancée*.

C.J. sauntered to the bar, Mackenzie and Boyfriend Guy shimmied onto the dance floor, and since Annabelle was pregnant and rarely came out anymore, Jen had moved downtown and Greg was hiding out from warrants for speeding tickets he refused to pay, Cara was left with Kevin.

Maybe the nausea would turn in to full-on too-much-to-drink, and she could throw up on him.

"So, I missed why Lindsay isn't here," she said, in hopes of wiping that all-too-knowing smile off his face. So, he'd seen her naked. As if that made him special. The ass.

Kevin's gaze was steady on hers. Steady and smarmy, that half smile she used to think was oh-so-hot made her want to throw ice cubes at him.

He leaned forward, languid grace, and, yes, okay, he was hot. But he was a douche.

Her type leaned toward douche, but not lying, cheating douche. Then his palm rested on her knee, a hot, heavy weight.

"You know how she gets."

Once Cara fully comprehended that he was actually *touching* her leg in an *intent* manner, she moved her knee away. "Ew."

Kevin only laughed. "It's okay. She's not coming." He tried again, this time his palm sliding from knee halfway up her thigh before her pushing his hand away morphed into actually slapping it, because apparently that was the only thing that was going to get him to stop.

But he didn't seem to get the picture because his hand was coming at her again, so she pushed out of her chair. "Stop touching me, ass-hat."

"Come on, Car, don't pretend you don't like it." He grinned, and it made her sick she'd once *liked* that grin. "I don't mind a *little* hard to get, but your normal ready and willing is way more what I'm after."

Your ready and willing. The words made the alcohol in her system slosh uncomfortably around in her stomach. It reminded her of everything he'd done, and everything everyone expected her to overlook for the sake of the group. Because sure, she was just easy Cara. She didn't have any *feelings* when it came to sex.

This was all his fault. This whole dissatisfaction she felt doing something she usually enjoyed. He'd ruined any easy or happy she'd had left by lying and cheating and messing everything up with her and her friends. And now he was trying to molest her.

So, she did what she should have done the second he laid a hand on her. She grabbed her glass of ice and tossed it in his face.

He had the gall to smirk and fold his arms over his chest. "Being a little overdramatic, don't you think?"

"Keep your hands off me. I do not want you to touch me. Ever."

"Ever again, you mean."

She gave a long thought to hurling her actual glass at him, wondering how much pain that could inflict.

"Oh, my God, Cara, what are you doing?" Mackenzie demanded, pulling Boyfriend Guy off the dance floor and toward her.

"I'm leaving." She slammed her glass down, not bothering to look at Kevin, since he was probably still smirking.

"Come on, Cara. Calm down. Come back to the table. We can talk about it."

She walked away from Mackenzie, who kept

pulling Boyfriend Guy behind her as she followed. Right, she was going to calm down and spill her guts to her best friend in front of some random guy.

"He won't keep his nasty hands off me. I'm not coming anywhere near him again."

"Well, you let a guy screw you once—"

She whirled on her best friend in the world, aside from her sisters. She was…so tired of Mackenzie excusing everything Kevin had done simply because she'd let him. Once. "No! No. He can't… no! You guys are all being so… This isn't right, and I'm not going to sit around and take it." Because if she did, she was going to cry.

She could not think of anything that would be more mortifying than crying in front of her friends. Than them knowing how hurt she was by all this.

So, she stalked out of Juniors, blinking back the tears that were threatening. Whatever. It didn't matter. Kevin didn't matter, and Mackenzie's need to find The One *immediately* was wearing thin. So, maybe she'd outgrown her friends or whatever.

No. Big. Deal. She'd find new ones. Ones who didn't think she should *get over* some guy who couldn't take no for an answer, just because one time she'd said yes. Ones who hadn't known her for almost her entire life and still saw her as the things she pretended to be.

She started walking through the parking lot, feeling teary and exposed and stupid. When had her life become pretend? She couldn't even pinpoint a certain moment. It just seemed suddenly…

Bam.

Her apartment was only two blocks away, and hopefully, that would give her enough time to get herself together. Walk off the anger and more importantly, the hurt. It wasn't pretend. It was her life. They *were* her friends; this was just an unfortunate situation.

Really.

But why did they take Kevin's side when he was obviously the sleaze in this situation?

Before she could get halfway through the parking lot, a woman's voice called her name. She turned to see Lindsay getting out of the car. Great. Well, good thing she'd walked before Lindsay had walked in and witnessed Kevin being gross.

Of course, Lindsay definitely knew what Kevin had done, and yet that ring was still on her finger, and their undetermined wedding was still topic du jour whenever Lindsay was around.

"Leaving so soon?" Lindsay craned her neck, looking around the parking lot as if she was expecting someone else.

"Yeah, your fiancé is being a dick." Which was not her smartest move, as they'd spent the past year pretending they *hadn't* both slept with the same guy.

Lindsay took a not-nice step toward her. "*Was* he, or you threw yourself at him and he declined?"

Cara blinked at the woman who'd been her best friend in middle school. They'd talked about everything under the sun from crushes to getting their periods, and then something about high school had put them in some faux friendship. Where they pretended as if they liked each other, but they were constantly battling each other for something. A guy's attention, the right kind of rumor. Whatever.

Cara was inexplicably exhausted. "For the record, I tossed a drink in his face when he wouldn't keep his hands off *me*."

Lindsay sniffed.

"Is he worth it?" Cara asked, knowing the answer before the question was even out of her mouth. Obviously Lindsay thought he was.

"Was he worth it when you slept with him while I had his ring on my finger?" She waggled the dinky little diamond in the dim light of the parking lot.

Cara could tell her, *again*, that she hadn't known. That he'd said he'd broken it off. That she had actually made him work for it a little bit, and he'd romanced her into thinking maybe he really *had* been with Lindsay because he wanted to get closer to *her*.

You are the biggest moron to walk into that bar tonight, Cara Pruitt, and that is saying something.

She didn't want to fight with Lindsay. She wanted to go home to her dog and cry, so she turned on a heel and walked the two blocks home in the quiet darkness of a New Benton night.

When she walked in the door, Sweetness yapped and hopped, and people sucked, but dogs weren't so bad.

Of course, there was a little turd sitting on her living room rug, because of course there was.

"I can't even be mad at you," Cara muttered, scratching her behind the ears. "That is not the worst thing to happen to me today." Not by a long shot.

CHAPTER EIGHT

WES KNEW HE was an idiot. That wasn't the surprising part of this Monday morning. The surprising part was after years of learning how to silence that stupidity, or at least hide it effectively, he couldn't stop himself.

Not when it came to Cara Pruitt, and didn't that tell him everything he needed to know about this woman he should fire but was instead going to give more responsibilities to?

He rested his forehead against the tile of the shower, knowing he needed to hurry, so he was out of there before she arrived. Everything was taking twice as long. The morning training session with the dogs, because it kept him from thinking about work. Working out more than he usually did because it kept his mind off *her*.

Barely. Okay, not at all. He grunted and pushed himself from the wall. He had to get dressed and…somehow do this thing without turning into a muttery, stumbling fool in the process.

The thing about Cara was…sometimes he wasn't that person. Sometimes, interacting with her was oddly easy. She was so...*personable* and had a way of never making anything too... weighty. Like that first day she'd come out to his house and he'd dropped the dog container, and she'd simply grabbed it and swept into his life.

No questions. No pity. A few sidelong glances at his scars, but she didn't make him feel like a malfunctioning robot part of the time, and aside from his customers and suppliers, that was rare.

It made him want to try. Try to be a person again. The kind he was in the army, when he knew what was expected of him and could find enough comfort in that to be a person. Not some shell of one.

Wes blew out a breath as he stepped out of the shower. It was either an illusion or temporary, Cara's effect on him, but maybe for the first time in a few years he needed to push.

You know what happens when you push.

The pounding started the minute he grabbed his towel, thankfully killing off that line of thought. Toweling himself off hurriedly, he glanced out the little bathroom window that was high enough to keep people from looking in but allowed him to look out.

And see Cara standing on the porch, knocking on the door. More incessantly with every second.

As quickly as his not-quite-quick hip could manage, he shoved his legs into boxers and jeans and pulled them up. He worked to zipper and button his pants as he stepped into the hall between his bedroom and his kitchen. He needed to grab a shirt, but she started yelling.

"Wes, I swear, if you are trying to ignore me into hoping I quit, I'll—"

He lunged into the kitchen and swung the door open because that was the last thing he wanted her thinking. Her mouth dropped, arm still up in the air.

"Sorry. I was in the shower," he offered as Sweetness sniffed at his bare feet.

"Yeah, you were." She cocked her head, her gaze not meeting his. Not at all. No, she was staring at his chest. Not even at his arm where the white line of scars snaked up to almost his shoulder.

Wait. Was she…like…*interested* staring at him? Should he be…flattered?

Finally, her blue-green gaze slid to his, her mouth curving, slyly. "Well, this is a happy Monday morning." And then she muttered something that sounded suspiciously like *happy trail*.

"I…have to get a shirt." Because he didn't know what to do with…that kind of thing.

"Do you really *have* to?"

"Yes." Yes, it was imperative. So, he turned away from her and disappeared into his room, trying to find some calming center to the hurricane in his kitchen.

He was the boss, she was the employee. He gave the orders, and she would listen, and if she didn't, all he had to do was retreat to his kitchen and do *his* job.

And wasn't it just hilarious he'd been thinking he was *at ease* with her. He pulled a T-shirt over his head, then buttoned up a flannel shirt over it. His morning work would all be in the kitchen, and the long sleeves would likely be too hot, but he had the strange sensation of needing to cover it all up. Hide from any...

He paused at his door. She'd looked at him as if, despite everything she knew about him, she found his body appealing. His nonexistent way with people and bad temper wasn't obnoxious enough to keep her from flirting with him.

His mouth quirked. He couldn't help it. He *was* flattered. She was beautiful and nice and easygoing, and she thought he was attractive?

Yeah, she doesn't know the half of your weird, buddy.

Right. Had to remember that. He retraced his steps to the kitchen, but she wasn't there, so he went to the office. She was standing at his desk, flipping her way through a pile of papers that was probably an eighth of the size it had been when she first started.

But, it was his turn to cock his head at her, because...she looked different. It took him a while to unwind it, but she was wearing a gray bulky sweatshirt and some worn-down jeans, plus actual athletic tennis shoes, not boots or the bright flimsy canvas shoes she so often showed up in. Her lips weren't brightly painted, and there wasn't a line of black around her eyes. The only color on her was the actual iris of her eyes and painted on her fingernails.

There was an odd pang in his gut, something he couldn't quite name and definitely couldn't trust. He wouldn't ask her what was wrong or why she looked different, because as far as it concerned him, she didn't. She was here. She was talking and working. Nothing else mattered in the ways that they had to interact.

So, why are you going to do this?

Because *this thing* was different. It was work, not…personal. "I have a project for you."

She turned, all surprise and raised eyebrows. "A project?"

"Yes. I want you to name the dog treats. I printed out a list of what I make, and the ingredients, and you can do whatever you want." He picked the printed sheet up off the desk and handed it to her.

She frowned at it, not making a move to take it. "But…you said it was ridiculous."

"It *is* ridiculous." He shoved his left hand through his hair, trying not to let his frustration

with how badly he expressed himself pour on
to her. "I mean, it's ridiculous to *me*, but I'm a
grumpy hermit who hates everything. My customers are not."

She gave him a considering look and took the
paper. "You don't hate everything."

No, not everything. There were animals, and,
as much as it irritated him, he was having a hard
time hating her. "Okay, most things."

Her lips curved, just a fraction. This oddly unpainted, gray version of the woman who usually
blew in like a spring breeze, fresh and cool and
colorful.

Something was wrong, and it reminded him a
little too much of being a kid, of Mom trying to
put on a brave face after another boyfriend turned
out to be a piece of shit, another job got cut, another bill she couldn't pay surfaced.

"So, you'll do it," he prompted, because as
much as he'd been useless to his mother in those
days, more often than not making things worse,
she'd always perked up when he asked her for
help with his homework or with some problem
he made up.

He knew comparing Cara to his mother bor-
dered on insane, but what in his life didn't? And
she smiled at him, so…

But then she shoved the paper back at him, her
smile fading away as she shook her head. "Why

don't you do it? It's your business. I'm just an assistant."

He frowned down at the list of treats. Mostly vegetable names. *Him* do it? "If I did it, I'd call them all moron biscuits and be done with it."

She let out a sigh and sank into the desk chair, taking the piece of paper with her. She studied it. "Can they be really cutesy ridiculous names?"

"If you think that'll go over well. You'd know better than me about what normal people like."

"Do you really think you're *that* abnormal?"

He stared at her for a few beats, because, really, she hadn't picked up on that? That his life was a series of *abnormal* from as far back as he could remember. He'd never fit in. He'd kept to himself, and his brief forays into trying to understand people led him into ridicule and teasing that perhaps someone *normal* might have been able to weather.

His brain didn't function that way. It catalogued every comment and blow, every laugh at his expense, until that's all that echoed in his ears. So here he was. Isolated and, yes, abnormal, and that was all well and good now. Long as everyone he had to interact with understood it.

"I am asking you to do this as part of your job," he said, perhaps a little too brusquely, but it was easier that way. Easier to offer gruff orders than apply personal significance to any interactions with Cara.

It might be easier with Cara than it was with other people, especially women, but that didn't mean anything except she'd be an asset of an employee.

"I'll do it."

"Good. Now I have work to do." He turned and was almost completely safe and out of the doorway when her voice caught up with him.

"Can I watch?"

He had to take a careful breath to keep himself from choking a cough on his own surprise. Watch him work? "Uh."

"It might give me some ideas for treat names— to see how they're made." She smiled, and he supposed in her world it was an easy, simple smile, but the gentle curve of her unpainted lips, and the gray of her sweatshirt and everything about her being *off* was not in the least bit simple.

She wasn't simple. *He* wasn't simple. The thing that seemed to light up the air between them sure as hell wasn't simple, and if he'd learned anything in a lifetime of disappointment and failure, it would be that he needed to say no.

No, she couldn't watch. No, she couldn't invade his space and smile at him and somehow work her way around to mattering to him.

But of course the word *yes* tumbled out, because why wouldn't it?

IT WAS STRANGELY fascinating to watch Wes work. It was fun to try and provoke a smile out of him, sitting on the edge of the counter, which she knew he didn't approve of.

Nevertheless, she'd say something goofy, and his mouth would quirk into a smile. All the hair and beard obscured most of that smile, but there was a way his dark eyes lost some of that gloomy serious weight, and she felt like a million bucks for making it happen.

Which was incredibly addictive, considering that for the past two days she'd mainly felt horrible. Mackenzie had come over yesterday afternoon, dragging along Boyfriend Guy, and asked *her* to apologize to Kevin.

For the sake of the group.

Well, screw the group. She was not apologizing or swallowing down her feelings. She was tired of… She frowned at her ugly running shoes, the frayed hem of her laundry-day jeans. She couldn't put words to this new frustration.

Boys ruled. Girls followed them around doing whatever they could to gain their attention, including turn on each other. It had been her life, and she'd thrived in that lifetime, that group.

So why didn't that work anymore? When she finally looked up to see where Wes was in the process of dog treat making, she found him staring at her.

He immediately looked back down at the molds full of mixed dog treat batter. Which gave her the strangest sensation of Wes seeing through her a lot better than her friends had Saturday night.

Or you just want someone *to see through you.*

Irritated with herself, she looked down at the list of treats and the little notes she'd made in an effort to think up names. "I could make colorful labels for each bucket. On the computer. You know, if you wanted. I don't—"

"That'd be great." He didn't look at her, but he *sounded* enthusiastic. Maybe since she couldn't throw herself into her social life without wanting to tear her hair out, she'd throw herself into this.

After all, what was the worst thing that would happen if she failed? She let down Wes? *Wes?* He'd either be gruff and mean, or he'd stumble around blushing. He wouldn't be *disappointed*. He wouldn't tell her to feel something she couldn't.

He'd just…probably let her keep working.

"So, creek lunch?" he asked, fixing a piece of foil over the finished pans.

She hopped off the counter, easily moving into the little ritual they'd somehow created in only two weeks of working together.

Wes made the sandwiches. She collected the drinks. He whistled for the dogs, and they'd fall into line as they walked to the barn. Wes let Monster and Franco out, and Cara had gotten to the point where she filled water dishes while Wes refilled food for the sheep and the cats.

Silence had never been her favorite thing. Part of the reason she'd loved going to Grandma's as a kid was the constant drone of AM radio, the way the static crackled when the weather changed. In the woods, the rare times she wanted to be alone, she could get lost in the sound of insects, the rustle of birds and squirrels, the gurgling water along the creek. It wasn't silent, and she was alone.

Silence with another person? She didn't believe in it. But, aside from a random dog bark, or a bleat of Shrimp the sheep, this place was a lot of silence, and this thing she'd always thought she'd hated wasn't so bad here.

Or maybe, the things in her life were making silence seem not nearly as bad as they once had.

They hiked down to his bench of a big slab of rock, and they settled in with their lunches. Ever since that first day, she badgered him with one question. Something personal, that irritated him, but if she limited it to one, he gave in. He let a little piece of himself slip. She found herself collecting those little morsels of information, stitching them together so she could understand the man next to her.

He'd wanted to be a veterinarian. He'd joined the army because he couldn't afford the college he wanted to attend. They were big things that told her a lot about his life, but for some reason it felt as if...it was all surface stuff. It explained bits and pieces of his life, but it didn't explain *him*. Any more than her desire to make pies might tell him anything really about her, even though it was...a huge part of her.

That you're ignoring.

She wanted nothing to do with that thought, or even with trying to figure Wes out. Today, she had no question, no real desire to ruffle him. He was being nice-ish, and she was too mired in self-pity to...

Oh, hell, there really was something wrong with her, wasn't there? She hadn't felt like getting dressed or putting on makeup or looking in any way presentable this morning. She didn't want to mess with Wes. She'd told her best friend to leave her alone. This might actually be a...problem.

"So, what's your deal?"

She turned her gaze to Wes, surprised he was breaking the silence with anything—let alone a question that pried into her business. "My deal?"

He shrugged, dropping his gaze from hers. "You're weird today."

She blinked at him, but he stared at his sandwich and ignored the fact she was staring at him. "*I'm* weird?"

"Today." He looked up, most of his gaze hidden by unruly hair, but she could feel the weight of it. How did he…do that? She didn't understand him, and that naturally curious part of her that had once stuck a utensil in an outlet as a child, that walked outside during tornado warnings and occasionally badgered the wrong person into an outburst, found him fascinating. Even when she didn't want to.

"What is wrong with you today?" he repeated, that weighted gaze still on her, the curiosity in her chest winding around some other feeling that wasn't quite so familiar. It reminded her of sexual tension, but there was something *more* to it than that. This wasn't just a will-he-or-won't-he-ever-make-a-move feeling.

It was a heavy, beating thing, a sense of being magnetized, drawn in, stuck, and the result was both frightening and exhilarating. Actually, a lot like being outside when the sky turned green and the trees bent to the ground and the air was charged with danger.

Electricity.

The powerful knowledge something was going to blow through and leave everything changed.

Okay, yeah, there *was* something wrong with her today. She didn't have any idea how she'd ever express it to him.

She blew out a breath, trying to blow the

tension—sexual and otherwise—out with it. This was just lunch with her boss, not tornadoes and lust.

Okay, mostly not lust. She wouldn't soon forget the look of that chest or those abs or the absolute male perfection of Wes without a shirt. The way a few stray water droplets had clung to the ends of his beard and hair, and one had traveled the delicious path from collarbone to waistband. A much happier thought than *you're weird today.*

She was, though. Her life didn't…fit her anymore.

"Have you ever felt like—" she toed a dent in the rock with her shoe "—you've woken up in…a different place than you went to sleep in? Figuratively. Like…one day your life was fine and happy, and the next day everything's all…wrong. Too small or too big or…something."

He was quiet for a few humming moments. Humming moments where she felt like an idiot for voicing her stupid feelings. Hadn't she learned a long time ago to keep the deep ones way, way undercover where they couldn't make her worthy of anyone's…disappointment?

"Well, I have been blown up by a bomb, so in a manner of speaking…"

A laugh was wrong, and yet she laughed. Because, of course. She was talking about… stupidity, and he'd had real problems. Real blown-up-by-an-*actual*-bomb problems. "I was being metaphorical. But your literal wins. Congrats."

"I'm not trying to win." He cleared his throat, collecting her trash with what she was sure was an unplanned brushing of hands. Unplanned because he jerked his hand away as if she burned him. Oddly, she felt the heat, too.

She'd never much believed in…this kind of potency of attraction before. Usually she could find enough about a guy to like to find him attractive. It didn't have to be physical, it didn't have to be feelings, they just had to have something that made her feel good, and voilà, Cara would drop her pants for something else that felt good.

But this…energy between her and Wes was not like that. It was something beyond her control. Unless this was all part of her life no longer fitting the way it once had. "But it did mean I woke up, and things were different and it's a hard row to hoe to get back to where it felt like…life. Same as adjusting from military to civilian life. And starting a business and—"

"Okay, you can stop with how much harder your life is. I get it. I always get it. I had nice if crazy parents who stayed married. We struggled without being poor. My life is pleasant and easy, and my failures are all on my shoulders, and I should just…" She snapped her mouth shut because she realized she was saying a lot more than she meant to.

Way more than anything that Wes, of all people, would want her vomiting at his feet. "Wait. Did you just badger me into sharing something about myself?"

He stood to his full height. "I don't badger."

"You do. Just in a different way. It's sneaky. Hidden underneath beard and hair. But it's badgering, nonetheless. You just got me to spill my beans. I demand a reward." Because when she was off-kilter and spewing her guts—not that *that* ever happened—she would regain even ground and the upper hand by throwing in what she did know how to control.

Sex appeal.

"A…reward," he repeated, because, no, she certainly hadn't hidden her intent in the way the word had rolled off her tongue.

Cara wasn't known for her subtlety. *Easy, Cara.* Maybe she was sick of being easy. Maybe she wanted to be *difficult*. Her parents had thought she was, but they'd long since given up on changing that.

Everyone had given up on her being more than a flaky party girl. So. She was going to do what *she* wanted.

"Come on." She pulled off her shoes, then her

socks and stuffed them into her shoes. Screw work and impulse control. She was going to splash in the damn stream.

CHAPTER NINE

Wes...did not know what was happening. Maybe the world had spun off its axis, and this was an alternate universe where he asked people how they were doing and felt compelled to take his shoes off and follow Cara into a creek.

Because this was not...him. In the least. He didn't do impulsive things, and he didn't...ask women about...things. Without even *stuttering*.

And he most certainly didn't allow himself to think about what kind of *rewards* she might be looking for.

Figure of speech. Move along, idiot.

"Come on, Wes. Live a little."

He'd lived plenty, and he meant to say that, too. Except somehow his fingers were at the laces of his boots. What was the harm of walking through the creek with her?

He couldn't embarrass himself here. If he kept his mouth shut, his responses grumpy at best, they'd have a nice little walk, and that was it. There was something nice about these lunch breaks with her.

He didn't have a lot of *nice* interaction. Surely he could handle this. Cara made it a lot simpler than most people, even when she complicated things.

Before he knew it, his shoes were off. Because Cara was *splashing* like a kid in the creek, and the dogs were yapping around her—Monster and Flash enjoying the water, the rest of the dogs barking restlessly from the banks.

Franco jumped in as if he couldn't stand to be parted from his partner in crime, and Wes took a step toward the bank—feeling much the same. She was like those sea creatures that lured sailors to their deaths.

"Why are we doing this?"

She grinned, and though she wasn't wearing any color, that smile somehow brightened everything around her and reflected in her eyes. "Why not, Wes? Why. Not?" She crossed to the bank he was standing on, grabbed his hands and tugged.

He could have stayed where he was. But…he found himself being pulled.

He made a not quite manly sound as his feet sank into the cold water, and she laughed. The cloud that she'd been shrouding herself in seemed to have lifted. She was smiling and bright again.

He wanted to say something about not thinking his problems were worse, necessarily. They *were*, truthfully, but it didn't mean she couldn't have the same feelings. He wanted to find some way to explain that.

But words were not his strong suit.

She hopped up on a fallen log, holding her arms out as if she were walking a balance beam. The sun filtered through the trees, teased out the red in her hair, and she glowed.

Whatever had been bothering her was washed away by fresh air or fresh water or both.

He'd felt that before. Not quite as joyously or effervescently as Cara, but it was amazing what a walk in the woods could do for a heavy soul.

He was drawn to it and her, and his mind didn't even have the decency to kick on and be scared— none of the usual insecurity, none of those old voices. He just…moved toward her. Until he was close enough to her his knees brushed soggy bark off the log she stood on.

Putting him eye level with her chest when she turned to face him, and only a few inches away. The normal boss-to-employee space ratio was much…wider.

He shaded his eyes against the sun and looked up to find her gaze on him, something considering in the angle of her cocked head.

She slid off the log, so now they were legitimately too close. Her toes were on top of his. Their thighs touched, her chest was most definitely pressed to his, and her mouth was right there.

His heart thudded heavily in his chest, and his throat seemed to close. The brain that had been pleasantly unaffected before went into its normal hyperdrive. *Idiot. Loser. Weirdo.* He tried to find some center of calm. So they were close? She didn't mean anything by it. He wasn't going to panic. Something about being around Cara was… not as bad as it was with other people.

What is wrong with you?

No. This was fine. Because he was just…beyond it. Women weren't ever going to be a thing for him. He didn't need to freak out, because there was no possibility here.

It was all an accident, he decided. He managed to clear his throat and forced himself to speak. "I don't know…what you want from me." He wasn't sure he'd ever admitted that aloud to anyone before, even though it was always in the back of his mind. What did the person he was talking to want him to be?

If he could only find out, then he wouldn't have to be afraid of ridicule or sympathy or need. That's why the army had worked. Why couldn't Cara be like the army?

Was it his imagination her mouth was getting closer?

"You could kiss me."

Any of the dazzle or sparkle, or whatever it was that emanated off her, dimmed, disappeared.

The magnet that had kept him from moving away from her lost its strength. This was outside the safe zone, and as much as he'd like not to make everything inside him seize up, even Cara didn't have that kind of magic.

For a second he thought she might. He cleared his throat again, taking a careful step away. "I cannot kiss you." Look at him being all firm and decisive. Not a stumble of words.

This was progress. Growth. So why did it feel like the same old running away shit?

"Why not?"

"Because." His steps away weren't careful anymore, because the panic was building. It was becoming that bigger thing he couldn't control, and since he hadn't kissed her, he was damn well not going to let the panic win. He stalked to the rock and his socks and boots.

But she followed. "Married?" she asked, still so...light and easy and wonderful. *Not for you. Light and easy and wonderful will never be for you.*

"No." His head pounded. His heart pounded. Everything in him was on a narrow path to panic. Talking to her, working with her, it might not make him have all those old feelings, but the thought of kissing her did.

He'd do it wrong.

She would laugh. Or, barring that, she would

pity him, which was equally as bad. Laughing made him want to disappear, and pity made him want to rage.

No, he couldn't kiss her. Whatever Cara thought of him was some false impression. The mask of grumpy, bearded man. It worked on the surface, but it didn't work when you added *this* to the mix. He laced his boots with extra force.

He couldn't do it.

"You're heartbroken and in love with someone else? Although, really, you could still kiss me. I hear I'm good for that kind of—"

"No, Cara. No. I can't."

She smiled. "You can't kiss me. So, technically speaking, I could kiss you."

Don't look at her.

"You don't want to do that. Trust me." He grabbed the little bag of trash and whistled for the dogs. "Forget it. L-let it go." Hey, only one stutter. An accomplishment.

See? He was getting better. He might never have sex with a woman, but at least he'd learned how to extricate himself from meltdown embarrassment *before* it happened.

Gold star for him. Goody.

CARA SLOWLY LACED her shoes, double-checked to make sure there hadn't been any trash left behind. Mostly she was giving Wes some space, and herself some space, at that.

It certainly wasn't the first time she'd been the one to initiate a flirtation with a guy and suggested a kiss, but it *was* the first time she'd been rejected.

She wasn't oblivious enough to think this had something to do with her. *I can't.* He hadn't rejected the idea there was attraction buzzing between them. He hadn't stepped away when she'd first dropped from the log to all but press against him.

No, some part of him had wanted that. Whatever thing kept him from *taking* it had little to nothing to do with her.

She blew out a breath and took her time walking back to the cabin. She'd had a brief flash of… peace. Her life not fitting her didn't matter, because she was splashing in a creek with dogs and Wes, and he had looked at her like…

Even with him long gone, the feeling swept over her again. Like she was the center of something good and useful. Like she wasn't just *easy* Cara, but elemental. Important.

She stopped in the middle of the expansive yard around Wes's little cabin. She had *never* felt that before. Not even when she was helping Mia. This wasn't help, it was…

What does it matter? The man won't—can't
kiss you.

And she wasn't in a good space for that kind of
thing, anyway. Moping around in her ugly clothes
and laying all sorts of extra baggage on a guy
who had way bigger baggage. Way, way bigger.

So.

So?

There was nothing to do but go inside, get her
work done and stop this *feelings* nonsense. Sure,
it might be irresistibly amazing in the present,
but it was sure to only bring pain and hurt in
the future. Bracing herself, she walked casually
back into the cabin. Wes stood over his treats on
the counter, focusing on getting them into the
oven. She gave Phantom a pat as she passed, but
she didn't say anything to Wes. Best they pretended these moments that transpired between
them didn't exist.

Best she leave it alone. What else could she
do? Push? Fail? Be same old Cara? No, and Mia
or Wes pushing her into pushing was…done. Because she was left with this feeling that her life
didn't fit. She needed to go back to skating by.

She reentered the office section, which was
looking decidedly less like a disaster, though not
completely fixed. She still had work to do, and this
was work she *could* do. Organizing and naming

silly dog treats. This did not require any special… thing she couldn't be.

She threw herself into it wholeheartedly. So much so, she didn't even notice when the room glowed orange.

"Cara."

She started, looking up to Wes looming in the doorway, scowling.

"It's five-thirty," he offered.

"Oh." She glanced around, realized the room was glowing from the sun setting outside the window. "I…lost track of time."

"I can see that. I think you've worked miracles."

"Organizing isn't a miracle."

"It is for some of us."

You aren't doing this again. He can look at you like that for hours, but you aren't going to throw yourself at him. Because you have some self-respect. Oh, if only her heart and her brain could get on the same damn page. Always the problem. Her brain did have sense, but her heart always hoped, always ended up hurt and she always struggled to patch it back together. She had no fortitude.

She had to get out of here. "I'll be a half-hour late on Wednesday, then."

He inclined his chin, some half approximation of a nod.

She began to collect her things, glanced at the calendar she'd made up for him. She tapped Tuesday with her finger, not wanting him to forget. "Good luck at your doctor's appointment tomorrow."

It was silly to think the room's temperature dropped a degree, but she supposed if he *could* control that, he would. And freezing her out would be exactly what he'd do.

Still, she thought of him calling himself malfunctioning, and she couldn't quite be blasé about it.

"If you need anything—"

"I won't."

She shook her head. What a lie. Of course he needed something, someone, but she had the presence of mind to know that the something, the someone was not *her.*

"I'll see you Wednesday." She clipped on Sweetness's leash, grabbed her bag and made sure to make eye contact as she offered him a friendly smile. She would not let the moment at the creek make things *weird.*

"Thank you," he said, his voice barely above a grumble. "For your work."

She quirked an eyebrow, very much *doubtful* that's what he was thanking her for. But, if that's how things were going to be, well, that's how things were going to be. She was not going to make any more mistakes with him.

She sure as hell hoped.

CHAPTER TEN

WES HAD TO focus to not grind his teeth as the doctor explained the procedure. Another damn surgery.

"It's not terribly invasive, but it will decrease your mobility for a bit. It could alleviate the worst of the symptoms, though."

The worst of the symptoms. Could *alleviate.* Not words he wanted to hear. He wanted to hear *fixed* and *good as new* and *normal.*

"Here's your paperwork. You'll want to call to schedule soon. Since it's not a pressing issue, the wait time can be months out."

"Fantastic." He clutched the paperwork and stood, the pain of a headache digging deeper, sharper. "I'm running late for an appointment. I need to go." He gestured at the door.

The pretty doctor looked at him sympathetically, nodding. "Of course."

He turned away, so tired of pitying nods and looks today he could... Well, that was the problem. He didn't know what to do.

Except go home. Go home far away from pity

and concern and bad news. Even when he was
screwing things up with Cara, there wasn't *pity*.

But Cara wasn't there. The only thing that
waited were animals and... Mom's call. His gut
clenched. No. He couldn't deal with that tonight.

He left the doctor's office, making sure to avoid
the hospital section. The migraine sliced behind
his right eye, but he forced himself to focus on
his phone and type a text to Mom.

Not going to be home till late. Will talk next week.

He walked to his truck, and as he reached for
the handle, a sharp pain shot down his arm. He
cocked his good arm as if to punch the truck.
Maybe kick it. Maybe beat it till he was bloody,
but a little old lady with a walker was shuffling
past him.

So, he took a deep breath and opened the
door and hefted himself into the driver's seat.
He grabbed the bottle of aspirin off the console
and the lukewarm bottle of water from the cup
holder. It wouldn't kill the migraine or end the
arm pain, but it would dull everything enough
to get home.

He glanced at his phone and saw the little icon
that showed Mom was typing a response. The
weight of the lie was nothing new. He couldn't

remember a time where he hadn't had to tell lies. *No, I'm not hungry. No, school is fine.*

I don't need help.

He rested his forehead on the steering wheel and tried to fight off the memories, but they were all there. As a kid, he'd tried to find a way not to get bullied, so at least that wouldn't be a lie. He'd tried to find somewhere to belong. But as the poorest kid in school, riddled with anxiety, he'd been such an easy target.

The lie to Cara was so similar. Trying to spare her feelings, because he'd only ever hurt his mother's. Even when he'd tried so hard to avoid it.

Wes sat up straight and maneuvered out of the hospital parking lot. His head hurt, and he was nauseous. He needed something to eat. He didn't handle all those old memories as well on an empty stomach. He'd been anxious all day about the appointment and had barely forced down a bowl of cereal this morning. That was practically eight hours ago.

He didn't feel like cooking or going to a drive-through, but real restaurants meant sitting down surrounded by *normal* people with *normal* functioning parts. Maybe he could pick up some carryout from Moonrise. Might take him enough time so he wouldn't feel 100 percent guilty about missing Mom's call. And it would help with the headache, too.

His phone chimed, but he ignored it as he drove from the sprawling suburban city of Millertown back toward New Benton's tiny epicenter. Moonrise was an old diner frequented by locals. Usually he avoided it, but they had the best hamburgers around, so once every few months he'd stop in for some carryout.

Waiting with his head down and phone out usually kept anyone from talking to him. Besides, if he didn't deserve a decent meal today, what day did he? And if he didn't get a hold of his swirling emotions before he got home, he'd lose it altogether. He pulled the truck into a spot at Moonrise. It was early enough the dinner crowd wasn't overwhelming. Wes pushed into Park and finally looked at his phone and the message from Mom.

Sure, honey. Plans with friends?

Wes walked into the diner. Well, he was going to take the food home and eat on the porch with the dogs, so, *yes*?

That would be lying to your mother. Dick move. He stepped up to the counter and ordered the same meal he'd always gotten at Moonrise. A double cheeseburger and fries. It still felt like a luxury, all these years later. Going out to eat. Having the money to pay for whatever he wanted, not just something off the McDonald's dollar menu on a special occasion.

He tried to focus on that, that they'd both come a long way from a birthday meal of French fries. There was accomplishment in that, there should be *pride* in that.

He glanced at his phone again, trying to determine how to answer Mom. But then someone called his name. He glanced up at Cara grinning and waving at him from a seat at the far end of the counter.

Cara. Was she…everywhere? He should turn around and walk away. Pretend he hadn't seen her, but the thing he *should* do around her never seemed to happen until he was forced into it.

Still, he'd use her to make his lie the truth. Stiffly moving toward her, he typed the message into his phone. Yup. Dinner with friends.

"Hey," Cara greeted him as if yesterday's… moment had never happened. "I didn't know you ever left your hermitage."

"I don't. Usually."

She glanced down at his arm, presumably because she remembered it was doctor's appointment day. That she'd offered her help and he'd shut her down.

"Sit down." She patted the chair next to her. "Eat with me. I was keeping Mallory company before the dinner rush." She gestured to the waitress behind the counter.

"I ordered some to take home. The dogs have been shut up for too long."

"Oh, right." She looked down at his arm again. A brief glance before she seemed to catch herself. "Anyway—"

"Wes? Wes Stone?"

He didn't recognize the voice, but as soon as he looked at the woman approaching, the pain in his head that had dulled to a tolerable ache went full-throttle throb.

"It's me. Liz? Liz Fetter."

Yeah, he knew who she was. Did she honestly think he'd forget? The initial domino flick in a lifetime of little disasters.

"How are you?" She touched his arm, and before he could temper his reaction, he jerked it away. This woman he hadn't seen in years was touching him, and it took him back to a person and a place he never wanted to be. To those things he thought he'd never have to be again.

She blinked in surprise, then that look he knew so well claimed her expression. Pity. "I had so hoped you were doing...well." She made a little *tsk* noise. "I heard about your time in Afghanistan and—"

"I have to go," he muttered to Cara. Not to Liz.

He could give a flying monkey about Liz Fetter and what she thought of his time in Afghanistan.

Food forgotten, he pushed out of the diner. He felt sick to his stomach now, anyway. Beyond hunger. It was the migraine. Not memories. Not *her*.

He squeezed his eyes shut against the old voices, the old laughter. Sure, he should be over it by now, but he wasn't. He'd only kept it away by hiding from it.

The pain in his skull was slicing away at him until he could barely walk, let alone drive. He couldn't get his hand to open the truck door.

I'd so hoped you were doing well.

"My ass," he muttered through gritted teeth. He had to get out of here.

CARA STARED OPENMOUTHED as the door swung shut behind Wes, then she glanced back at Liz Fetter. She generally kept her opinions about Liz to herself because it wasn't any of her business, but after seeing Wes's reaction…

"Still a bitch, I see," Cara said sweetly. Someone needed to stand up for the poor guy.

Liz's head snapped back. "Excuse me?"

"Remember making my sister cry her freshman year of high school? Bitch city."

Liz's horrified surprise morphed into a sneer.

"I don't know where you get off talking to me like—"

"Hey, Mal? Can you pack up my food to go and put that guy's order on my bill? I'll be right back to pay and pick them up."

"Sure thing, Cara."

While Liz sputtered behind her, Cara ignored her and rushed out to where Wes had gone. Luckily, he was still there, leaning against his truck, forehead pressed into his good arm above his head.

He was tense and looked to be in pain. She didn't know what Liz had ever done to him, but, considering the way Liz had bullied Mia, Cara wouldn't be surprised by anything. Cara figured Wes hadn't had it much better than her sister. He'd possibly had it worse, judging from how he'd acted.

She slowed her approach. Not sure what to say. Her normal response to real pain was a joke, and that seemed so wrong right now. Why had she thought to come after him? As if she could do anything.

Well, she was here now. She had to *try.* "Wes."

"Go away, Cara."

"You don't want to forget your food."

"I want to forget every second of this day."

His doctor's appointment couldn't have gone well, then. "Will you let me help? Please." Usually her kind of help was of the take-the-sad-party-out-drinking variety, but what she really wanted to do with Wes was wrap him up in a hug and tell him it was okay. Which he would reject. Wholly.

"You wanna drive me home?"

His question came out of nowhere, enough her mouth dropped open. He was *accepting* help? Oh, jeez, this was really bad. Really, really bad. But how could she say no?

"Sure. I can drive you home, no prob." Which actually made her nervous. Chances were she'd screw this up, but what other choice did she—or he—have? He didn't seem to have much of anyone in his life. At least anyone human.

"Do you…" He dropped his arm and slowly turned to face her before he cleared his throat. He didn't make eye contact, but he pushed his shoulders back. Any pain morphed into something else. As if he was deciding to do something. Something important.

She waited…holding her breath.

"Do you want to stay and eat your dinner with me?"

Her breath whooshed out. She wasn't sure if there was more to what he was asking, but she couldn't say *no*. Or ask him what he meant. Not in his current state. "O-okay." He still wasn't looking at her, but his voice had been all intense. "We'd have to swing by my place and get Sweetness."

"All right."

"Here." She pulled out her keys and pointed to her car a few spaces down. "Make yourself comfortable, and I'll grab the food."

He shook his head, pulling out his wallet, then shoving some dollar bills at her.

"No, I can—"

"I'm buying you dinner," he said firmly, in a voice that she wouldn't have argued with even if he didn't seem as if he was halfway to a mental breakdown. When his gaze finally met hers, she could only nod.

Yeah. Fierce, determined.

Hot.

Shh, brain.

She hurried back into the diner, and Mallory pointed to a bag of food by the cash register. Gary rang her up, and when he handed over her change and she turned to go, there was Liz again. All pinched and evil looking.

"I have one thing to say to you, Cara Pruitt. At least I'm not the town slut."

She looked so pleased with herself for the insult that, even though it cut a little bit, Cara would *not* give her the satisfaction. "Yes, you're right. I spread love, not hate. Ask your boyfriend." The parting line was too perfect not to use. She left, head held high. When she hopped into the driver's seat of her car, she plopped the bag of food in Wes's lap.

"I don't know why you hate her, but she's nothing but a bully. Always has been. She used to make fun of my sister till she cried. For weeks on end."

"Sounds about right."

"Did you... How do you..."

"I don't want to talk about it right now."

"Oh, sure. Yeah." She pushed her car into Reverse. Well, her plan for a distracting dinner at Moonrise had certainly come to an abrupt halt. But, she was...glad she'd been there. Glad he could have someone, even if it was her. Maybe she knew enough to be the kind of person he would need for a brief few hours.

Please, God, let that be true. "So. You know, we can eat at my place. Food will probably be cold by the time we get all the way out to yours."

"I need to let the dogs out." He scrubbed his hands over his face and let out a mile-long string of curses.

"Are you okay?"

"I think it's pretty well established that I'm not."

She hesitated and then decided it was best if she asked, if she was honest and straightforward. "Are you crying?"

"No." He dropped his hands from his face, and

his denial looked to be true. "Although I wouldn't put it past me."

She pulled up to her apartment complex. "This is me. I'll grab Sweetness. Maybe a pie, and I'll be right out. Unless…unless you want to come inside and help me?"

He looked up at the doors to the complex, then shrugged. "Eh, why not?"

WES FOLLOWED CARA into her apartment. He wanted to go home, but he'd been curious enough about what her place might look like that he could put it off for another few minutes. He wanted to see what it was like to be normal and happy.

He wanted to see what her life looked like when it wasn't skulking around the edges of his, and mostly he wanted to see her. To understand *her*. Why she kept showing up, why she gave him the sense that he could rise above…

I had so hoped you were doing well.

She jiggled her key into the lock, then pushed inside. Sweetness greeted them both with yips, jumps and spins.

"Aw!" Cara bent down and snuggled the white ball of fur. "A dog's greeting when you get home is certainly an ego boost."

In an easy movement he didn't want to be jealous of, she stood and hefted Sweetness with her.

"There are a couple pies in the freezer. They're labeled, so pick a flavor. Be right back."

She disappeared down the dark hallway, and he moved into the tiny kitchen. Pie tins hung in a scattered pattern above the sink. Pictures littered the refrigerator. Mostly of Cara and her sisters. Cara at bars with smiling, probably drunk, groups of the same people over and over.

A menagerie of fun and freedom and all things he'd never had.

He wrenched the freezer open and pulled out the first pie he came into contact with. He was done being morbid. Done feeling sorry for himself.

Liz so hoped he was doing well? Well, he was. He was doing fantastic. He was going to go back to his house and have dinner with a gorgeous woman and not fall all over himself like an idiot because he didn't do that with Cara. Sometimes he was too harsh and sometimes he stuttered, but he functioned.

He'd *told* her he couldn't kiss her, hadn't he? That wasn't panic or stuttering or falling apart. He was in charge of himself. Maybe he needed surgery, maybe his health was a joke, but him? He was functioning just fine and dandy, thank you, Liz Fetter.

Cara didn't laugh at him. She wasn't *using* him.

So…he was going to do something. He was going to *prove* something. Somehow.

Cara returned with a big purse on one arm and Sweetness still in the other. "All right. Ready?"

He nodded. A row of bottles in her pantry caught his eye. A bottle of whiskey, partially empty. He didn't keep alcohol at his place except for the occasional six-pack of beer. No point in having bottles of the stuff when you never entertained or had people over, and he still hadn't gotten used to having the kind of money to spend on something as frivolous as a bottle of booze. "Are you saving this for a special occasion?"

"Um, no."

"Wanna bring it?" Liquor might help. Couldn't hurt. He didn't think.

Her eyebrows shot up, but the nicest thing about Cara was she didn't press. Sometimes she'd ask an unwanted question, one time, yes, she had *pressed* her body to his, but she didn't pressure him to answer, pressure him to move forward. Didn't keep at him or look hurt if he didn't answer. She let it go. He'd said he couldn't, and she'd pretended as if nothing had happened.

She shrugged and said, "Sure."

He grabbed the bottle and followed her out the door and back to her beat-up little car. He had no idea what he was doing, but he'd figure it out once he got home. On his own turf.

CHAPTER ELEVEN

CARA DROVE HER Camry over the bumpy path of Wes's drive. Sweetness yipped happily in Wes's lap. The sun was setting behind the trees that surrounded Wes's cabin.

It was all very weird. Which seemed to be the theme of her life, since Wes had crashed into it. Or vice versa. Or something. Why couldn't she know what to do? With him? With everything?

She rolled to a stop, shifting into Park, and Wes and Sweetness were out of the car without a word.

This was not about her. This was about him. Obviously his doctor's appointment had been bad, and the run-in with Liz had made him...angry. She wasn't quite sure what to do with angry Wes, but...maybe she could figure it out.

Feeling more than a little uncertain, Cara grabbed the food—and the whiskey—and followed Wes to the barn out back.

He shoved open the door, and Sweetness yelped and danced as Wes's dogs rushed out to greet him and her. Even though she was feeling uncertain, she couldn't help but smile. No wonder he surrounded himself with animals.

"All right, all right. Calm it down." He pushed through the tail-wagging throng and into the barn. She stood, arms full of stuff, while Wes checked bowls and petted cats and Shrimp.

He walked back to her, taking the bag of food and looping it on his arm. "Just need to put Monster and Franco out on their lines."

She nodded, watching as he did so. Then he whistled, and the other dogs fell into line behind him, including Sweetness.

Cara felt compelled to get in line, too, but instead she walked next to him. In silence. Heavy, awkward silence.

He unlocked the door, pushed it open, then gestured her inside. He turned to the dogs standing expectantly on the porch.

"Stay," he instructed.

The dogs wagged their tails and obeyed the command, and Cara felt herself obeying it, too, standing perfectly still in the kitchen as he dropped the bag of food on the counter. She watched while he grabbed a handful of treats from a bin by the door and tossed one to each dog.

Then he turned to her, Mr. Fierce-and-Determined once more. Mr. Oh-Please-Get-In-My-Pants. *Do not think like that, Cara Pruitt.*

*This is an injured, broken man, and you have
no business trying to heal him.*

Oh, but she wanted to, and that was a shock.
She hadn't realized that's what that feeling was.
Wanting to help. *Wanting* to heal. So much so that
it blossomed through all her usual determinations
to hide from the hard.

"I'm not an invalid," he said, bursting her from
her reverie.

She frowned. "Have I ever said that?"

"No, you haven't." He took a step toward her,
a halting, uncertain step—but a step nonetheless.
There was something about the way he was looking at her, something…different. As if…

"My life is just fine," he said with another odd,
resolute step toward her. "*I* am fine and doing
well. Really damn well."

"Oh, this is about what she sa—"

His last step put them standing much as they
were at the creek. Yesterday. When he'd said he
couldn't and stomped away.

But he was staring at her now, and she had to
swallow. She should…look away. Remind him
that he…couldn't. She should remind him that
he'd said that. And she would remind him. Once
she could catch a breath through the heavy beating of something against her chest, squeezing out
all the space for her lungs.

"I *am* well," he repeated in something little

more than a whisper, a *determined* whisper, but a whisper. Then he swallowed, straightened his shoulders. "Well enough to—" And then he kissed her. Totally out of the blue. He grabbed her face, not all that gently or with any kind of finesse, and his mouth was on hers.

Frustrated angry kissing. At first it was a little strange and not quite smooth. His body shuddered against hers, but once she stepped into it and angled her head a little—oh, yeah, smooth. He was all hard, tense muscle, but his lips were soft in contrast with the beard scratching her chin.

A really nice contrast. And his hands—big palms covering her cheeks, long fingers curling into her hair. It hit all those buttons, the ones that made her skin feel like velvet and her heart feel full and every delicious flipping feeling south of the border.

All she could do was hold on to the sides of his shirt and hope losing clothes was next. That was comforting she knew how to do. If he'd gotten over his "can't" regarding kissing her, maybe she could offer—

But he stepped back, releasing her completely. He ran a surprisingly shaky hand through his shaggy hair, and she had to press a hand to the wall to right herself from being released so quickly.

"Th-that is how f-fine I a-am," he said, pointing to the ground.

"You're stuttering."

He glared. "Well, you're breathing hard."

"It was a really good kiss." And surprising. And over. Boo.

He turned abruptly, grabbing the bag of food. "I'll heat this stuff up." He unceremoniously dumped her food onto a plate and shoved it into the microwave. When it was done, he handed her the plate and nodded to the table, then repeated the process with his own food and took a seat across from her.

She went with it, because what could she do? Demand an explanation? She didn't need one. She knew exactly what had happened. He was trying to prove something to himself, and it hadn't… quite rocked his world the way it had rocked hers.

She swallowed thickly, trying to work up any enthusiasm for her hamburger when she was dealing with the heavy weight of surprise rejection.

After a few ticking minutes of silence and chewing, he opened his mouth. At first no sound came out, and he shook his head. "I'm sorry I k-kissed you like that."

She studied him. Maybe…the step away wasn't rejection after all? Maybe he was simply…bad at this. Huh. "Like what? Like awesomely?"

He blinked at her with his mouth hanging open before he shook his head. "Grabby and without permission."

"I don't want polite kissing. I want that." She pointed to where they'd stood. He might be sending mixed messages, but she didn't think he *meant* to, and more…she wanted to kiss him. She'd wanted to kiss him yesterday, and after that she wanted to kiss him again.

And since kissing and flirting and seducing were the kinds of things she *knew* she was good at, it was easy enough to smile. "Grabby and fierce and *mmm*."

She tried to read his expression. Blushing? Check, but if she wasn't totally reading into the little quirk of his mouth, he was at least a bit pleased with himself.

Which was nice, but where had it all come from? She hated the idea that it might be because of Liz and nothing much to do with *her*. "But you were mad at her. That's why you kissed me." The run-in with Liz had prompted it, but this wasn't simply her being the easiest target.

Right?

He shrugged, focusing on his sandwich. "So to speak."

She swallowed away the disappointment. Why should she be disappointed? If he'd wanted to do it, he would have done it yesterday. Not given her *can'ts*. So, she'd focused on what had happened. Liz and the doctor, not…the little kiss he had to get out of his system. "You two dated?"

"We sort of went on a date. I guess. It was high school."

"So…"

"Let's open up that whiskey." He pushed back from the table and grabbed the bottle and two glasses, then plucked two cans of Coke from the fridge.

She studied the bottle he slapped on the table. Well, honestly, if Wes didn't deserve to get a little drunk to deal with all his issues, no one did. "Doctor appointment didn't go well?" She wanted to reach out and touch him, but everything inside of her was…confused. He was confusing her, and…she'd keep some kind of platonic distance.

Maybe.

He grunted and poured a generous splash of whiskey into his glass before adding some of the soda.

"So…"

He shrugged. "You want some?"

Cara nodded, and he repeated the process with her glass. Honestly, if she didn't feel so bad for him, she'd probably think he was a giant jerk. But he was so wounded under all that jerk. Maybe it had been a while since he'd been with a woman if his hermit ways were any indication. "Are you going to get drunk and *then* tell me all your deep, dark secrets?"

"No." His expression was dark, unreadable. "Are you?"

Only pride kept her from leaning away from that look, kept her from dropping her gaze from that…really intimidating question. "I don't have any secrets."

"Everyone has secrets. Or at least things they don't want anyone else to know."

"I'll show you mine if you show me yours." She grinned, but he only stared. Stared as if he could see her secrets, *whatever* they were, without her even spilling them.

Okay, so, coming here might not have been her best choice.

"How about this. Truth or dare?"

Two drinks in and Wes was relaxed but not drunk or stupid. "No."

Cara pouted. A sexy, enticing pout. *It was a really good kiss.* Yeah, as relaxed as he felt, it was not good to think about that. To wonder if he could do it again. Without stepping away, without stuttering. He'd never done anything like that before. Apparently, driven by anger, he could do anything.

Dangerous line of thinking, considering she was in his house. Alone with him. *Not* for work.

"You have to play," she whined, finishing off the last of her drink.

"No. It's my house. My rules. And I'm the boss." Also a dangerous line of thinking. Because this might be his house and his rules, but he knew he wasn't in charge of this. Whatever was happening.

"Ah, but it's my whiskey." She pulled the bottle to her side of the table, grinning.

"I've had enough," he said with an easy shrug. How had he not tried this before? Everything seemed easy with a little bit of whiskey under his belt. He could stare at her and shrug and pretend he hadn't kissed a woman for the first time in two years. The first time since high school he'd done so without therapy directly beforehand.

He'd kissed *this* woman. This beautiful, confusing, wonderful woman whom he should tell to get out. He was fine. He should open his mouth and tell her to go home. He was fine. Really. He'd drink away his anger at Liz, and she didn't need to be around for that.

"And it's my pie." She hugged the pie pan to her chest.

He looked at the remnants of his first piece on the plate. She made really good pie, and something about the combination of liquor and sugar was drugging him into some sense of normalcy. "Damn. I really want some more of your pie."

She giggled and he blushed. Because, yeah, whiskey wasn't a cure-all for everything.

"How about this?" she began, still holding the pie and whiskey. "In my version of truth or dare, you get to choose knowing what both choices are. I set out the dare and the truth and you get to pick. And if you play, you get another piece of pie." She held it up, making "mmm" noises that did *not* make him think about eating.

"What are they?"

"What?"

"The truth. The dare. I'm not agreeing to play. Yet. I want to hear what they are."

She set the pie down and clapped. "Yay! Okay. Truth. What happened with Evil Liz? Dare—" she tapped her chin, eyeing him "—you take off your shirt."

He choked on his own spit. "What?"

She opened her eyes extra wide. "What?"

"I don't…"

"What's your best option, sweetheart?"

He thought about Liz's *tsks*. He thought about Cara kissing him. No, him kissing her. He had definitely kissed her, and she'd kissed him back and thought it was awesome. Her words. He thought about all the ways he *hadn't* screwed things up tonight. And how telling her what happened with Liz would. And how refusing to play would. Now he wanted to push until something *gave*. He couldn't push his nerve damage. He couldn't drive back to Moonrise and somehow prove to Liz he was a well-adjusted, successful man, and the torment she and her friends had put him through didn't matter.

Partly because it wasn't 100 percent true and partly because how did he prove that? How did he prove his life was good? It was good. He had this job, this house, his dogs.

And Cara, who might be here out of pity but wasn't *acting* as if she pitied him. She didn't look at him like the doctors and the nurses had, certainly nothing like Liz had.

So, he would act. He would *act*. He couldn't prove shit to Liz, but he could prove something to himself. He pulled off his shirt. "Your turn."

Her eyebrows shot up, and much like when he'd opened the door to her shirtless, she didn't try to hide she was staring at his chest. And enjoying it.

Because they were attracted to each other, and he couldn't deny that. It looked as though he couldn't keep pushing it away, either. So, he was going to try. And the voice in the back of his head telling him he was going to go down in flames could shut up.

She leaned forward against the table, which, not that he noticed or anything, kind of pushed her breasts up against the neckline of her shirt and, um…

"So, what's my truth or dare?"

"Uh. Um." This was flirting. He wasn't good at flirting. He wasn't good at women. What was happening?

He finished the last gulp of his drink, taking the moment to rein in the panic. The ancient memory of laughing. It wasn't going to happen here. He was pushing. "Pie first."

She nodded, slicing another piece of pie and maneuvering it onto his plate. He picked up his fork. "O-okay. Truth." He stared down at the pie. *Think of something.* "Why did you get your tattoo? I mean, why a bluebird?" Because of all the things he knew about her, he knew that the bluebird was some symbol to her, and it would give him a clue. A clue to deeper.

You should not push for deeper.

He found he didn't care what he *should* do right in this moment. Not when she smiled at him, an inviting, *sexy* smile.

"And for a dare?"

"You could... You could..." He cleared his throat. Okay, he could do this. "I have no idea." God, he was an idiot.

"No tit for tat?"

He somehow managed to not choke on the bite of pie in his mouth. He somehow managed to swallow despite all the things *tit for tat* brought to mind. "That doesn't seem very gentlemanly."

She wrinkled her nose. "You're an interesting

guy, Wes. I don't know a lot of guys who would pass up the opportunity to get my shirt off."

"I didn't say I was passing it up," he muttered.

"Okay, so what's your dare?"

He shrugged. Whatever control he thought he'd harnessed petered out. It evaporated, because he knew this feeling so well. The complete and utter inability to know what to do next. What was she after? How could he do anything she'd ever expect or want, when he was always going to be the weirdo who couldn't seal the deal?

Sure, he'd been able to afford Cara's dinner tonight, and he'd kissed her without bumping noses or teeth. But that didn't mean he could suddenly ignore the first eighteen years of his life as the butt of everyone's joke. He couldn't forget that even after the army, and therapy, he had tried and failed at this kind of thing.

Yeah, he didn't feel much like playing games anymore. Sitting around with his shirt off like an idiot.

"Well, I pick truth. I got the tattoo after my grandma died. And, oh-em-gee, you should have heard my mother's freak-out. But, see, my grandma had all these bluebird houses on her property, and we'd watch for them in the spring, and, I don't know. She taught me how to make pies and somehow *I* was her favorite. Me. With two perfect, interested-in-farming-and-school sisters, somehow she liked me best."

He glanced up at her and saw she was rubbing her index finger behind her ear where the tattoo was. "It made me feel like she was with me, even though she wasn't." She gave him a sheepish look. "Not a deep, dark secret."

He couldn't believe she'd be surprised someone would like her best. This bright and funny woman sitting across from him, putting him almost at ease. How could she not see herself for what she was? "If it makes you feel better, I don't like anyone, and I tolerate you well enough. And I like you much better than your younger sister, though I suppose I haven't met the older one formally."

She chuckled. "Well, then, you'll never meet her and know how much better she is than me. They both are, really. Smart and successful. They make all the right choices." Somehow her voice managed to sound proud and wistful and sad all in a few sentences.

"You shouldn't be so hard on yourself. School isn't for everyone. And neither is farming, I wouldn't think. You're very smart. Look at my office. If that organization miracle isn't successful, I don't know what is."

She stared at him, an oddly awed expression on her face. For a second, he thought she was going to smile, but then she shook her head, poking at the filling streaks on the bottom of the pie pan. "I still haven't talked to Sam."

"Who's Sam?"

"The guy with the restaurant and the pie needs. He's probably already found someone else. But I can't pull the trigger."

Failing to pull the trigger. Yeah, that sounded familiar.

"Don't yell at me this time. I already know I suck."

"I'm not going to yell at you." When she'd told him about it last time, all he could think was she had a functioning arm to do her dream job and he didn't, but now things felt different.

He had a functional penis, and he wasn't exactly using that. At least not in any way that counted.

"What changed? Last time I hinted I couldn't do what I wanted to do, you said, and I quote, 'try harder.'"

He shrugged, feeling like an ass. Well, nothing new there. "Maybe I get the not-being-able-to-pull-the-trigger thing."

She looked at him. "You know what? We're both kind of pathetic."

"I can't argue with that."

"So, let's make a pact. An un-pathetic-ourselves pact. I'll call Sam." Her eyebrows drew together as if she was already regretting saying it, but then she shook her head. "And you'll do whatever thing you've been holding back on, and we'll keep each other accountable." She held out her hand to shake.

He stared at it.

"Come on. Whatever it is. You want it, right? And you can have it?" He nodded. "Then shake. Because you should get something you want, Wes. You really should. And if I know you'll be all cranky with me, maybe I'll suck it up and get what I want."

He swallowed. She was right. For some baffling reason he thought maybe he could overcome this. Maybe with Cara. Okay, maybe not. But maybe he could try.

The worst that could happen? He failed miserably, she quit and he hid out in his cabin like he already did. Was there something to lose here?

Her.

Well, hell, maybe he should lose her if he couldn't suck it up and stop yo-yoing her all over the place.

"Okay." He shook her hand firmly.

"Yay." She started clearing things off the table, so he got up to help. He was still shirtless. Should he put his shirt back on? Leave it off?

She glanced at the clock, then at her empty glass as she placed it in the sink. "I feel like I should go, but…"

"You can crash on the couch if you need to."

She smiled. "Thanks." Then, with no warning at all, she flung her arms around his neck and gave him a quick peck, right on the mouth. Maybe she did that with everyone. And, well, he had kissed her before. So…

She released him, trailing her fingertips over the ends of his hair. "You need a haircut."

"Yes." Her arms weren't around him, but she was close. Really close. Like see-all-her-eyelashes-and-feel-her-breath-on-his-neck close.

"So, that shaggy look isn't for fashion? Or some anti-military protest?" Her hands were on his chest. Just resting there.

"N-no, it's to avoid chatty hairdressers."

"Ooh, I know!" She hopped back, clapping her hands, and he couldn't help but be a little disappointed, even knowing he should tell her to run in the opposite direction. "I'll cut it. I watched people cut hair for *years*."

"Watched, not did?"

"I can't make it any worse than it already is."

Yeah, she had a point there. But the hair, the beard—it was his thing. The beard hid his scar, and the hair, okay, it wasn't his thing, but cutting it—her cutting it—seemed like a big deal. "You're drunk."

"I'm not *drunk*. I just don't want to risk driving."

He shook his head. "I want the person cutting my hair with *scissors* not to be impaired, either."

"Steady hand wins." She held out her hand, palm parallel with the floor. When he stood there, she nodded at him. "Go on."

He held out his left hand, and while it was steady, this whole thing was idiotic. He should tell her no and go to bed.

"Okay, fine, but leave the beard alone."

She let out a little squeal of delight. "What about a teensy tiny little trim?"

He groaned. He was sunk. She'd put her hands on him, and he'd do whatever she wanted.

And her hands would be on him again, so there was that.

CHAPTER TWELVE

"Scissors." Cara held out her hand, but Wes only shook his head.

"I can't believe I'm letting you do this," he grumbled.

They had wedged one of the kitchen chairs between the vanity and bathtub of his bathroom with just enough room for Cara to get around him. He was still shirtless—*hello*—and she'd draped one of his sad brown bachelor towels around his yummy shoulders.

Man, she had issues, but she had the feeling she might—just might—be helping Wes with his, and that somehow made anything worth it.

But, finally, he slapped the scissors into her palm. "Try not to maim me. I have enough scars."

"Speaking of scars…"

She trailed off because she expected him to do the curt "no" thing, but then he didn't say anything. "Maybe you could tell me now how you got them." She held her breath, not sure why. It wasn't as if he was going to rage at her for asking, but the way he wasn't saying anything was new. It wasn't a shutdown or a refusal.

"If I remember correctly, one of the rules was don't look at or ask about my scars."

"It's not work hours." She knew helping him get over the Liz thing wouldn't be aided by things he didn't want to talk about, but she felt as though she had to know this. Had to understand...something deeper about him to be able to handle this right. God, she hoped.

He made a *humph* sound, and she began to comb his hair. She was cutting his hair. She had somehow offered—insisted—on doing it. She'd blame the alcohol, but it had been a long time since two whiskey and Cokes had ever done much damage.

"I was part of a bomb sniffing dog unit, and we were defusing one when it...well, didn't defuse."

Her hands dropped. "You were *defusing* it?"

"It was Afghanistan. What exactly were you expecting?"

"I don't know." She took a slow, deep breath. She hadn't a clue what to expect, but actually picturing him being knocked flat by a *bomb* he'd been *defusing*. It made her eyes prick with tears. Foolish, stupid tears. She blinked them away, breathing again as she focused on making the first snip to his hair, trying to emulate all the hairdressers she'd watched over the years.

"Anyway, I wasn't actually working on the bomb when it went off. We were clearing the area, so I was far enough away it was mainly the blast knocking me flat. Landed on my hip and arm. Got some shrapnel. *Boom.* Pin in hip. Nerve damage in arm."

He'd been injured by a bomb. There was no way she'd ever be able to say the right thing or do the right thing when it came to that. Especially when, much like in the parking lot tonight, she only wanted to wrap her arms around him and hold on. Somehow hug it all away.

Which she was smart enough to know wasn't possible. So, she kept cutting his hair, hoping he'd continue.

"I have to get surgery again." He said it so quietly she didn't think he'd meant to tell her that.

"I'm sorry, Wes. That sucks." Such a lame response, but what else could she say?

He shrugged.

"Soon? I can help out however you need." She hoped she could help. She could help with business stuff, surely. But hopefully, he wasn't expecting… emotional help. *Unless it's physical comfort.* She closed her eyes for a second. Thinking with her lady parts would not be the best thing to do here, but it was the best thing she knew *how* to do.

"I won't need help." There was that curt refusal she was used to. "I probably won't have it done until the end of the market season. It's not too bad, but I need my arm for market stuff, and it's not pressing." He stared at his hand, the one with the scars on it. "Or a guarantee."

Her heart ached for him. Absolutely hurt. She didn't know what to do with that, with the lump in her throat, or the feelings jostling around in her chest, so she worked silently.

To do the front parts of his hair she had to stand in front of him. Which meant she had to, like, actually look at him and, at times, have her boobs in his face. She would try to be good about it, she really would.

She combed the hair at the peak of his scalp straight up, judging what was the right length, snipping and letting the cut hair fall onto his back and the floor. She worked through the rest of his hair, occasionally sneaking a peek at him.

Always he was completely still, staring at some point beyond her. It made him seem very soldiery. All ramrod straight posture and complete stillness. Although once she did think she caught him staring at her chest. But it was such a quick flick of a glance she almost wondered if it was wishful thinking.

"All right. I may be done." She crouched a little so she could be eye level. Luckily, his hair was thick and wavy, so being perfectly even hadn't been a total necessity. She made a few more snips, her heart rate accelerating when she realized he wasn't staring at some point behind her anymore.

No. He was staring right at her. Intensely, though not frustrated, as he'd been earlier when he'd kissed her. His eyebrows were drawn together in something like confusion.

She swallowed, setting down the scissors on the sink and brushing stray hairs off the side of his face. The fact of the matter was, she liked being close to him. Touching him. Sure, it made her feel all jittery and squirmy, but it was a *good* jittery and squirmy.

She kind of ran her hands over his hair. Okay, there was nothing *kind of* about raking her fingers through his hair. She was totally feeling up his hair. But it was coarse and some pretty color between blond and brown. All different highlights. "I think I did okay."

His head had fallen back, and he looked up at her, her fingers still in his hair. He was handsome under all that shag. How much more handsome might he be if she could see more of his face? A square jaw to go with the sharp nose? A chin with a cleft? Razor-sharp cheekbones?

Would those eyes always look troubled and a little haunted, or was there some joy to be had in his life?

Well, a few drinks, a haircut, a little scalp massage and he actually looked more relaxed than she'd ever seen him. Maybe she could relax him a little more. She shouldn't, she knew. She should keep this friendship hands-off. They were boss and employee, too.

But the man needed something. He needed to be touched, held. He needed to feel something other than painful memories and frustrated dreams, and sex wouldn't cure anything. Not a damn thing, she knew, but it might take his mind off it all for a bit.

So, screw it. She was already almost in his lap, her fingers claiming ownership to his hair, and he was watching her with some internal war she'd never understand going on in his head.

She kissed him. Because she didn't want him to be warring, internally or otherwise. He'd had enough war and getting blown up by bombs. Somehow, someway, she wanted to soothe, and this was the only way she could.

It took him a few seconds to catch up, but when he did, his hands rested on her hips. Almost hesitantly, but, seriously, how had she not noticed before today how *big* his hands were?

She leaned into the space between his legs, tracing his bottom lip with her tongue until his mouth parted. She'd hoped he'd move his hands, feel her up a little, but they remained at her hips.

Which wasn't bad. It was kind of sweet. Not trying to hurry things along. Just enjoying. The contrast between lips and beard, the heat of his palms on her hips, the tentative way his tongue brushed hers. The little catch in her chest when he sighed against her mouth.

She pulled away, just a hair. "*I'm* not sorry for kissing you, by the way."

His head fell back, and those intense eyes studied her. "You might be sorry. Eventually." He said it so earnestly, any of the happy left from the kiss petered out.

She'd never known pity to be a turn-on, and maybe that was it. What she felt wasn't pity. It was more like empathy. She *felt* for him. Wished his burdens were a little lighter.

Well, she couldn't lift any burdens, but she'd always been good at distracting people from their burdens. Alcohol and pie had worked briefly. The last option she knew of was…tempting.

Obviously he'd changed his mind about not being able to kiss her, so maybe…

"You know what you need?" she asked, her fingers finally leaving his hair, trailing over his neck, brushing the remaining strands of hair off along with the towel. She traced his collarbone, then dragged her index finger down the center of his chest.

He didn't make a move to stop her, and he didn't look away. So, she didn't stop. She'd keep going until he wanted to stop. If that meant doing something she'd regret in the morning, well, it wouldn't be the first time.

"What do I need?" he asked hoarsely.

"A little…" She knelt in front of him. Strange, the way her heart hammered in her chest, the way nerves fluttered in her stomach. She'd propositioned a few guys in her day and had long since moved past the part of her sex life where she was jumpy with a guy, but something about Wes made her nervous.

But not nervous enough to stop. He needed this, she couldn't help but think. What better girl to offer? "A little distraction." She brushed the last few pieces of hair off his thighs and then flipped the button of his jeans.

IT WAS AS if he'd been knocked flat by that bomb again. He couldn't move, and there was a buzzing in the air.

She was going to…

He closed his eyes, ordered himself to focus. Maybe if he focused hard enough, he could fight off the panic.

He blinked his eyes open as Cara pulled the zipper of his pants down, the sound echoing in his ears like close-range gunfire.

She was going to touch him. She was going to touch him, and what if it happened again? Sure, Cara hadn't been teasing him all night, but this wasn't out of nowhere, either. She'd had an effect. He was hard, and she had done this before. Often. She'd expect things of him he didn't know how to do and then—*weirdo*. All those voices from years past. Giggling, taunting.

Can't seal the deal. Liz making it all a joke.

Or two years ago, when he'd gone to therapy again and had come out certain he'd been healed. Absolutely ready, because therapy was supposed to solve everything. The woman he'd picked up at the bar had backed away from his panic like someone tiptoeing away from a sleeping child. *What's wrong with you?*

Cara's fingers brushed the waistband of his boxers and... He couldn't do it. He couldn't bear her touch, her sweetness, whatever pity she was enacting. He couldn't *take* it.

Weirdo. Weirdo. Weirdo. What's wrong with you? Who can't keep it together for a few seconds? Some kind of creepy pervert.

He pushed at her shoulders and stood up abruptly. The chair tipped toward the bathtub. Cara knocked into the vanity.

"Ow."

"Oh, no, I h-hurt you? I'm s-so sorry. I'm sorry. I'm sorry." He was losing it. Hurting women and pushing away from something he wanted.

"I'm okay. Wes, are you—"

"I have to go." He couldn't be in this tiny room

anymore. Not with her. The smell of perfume and pie and…

He turned abruptly, tripping over the chair but catching himself against the door frame before he fell completely.

He managed to climb over and get out. In the hallway he sucked in a little breath, but not much of one until he was in his room. Door closed. Safe. Safe.

With Cara still out there. And he'd hurt her. And… He pressed his fingers to his eyes to alleviate the stinging there.

So, he couldn't. Couldn't pull that trigger. Couldn't get over some dumb thing that had happened half a damn lifetime ago. He could kiss a woman, but he couldn't let one proposition him. He was pathetic. And a total dick, to boot.

He jerked open a drawer and yanked on a T-shirt, ignoring the itchiness on his chest from the hair that hadn't fallen off. Then, because he could think of no better way to deal with the overwhelming tide of frustration and self-disgust, he slammed his fist into the wall.

Then he let out a string of curse words under his breath because it *hurt*.

His windows were open, and he could hear Phantom whining outside on the nearby front porch. He needed to let him in, but that would mean passing the bathroom and possibly seeing Cara and how could this have *happened*?

Where had everything veered so off course? *When you let her in.* Or maybe when he'd offered a hand to help her up at the market. Or maybe when he'd stopped his truck that day to ask her if she was okay. Or maybe a million little curves away from his path of solitude and isolation.

Curves that hadn't felt bad when he was doing them. For a few sparkling moments, walking in a creek, making pacts and playing truth or dare and letting her cut his hair, he thought he'd been making some kind of progress. Some kind of forward movement he hadn't made ever.

Because she was somehow special? What a fairy tale. It was all a mirage, a warped hallucination. He was still him. The him he'd always been. Always ruining everything.

Always.

Bringing the strays back to apartments he knew they weren't allowed to have pets in and getting his family kicked out. Nerves ending the night with Liz early enough that she'd felt the need to tell everyone. Going into the military and ruining his chances to become a vet. The night after therapy with a girl he couldn't even remember as the final nail in his coffin. Wes Stone's path of never doing it right.

When would he ever get that through to his idiotic hope?

He needed Phantom. He hadn't had a downward spiral like this in a while, going all the way back to the beginning. He needed the dog and to calm down and remember that he was alive, he'd saved lives in Afghanistan, he'd built this business. There might be things he'd never get over, but failure was only part of him. Not the whole.

Not the whole.

He forced himself to the door. Even though his arms shook, he pulled it open and stepped into the hallway. Maybe Cara had left. Or...

He heard sniffles as he approached the open bathroom door. *No. Please, no.* When he dared look into the bathroom she was sweeping the hair into a dustpan.

Sniffling and wiping her eyes with the sleeve of her shirt.

No.

Propelled by the sheer wrongness of it, he stepped into the doorway. "You don't have to—"

She was crying. She was cleaning up his bathroom, crying and, well, apparently things *could* get worse.

"I'm sorry," she said in a high voice. "I'm an idiot. This was such an... *Ugh.* I'm sorry." She rubbed a palm against her cheeks.

"No. It's so not you. None of it. It's me. Please, don't…" He couldn't even say it.

"I know you kissed me and all, but that does not automatically mean you want anything more than that from me, and that's my fault. And—"

He pressed his fingers to his eyes. Her words caused little pricks of pain on the base of his scalp. This was wrong. He couldn't let her blame herself.

"I'm an idiot and I'm sorry and—"

"I'm a virgin!"

He didn't want to look at her, didn't want to see her reaction, but he was coward enough most of the time. So, he forced himself. Wide eyes, mouth hanging open. Well, at least she was surprised. Probably be worse if she wasn't.

No. No, not much was worse than this.

CARA TRIED TO wrap her mind around that statement. Virgin. He'd freaked out like that because he was a virgin? That didn't seem right. Wouldn't a virgin be eager to get the deed done?

Besides, even with the hair and the beard and the grumpiness, he was so sweet and good. How could he have never…?

Maybe his injuries had done more damage than just to his hip and arm.

But she could have sworn he was hard. Sure, it was hidden under the denim of his jeans, but she'd *seen* it. It wasn't some wishful thinking on her part.

"So, um, is it okay to ask why?"

"Cara—"

He was going to shut her down, and she wasn't sure her curiosity would allow her to live if she didn't push, just a little. After all, he'd freaked out on her. Didn't she deserve something? "Like, religious reasons? Or philosophical? Or health?"

"No. None of that."

"It never happened for you? That's not something to be ashamed of, Wes. You're a little shy around women. That's okay, I—"

"I just *can't*."

"Something happened during the war? Or when you were a kid?" Her stomach churned at the thought.

He pinched the bridge of his nose. "There's no good reason. I panic."

"Like every time? And you don't know why?"

"No." He pressed his lips together. It was strange how different he looked. His hair was still shaggy, but it was so much lighter. If she'd had a chance to trim his beard a bit, he'd be…

Not the time to think about that, fruitcake. She hadn't known it was even possible to screw up propositioning a guy, and she had done it.

"Wes, I hope you know you can tell me. Whatever it is. I like you. Maybe, selfishly, I need to know it wasn't me." Because if it was, she wasn't sure she'd recover from that.

He dropped his hands from his nose. "It wasn't you. It wasn't." He shook his head. "You're beautiful and perfect, and you shouldn't cry, because this is all me."

"Well, I'll take the beautiful compliment because I'm vain, but we both know I'm not perfect."

"It feels that way. Right now."

She rested the broom against the wall and moved the chair out of the way. She approached him, though she held off touching him. Part of her wanted to, to offer some kind of physical comfort, but it seemed as if any touching from now on needed to start with him.

The way he'd pushed her away. Yes, it had been panic, but she wouldn't forget the shock of such a visceral rejection anytime soon. That she'd been so completely, utterly wrong to kneel in front of him. Touch him.

"Please, tell me," she croaked. "Whatever it is. How can I not think it's me if I don't know why that happened?"

He swallowed. "You can't take my word for it?"

The old feeling of failure crept into her bones. Maybe it was his panic, but she'd driven him there.

"Liz." His voice was little more than a creak.

Cara tried to make sense of it. "It has to do with Liz?"

He nodded. "Um, when we went on a date." He ran a shaky hand through his hair and seemed confused when his hand went through a lot faster than it used to. "A-anyway, we were going to have…"

"Sex?"

"Yeah. Yes. That. S-sex." He said it so determinedly, as if he was not about to let her be the only one who could say it. "It was a failure from the start. She asked *me* out to make some other guy jealous, then I couldn't pay for the expensive meal she ordered, and… But she said she wanted to. All night, she talked about what we were going to do, and I hadn't before, and when it was time to… I couldn't. I mean, I—" he made a motion around his crotch area "—too soon. So, we couldn't."

"Wes, you were, like, sixteen or whatever. My God, if I had a quarter for every time a guy got a little too excited, I'd…" *Sound like a hooker*, so she let that sentence trail off into nothing.

"The kids at school did not share your cavalier attitude."

"Kids at school? Why would they— She *told* people?" It was bad enough to be a bully, which Liz had been to Mia, but spreading Wes's secrets was even worse. "I should have punched her. I should have—"

He rested his hand on her wrist. It was the lightest of touches, but she stopped raging.

"It's not her fault. Not really. A normal guy shrugs it off and finds some other girl and gets over it. But I've never been normal. I've never been able to shrug stuff off. Anxiety. Turns into migraines. Ever since kindergarten when Greg Sampson made fun of my mom's sad attempt to make my clothes. I hide from people because I can't deal. I'm all malfunctioning parts, Cara. I thought maybe I could fix this. That was the thing in our pact. My trigger to pull, but I can't. It's in my head, and it's not coming out."

She wanted to tell him that he was wrong. But what did she know? She dealt with her mother's anxiety by avoiding her. She'd helped Mia break out of her shell by being straightforward about what Mia needed to do.

Wes didn't deserve either treatment, but Cara didn't have a clue what the right thing would be.

"Please, don't feel bad or cry. This was all me. Let's forget tonight ever happened. It's okay. I'm okay. My life is okay without this. We just have to stop pretending it's ever going to be a possibility."

Because his hand was still resting lightly on her wrist, she touched her palm to his cheek. Forget? When he… Oh, the poor guy had made *progress*.

He was letting her in—why, she couldn't guess. "Oh, honey, no."

He stepped back, away, which had her cringing. "No?"

"We had a nice night. And we made a pact. You held up your end. You tried. Maybe you didn't make it all the way, but, hey, you told me what's holding you back. So I am going to do the same. Make my step with the pie stuff."

"Cara—"

She didn't know what to do, so she kept going. Speaking her heart. Which was scary. But it certainly couldn't be any scarier than the stuff Wes was dealing with. "Nothing that happened or anything you said changes how I feel about you. I like you. I'm attracted to you. I'm not running away scared." She should. Not run away scared, but run away because she was bound to make this worse.

"B-but you should."

She wanted to cry that he would echo her thoughts. That he thought *he* was the problem. No, it wouldn't stand. She was going to do something right. She was going to help him make this step—if not with her, with somebody.

She ignored the twisting in her gut at the thought of priming the pump for someone else. She forced herself to smile, sassy, easy Cara. The girl who didn't take things seriously. That was exactly what he needed.

"Never been very good at doing what I should. Now, if I'm crashing on the couch, I'll need a pillow and a blanket."

CHAPTER THIRTEEN

WES DID NOT SLEEP. How could he when he was re-living every second of the moments from kiss to meltdown to confession? When Cara was asleep on his couch?

Assumably. Unless she couldn't sleep, either. Which he told himself not to think about approx-imately two million times over the course of a completely miserable night of nonsleep.

He had freaked out. It was only one step above the original infraction with Liz, maybe two above the night after the therapy thing, and while Cara had a point that he probably wasn't the first teen-ager to get too excited too early, it couldn't re-verse the fallout from that incident.

Even with a woman who put him at enough ease to talk, to truth or dare, to kiss. Nothing stopped the inevitable fall.

This was hopeless.

I'm not running away scared.

He pulled his pillow over his face to muffle the groan. *Why* for any reason under the sun would she want to stick around?

I like you. I'm attracted to you.

And if he were normal, he supposed, that would be that. Dates. Sex. Fun. Maybe even a relationship. But he wasn't that normal guy. He couldn't be.

He rolled over and glanced at his alarm clock. Four thirty. Late enough. As quietly as possible, he got ready for his morning chores, sneaking out to the barn with Phantom, hopefully without waking Cara.

It was dark outside, and the dogs wouldn't expect him quite this early. "Let's go for a walk, Phantom," he said into the heavy silence of morning. He detoured to his truck and grabbed a flashlight, though he wasn't sure he'd need it.

The path to the creek was as familiar as anything in his life. Comforting. He stood with Phantom next to the rock that had gone from his to his and Cara's and wondered how all of this had crashed together in a few short weeks. A month ago, he'd barely known she existed, and now he couldn't seem to get rid of her.

Couldn't seem to want to.

"I should want to," he said aloud, and Phantom leaned against him. He had to…scare her off.

Only he couldn't at all stomach even the thought of it. She'd infused his life with something he'd been missing.

Company. Color. Comfort.

He'd never made any best friends in the army, but he'd been surrounded by a certain camaraderie. Losing that had been hard. But inevitable.

He was made to lose.

Phantom let out a low woof, then began trotting back up to the cabin.

"Phantom. Heel."

Wes hurried after him; it was so rare that Phantom disobeyed a command. Something must be wrong.

Oh, God, Cara's in the cabin. Alone. He ran back to the cabin, ignoring the pain in his hip, but he came to an abrupt halt next to the porch.

There she was, wearing his coat. How did the sun always find her? It was barely above the horizon, and yet it lit her up and made her seem like some kind of reachable fantasy.

She wasn't. She wasn't.

"'Morning," she called, patting Phantom, who was happily thumping his tail by her side. No emergency. No reason to disobey. Just...*her.*

"'Morning," he replied gruffly. "I have chores to do yet."

"I'll come with you."

She was down the stairs before he could protest, petting Phantom's head and falling into step next to them. He should be short with her. Tell her to leave. Instead, she broke the silence first.

"I've been thinking."

"Don't."

She slanted a look at him.

"Don't think. Don't try to fix. Go home, get ready for work and come back forgetting last night ever happened." He kept his gaze on the barn no matter how much the sun licked her face and made everything inside of him hope and want.

Don't do it. You will lose. You always lose.

"I already told you no," she said, so resolute he wanted to yell in frustration, much like he'd done into his pillow earlier.

"Well, I don't agree with you."

She shrugged. "Too bad, so sad." She smiled at him as he jerked open the barn doors, a herd of animals greeting him. Greeting *them*.

"Like I said, I was thinking. All night, really. You talked about therapy and stuff you did with the army. Did you ever talk to anyone about this?"

He glared. "You're going to push this no matter what I say."

She grinned. "Yup."

Impossible, infuriating woman. Yes, those were the feelings she brought out in him. Nothing warm or hopeful. She was a pain.

"So, when you were talking to professionals about your anxiety for army stuff, did you mention this?" she prompted, checking water bowls and going about their lunchtime routine this morning as if this was also routine.

Well, fine. Let her. Because he was about to burst her bubble. "Yes."

She paused. "And it didn't help?"

"Nope." He'd been hopeful it would. About two years ago, armed with a therapist's stamp of approval, a growing business and mostly healed injuries—aside from the lingering pain. He'd gone to a bar downtown.

All the therapy and calming techniques and antianxiety medication hadn't done anything to make him not panic once the poor unsuspecting woman had taken him back to her place.

What is wrong with you?

It hadn't been mean or ridiculing like Liz. She'd been genuinely, rightfully confused. And it had put a stop to him thinking he had a chance at ever doing this. If he thought he could and he couldn't, if he had professional help and he couldn't, he couldn't. He'd live.

"I'm sorry."

"I don't need your pity, Cara. Just give this up."

They worked in silence, feeding and watering and petting the animals. Normally he would do his exercises now, but maybe he'd just skip that today.

Cara whirled on him suddenly. "Wait! Did *she* know?"

He shook his head. *Give up. Give up on me. Please.* "Did who know what?"

"The girl you met after the therapy. Did she know that you had this...issue?"

"Of course not. I was trying to get *laid*. I was a twenty-eight-year-old virgin. Why would I tell anyone that?"

"Then that'll be the difference." She beamed, one hand resting on Phantom's dark head. The dog panted and looked so damn content Wes wanted to growl.

"The difference?"

"I know all about it. So, I'll be able to ease you through it. It'll work, because if you get a little... nervous, I'll know why. And you know I know, so...it'll work. We'll make it work."

"Why? Why would you want to do this?" Why couldn't she just leave him to his life and his misery? Monks and priests went their whole lives without sex.

She frowned, hand still resting on *his* dog's head, gaze somewhere off in the distance. "I'm not...good at a lot of things," she said, sounding way more sincere than he wanted her to.

He couldn't yell at sincere. He couldn't growl at it and tell it to go away. He knew too much what it meant when someone would listen to your sincere, and think on it, deem it important enough to consider.

"But…and I know what this makes me sound like, but I *am* good at sex. I've been around the block, and I know what I'm doing and how to put someone at ease. Those are things that you need to take a step forward in your life, and I like you enough to want to give that to you."

She blew out a breath, finally making hesitant eye contact with him. "I don't get to do a lot of things that help people, because I usually mess it up. I know how to give a makeover—so, that's what I did for my sister. I know how to have sex. So, that's what I can do for you. And, in return, I get to feel remotely good about myself."

"And if you fail?" She looked stricken. "Okay, if *I* fail and freak out—like last night—what then?"

Her eyebrows drew together, everything about her expression pained, but in the end she shrugged. "Then I failed. We can try again, or we can give up, depending."

"Depending on what?"

Her fingers smoothed down the top of Phantom's head, a rhythmic repeated movement, mesmerizing.

"Guess we'll have to play it by ear."

He knew what he should say, and just as he knew it was the smart thing to do, the right thing to do, the thing he *had* to do—he knew what words would come out of his mouth. "All right."

CARA BLEW OUT the breath she'd been holding. He'd agreed. Clear as day. *All right*. Of course, not before scaring the living crap out of her.

And if you fail?

She hadn't been looking at sex as a potential failure. But what if he was right? If a therapist couldn't fix it, why on earth would *she* be able to?

Her. Cara Pruitt.

Ha! It might be sex, but it was still important, and she didn't *do* important. She'd made him agree only to find out—

"Cara?"

She couldn't do this. She couldn't *not* do this. Trailing her palm over Phantom's head, over and over, letting it soothe her in the weird way it did. She forced what she hoped to God was a cheerful, easy smile. "Yeah. So, I'm going to go home and shower and get ready for the day. I'll come back. We'll do our work like we normally do, and at five, I'll make you dinner."

"You'll make me dinner."

"Yes. If all you eat is sandwiches and hamburgers, you obviously need a home-cooked meal. It'll be like a date."

"Yes, please, make this less appealing to me."

She didn't know how she could legitimately smile while she was panicking on the inside, but the dry way he made the date sound like something to dread made her feel less pressure.

Surely she could live up to his low expectations. She might fail, yes, but maybe if she kept *trying*, it would give him the confidence to get over the hump.

Or, they could both need therapy afterwards.

It certainly wouldn't be the worst thing. Maybe someone could explain to her the whole life-not-fitting feeling.

"Cara?"

"Right, then." She tried to act cool. Calm, cool, collected Cara. That was her! "So, I'll be back soon. For work. And then tonight we'll deal with the other stuff."

"You're sure—"

"Absolutely." She couldn't let him let her off the hook. Not on this. "See you soon."

She turned to go, but suddenly his fingers had curled around her elbow.

"You have to call the guy."

The words didn't make sense because words couldn't possibly make sense while a delicious trail of heat encircled her arm and spread across her chest. His grip was firm, his gaze was direct and blazing with that serious intent of his.

Maybe they could skip work? But he was talking about calling someone or something or… "What?"

"If I agree to this, it's our pact. You help me with…my thing, and you have to do your thing."

"My…" Sam. Pies. Disappointment. Add *more* pressure to this day. This was what she got for sticking her nose and her sad do-gooder tendencies where they didn't belong. "Oh. Right. That. He'll probably say no to a second interview. He probably already found someone else. So, there's no po—"

"The point is that you try. Maybe he says no. Maybe it is filled, but you won't know if you don't ask. And he may need pies some other time, and you calling and asking for a second shot means maybe he'll give you one someday. There's no way I pay you enough to have this be your only job."

Her chest was going to cave in. She was going to die right here of the crushing pain of absolute determined failure. He wasn't even going to argue with her that Sam would probably refuse.

And Wes wanted her to do it *anyway*?

"Having now actually eaten your pie, I know he would be crazy not to give you a shot."

She closed her eyes against the warmth of feeling. He'd probably seen how freaked out she was and just offered a placating compliment, but the thing about placating compliments was sometimes they worked. She opened her eyes and slid him a flirty glance.

He did one of those half smiles, the faint tell-tale smudge of blush right above his beard. God, he was adorable, and he was in her very wrong hands.

But they were the only hands she had, so she was going to have to suck it up and do it. Much like when Mia kept steadfastly refusing Anna's advice on how to dress, how to present herself. Cara had had to step in because she couldn't let Mia keep folding in on herself, when she was so much better. *So much better than you.*

So, she'd have to channel that again. She'd helped Mia. She could help Wes.

Hopefully.

"I'll be back," she offered, sliding her arm out of his grasp, a trail of goose bumps on her forearm.

That attraction they had was something. And if nothing else, she knew how to deal with that. So, that's where she'd start.

CHAPTER FOURTEEN

LUCKILY, WES WAS used to preparing for impending disaster. For nearly eight years, his life had been all about preparing for possible disaster. Preparing for war.

So, as they went through the day, him making and organizing treats, her pestering him to order new business cards and redo his budget to include an advertising section, inwardly, he prepared for war.

The problem with this war was that the enemy was himself. Dick versus brain. Not the most unique of wars for men, which was an odd kind of comfort. Hey, *part* of this was normal.

Don't get too ahead of yourself.

She wanted to magically cure years of trauma that he'd mainly invented in his head. Okay, maybe not *invented*, but… This was very much an in-his-head thing. He knew that.

He'd come to terms with it not being *his fault* per se. He hadn't *caused* Liz to run around school telling everyone he was some kind of pathetic sex freak—despite oh, never having had sex.

He wasn't even in total control of his reaction to that. Therapy had given him a certain…clarity. Enough to say he'd been dealt a shitty blow.

But it was a blow he hadn't been able to shake. *I know. That'll be the difference.*

He'd love to not believe her. To be certain she was an idiot for thinking *knowing* would make a difference. And a large portion of his brain told himself that. This was impending disaster. At the hand of a beautiful woman who wanted to help. Who thought she could. Who made octo-pies and lit up the air simply by existing. He scrubbed both hands over his face.

You should probably go back to therapy.

"Wes?"

He didn't jump out of his skin, but it was only military training that kept him immobile. Slowly, he turned to face her.

Her shoulders were thrown back, a smile that was just a pinch too bright to be genuine stretching across her mouth. "So, my famous enchilada casserole, or chicken à la Cara?"

It took his mind a minute to engage enough to realize she was asking what he wanted for dinner. Because it was five o'clock.

At her pleasant stare, he forced himself to concentrate. Mental preparation, he'd done it. All day. All. Day. He could do this. And if he didn't?

Well, at least she'd stop trying. "What's chicken à la Cara?"

"A surprise."

"The other one, then."

She laughed, going to the fridge and gathering the supplies she'd shoved there when she'd returned this morning.

"What can I do to help?" *Please, say disappear until it's ready.*

"Sit there and look pretty," she replied, nudging the fridge closed with her hip.

For a moment, he was so mesmerized by that hip and the possibility of seeing it without the skintight jeans she so frequently wore, he didn't even notice the aching pain in his.

Remember the plan. Which was to not think about sex until there was nakedness involved. And even then, a one-step-at-a-time type thinking. Because if he refused to think about it, it wouldn't build up in his mind.

Right. Because he had control over his mind. *That* was the exact problem. The rational parts of his brain didn't stand a prayer against the irrational ones.

Focus. Dinner. Conversation. Save the crazy for later. "So, um, did you call the pie guy?"

She opened her mouth, then turned away from him. "Do you like cilantro?" she asked conversationally, dumping what looked like already-cooked ground hamburger into the skillet she'd arranged. She added chopped onions, a can of some kind of red sauce, a few dashes of different spices she'd brought.

"Cara."

"It can be a very divisive herb," she said, keeping her back to him as she pushed the mixture around with a spatula. Which looked wholly unfamiliar. Had she imported her entire kitchen? "Some people won't touch a food that's even been in the same vicinity as cilantro."

"So, what you're saying is, no, you did not call him."

"I will tomorrow," she replied brightly, a fluttery wave of her arm before she started pulling tortillas out of a bag.

"You were supposed to do it today. That was the deal."

She tossed the tortillas in a dish and whirled on him. "I tried! I did. I called. Twice!" She threw her arms in the air. "But he answered and I just… blanked. I've never…begged someone for a second chance before. It's awful. You have no idea—"

At his raised eyebrow, she groaned. "Okay, you have every idea of everything, supreme freaker-outer of the universe. Happy?" She turned back to her dinner preparations, slopping the skillet mixture on to the tortilla.

He didn't say anything in return. What was

there to say? But there was something he could do. He retreated to the office, grabbing a pad of paper and a pen.

He returned to the kitchen with them, finding her grumbling to herself and filling tortillas. There were two routes he could take. The kind, careful one, or the jerk one.

His first instinct, the one he tended to fight off, was the comforting one. He didn't like to see people upset or hurt. If he *liked* that, he'd probably be a lot better off. But, he'd gotten in the habit of being a jerk to people because it was easier than trying to maneuver the complex pieces that went with a relationship of any kind.

So, he slapped the paper on the table. She looked at it and him over her shoulder as she poured cheese on top of the tortillas she'd put together. "What's that?"

"It's a pen and a piece of paper. When you're done with that, you're going to sit down and write out what you want to say. Then, you're going to call him."

She blinked at him, her mouth hanging open. Why should she be surprised? He talked to her like that enough. Granted, about work stuff, but...

"Why are you telling me what to do?"

"Apparently you need it. We had a deal."

"It's a stupid deal."

"Then you can leave your tortillas for me to

eat and head home and keep your hands off me."
He crossed his arms over his chest in an effort to
look intimidating instead of hopeful.

If she left, he might still be a virgin, but he
wouldn't have to deal with her knowing... Oh,
wait, she already knew everything.

Crap.

Without saying anything, she shoved the pan
into the oven, letting the door slam shut in a way
that shook her pan on the stove top. Then, she
marched to the table and sat down where he'd
slammed down the paper.

"Okay, Mr. Superior, what do I say to the guy
who has every reason to believe I'm a piecrust-
burning idiot who doesn't care when she fails?"
Her eyes met his, green with temper, or maybe
it was the purple top she was wearing.

If he understood why he wanted to smile, he
might have been able to stop himself from doing
it, which would have stopped her from smiling in
return, which definitely would have stopped her
from popping back out of the seat and pressing
her mouth to his.

Wait. How. What?

Her hands brushed over his beard, and he knew
he should either stop it or *enjoy* it, but mainly
he could only stand there frozen trying to catch
up. While her mouth slid against his, her hands
trailed down his neck.

Her mouth separated from his, but only a hair. Her eyes met his, her lips a pretty curve of smudged red. "All you have to do is kiss me."

Right. Sure. That was *all* he had to do. Easy. If he was just about anyone else. But he was him with all the bagg—

She trapped his face between her hands, all but forcing his gaze to hers. "Wes. All you have to do is kiss me back. And you can touch me if you want. There's no reason to panic. I'm not running. I'm not laughing."

She brushed a thumb over his bottom lip, then followed it with her tongue. Her hands sliding down over his shirt, then dancing along the hem.

"I—I'm not going to be d-distracted." He cleared his throat and focused on not stuttering. "We had a deal." Because, yes, instead of the kind of physical attention he'd been dying for for years, they should sit down and write out her phone call.

She laughed against his neck, her hands smoothing over his chest, still under his shirt. "I know. But you look so hot when you're telling me what to do. I can't help myself."

Hot. Him. Hot. Hot? His first instinct was to argue with that. Surely this was all pity. The compliments, the eager kissing.

But, hell, a woman like Cara could probably wrap just about any man around her finger; why would she harbor enough pity to have sex with him? Maybe the fact was, they were attracted to each other. And she knew.

I know. It'll be different.

So, he focused on what he could. The fact her lips were soft and patient, that even though her fingers tangled through his hair, she didn't seem frustrated with it. That *she* thought *he* was hot enough to jump up and kiss.

If he thought about it in those terms, and only kissing terms, it wasn't too hard to put his hands on her hips. To close his eyes and sink into her mouth, her warmth, the way she felt like a safe place.

"Mmm. Perfect," she said against his mouth, on something like a sigh.

It couldn't possibly be, but she almost made him believe it and it allowed him to enjoy. A few seconds of normal, *perfect* kissing.

"LET'S GO TO the bedroom," Cara said, against his mouth because she couldn't quite work up the strength to pull her lips that far from his.

"B-but...d-dinner."

He looked so perplexed and confused, and it twisted her stomach into a million knots. She had to finish this. Just to prove to him *he* could, because it wasn't about her. If she thought about it like that, she could...not run away herself.

Forcing a sassy smile, she flicked off the oven. "It'll keep."

"Right." He curled his fingers into his palm and then released them. "Right. Keep. Right."

"Wes." His eyes blinked to hers, and she had to breathe through the fact he looked a little panicked and it made her feel panicked.

Oh, God, she was going to be sick. But, she couldn't be, because she had to be the with-it one in this scenario. Terrifying.

Still, when she forced herself to lift an almost-not-shaking hand to his cheek, some of the rigidity in his shoulders eased. Which eased some of the fear jangling around in her chest. He needed this, and she could give it. She could.

"Everything is going to be fine," she said resolutely, letting her fingertips trace where beard met cheek.

"Uh-huh."

"It is. We're going to do this. And…it doesn't matter. Nothing you do really matters. You can't scare me off. No one's going to laugh. No one's going to tell anyone outside this cabin *anything*."

"Cara."

"If something doesn't work—you tell me. And if something doesn't work for me—I'll tell you. No drama. No worries. You are in very good hands." She hoped. "Now, smile."

He did something with his mouth. A kind of

teeth-baring grimace. "That's the absolute worst smile I've ever seen." Which at least got his mouth curving a little more naturally.

"It's going to be fine," she insisted, irritated her voice came out whispery. She needed him to believe she could do this.

And if you fail? She shook the thought away, pressing her mouth to his, because kissing him got rid of that voice in her head. Kissing him got rid of almost everything in her head when he gingerly combed his fingers through her hair, when his tongue tentatively touched hers.

They were going to do this. Everything was going to be *fine*.

CHAPTER FIFTEEN

IT'S GOING TO be fine. Wes let Cara's words echo in his head. The way she said them so solemnly, and suddenly he felt a certain kind of pressure to make it so. It wasn't a bad pressure. No, it felt more like determination.

The determination didn't flag through that kiss, or the next one, but when she pulled away, smiling and leading him into his bedroom, some of it deflated a little bit. The reality of the situation.

What if history repeated itself? Any of the histories? Getting too excited. Panicking. What if it was all too much no matter how determined they were?

Cara pulled off her shirt and let it drop to the ground, which was enough to silence the circus in his mind for a second. Her bra was something lacy and pink, like the one he'd caught a glimpse of that day she'd crossed her arms and unknowingly pulled her top down too far.

Even in the dim light of his room with sun-blocking curtains, her pale skin seemed to glow, each freckle a punctuation point to some dip or curve. She looked impossibly soft, and it was only fear that kept him from reaching out and touching her.

You will not be afraid. You are going to do this. She wants to do this, and so do you. He just had to get out of his own head. Somehow. The kissing helped. Maybe he should initiate it this time.

She pointed to his chest. "Your turn."

He gave an idiotic nod and then pulled the shirt off himself, letting it fall next to hers. Jeez. This was getting...real.

She kept smiling, her eyes staying on his as she unbuttoned her jeans, and then he had no idea where *she* was looking because *he* was watching her unzip and push her jeans down over her hips. And then she was standing in front of him, in nothing but her underwear.

She nodded toward his waistband. Right. Follow her lead. He could do that. He'd been a soldier for years. He could definitely follow a lead. With less-than-steady fingers, he unfastened his pants and awkwardly stepped out of them.

Standing across from each other in their underwear. He couldn't decide what would quell the raucous anxiety spiraling in his gut.

"You're beautiful," he forced himself to say, because at the very least he should offer her a compliment. A truth. Before all the insanity inevitably started pouring out of his mouth.

Her lips curved, and she crossed the room to him. "And you—" she placed her palms low on his abdomen and pushed them all the way up and over his shoulders "—are a work of art."

"Way to put my compliment to shame."

"Hush," she murmured, before touching her mouth to his, her body to his. It was a jolt, her soft skin against his, the warmth of her, the *ease* of her.

She had a way that made everything not easy but easi*er*, and for a man like him, easier was everything. It was…possibility. This might actually be possible.

Maybe. If she kept kissing him like this, her hands in his hair, his palms against the smooth warmth of her back, it wouldn't have to end up in disaster.

The tips of her fingers slipped under the waistband of his boxers, and he flinched, enough for her to stop kissing him.

"Tell me if you want me to pause, but I'm not going to stop unless you say you want me to stop." She kissed the part of his cheek not covered in beard, fingers brushing against him.

He tried to swallow again, but it was hard to complete the action with his mouth completely dry.

Her hand closed around him, and he sucked in a breath. The last time he'd done this, he'd finished on the spot. All Liz had done was touch him, and somehow it had made everything after impossible. And—

"Wes." Cara's voice. Cara's hand. Cara's arm pulling on his neck so she could press a kiss to his mouth, her hand never leaving him. "Okay, so how about you follow my lead?"

But he didn't want to just be a man along for the ride. He wanted to be a part of this. A willing participant. Who didn't stop. Who didn't freeze.

Anxiety and pleasure mixed up into one feeling, but slowly, as she kissed and stroked and occasionally said his name against his mouth, her perfume infiltrating everything, it morphed into mostly pleasure. Mostly good.

He worked up the courage to touch her hair, a gentle brush of fingertips over the silky strands at her temple. The slope of her shoulder, the curve of her back. She sighed, and he knew he should touch something more intimate, but…he couldn't get to that step quite yet. "Um…"

"Are you close, Wes?"

It was strange how something about her saying his name in that easygoing, take-everything-in-stride voice she had anchored the moment. Away from the thoughts and the panic, he could just enjoy. His hands could smooth farther down her back, to the lacy edge of her panties. He could kiss her temple and say "yes" in her ear.

"Do you want to get on top?"

On top of her. Did he want that? Hell, he didn't know. So he was honest. "I don't know."

"Or you could lie here beside me. Or I could try what I was going to do yesterday?"

"How about like…last night. A do-over."

Cara's mouth curved. "A do-over. I like that."

"Okay." He'd said it without stuttering. He was going to do this. And he wasn't going to panic. Because Cara knew, and she wouldn't judge him. It wasn't high school; there was no one to tell. And they'd gotten this far, and everything was going to be okay.

She tugged down his boxers. He didn't know what to do with his hands. He didn't know…

She grasped him again, and he tensed. But he didn't push her away. Not this time. Not with Cara. Still here. Still wanting this.

She stroked, then the heat of her mouth was on him. He watched through the shadowy dark, and he didn't even know what he didn't know but his brain had stopped functioning, so that was okay. All he could feel was her.

It was better than good. Fantastic. Amazing. "Cara, I'm…"

She pulled away. "Hold that thought." There was a rustling sound. "Do you have, like, a lamp or something you could turn on?"

"Oh, um…" He was aching, dying possibly, but

he moved to the bed and flipped on the little reading lamp clamped to his nightstand. Not much in
the way of light, but enough to see she'd taken off
her bra and climbed on to his bed.

There was an almost completely naked woman
on his bed.

She burrowed down into the covers. "Come
here."

He stared at her breasts, shadowed in the weak
light. She was gorgeous and doing this of her own
accord. Here because she wanted to be, even after
he'd been a total whack job.

He swallowed. Nerves, yeah, but not panic.
He kicked his boxers off. Awkwardly he strad-
dled her legs, her skin so smooth and perfect.
He didn't know what to do with his hands again,
but she smiled up at him all beautiful and sweet,
and then her hand wrapped around him, and she
began to stroke, her eyes never leaving his face.

"But I—"

"Shh." She smiled, all encouragement and
ease.

It felt so good. Someone else doing it. Her legs
brushing his, some strands of her hair brushing
against his hands anchored on either side of her
face.

So much better than being alone. All the time
alone. "Cara."

"It's okay, honey. Go ahead."

One more pump, and he couldn't hold back his release. The wave of pleasure diluted the panic that she might not have wanted him to do that, because she'd told him to. And, damn, that felt good.

She was all easygoing normalcy.

How was this even remotely normal? He collapsed on to the bed next to her, and when she snuggled in, some of the panic took hold again.

"D-don't you want me to d-do something f-for you?" What could he do? He didn't know how to do anything.

But surely she expected…

She kissed him on the shoulder. "Nope. That was all for you. Baby steps. Relax. Recover. We'll go eat and then move to the next step."

She had wanted to do that for him. *Had* done that for him. He didn't want to take baby steps. He wanted more. "Wh-what if I w-wanted to move on…n-now?"

CARA STILLED, NOT wanting her feelings on the matter to be too obvious. She was so turned on, she could barely move without whimpering.

"I want to try more," he said without even stuttering. Not that his nerves seemed totally gone, but he was managing them. He wasn't pushing her away, and he wanted more.

Yes.

"So." She swallowed. It wasn't the words so much as the actual implications that made them hard to say. "Actual sex?"

"J-just tell me what you want to do, and we'll try it." He watched her, his eyebrows drawn together and a scowl on his face. She liked that. Liked that he was talking to her. It might not magically make this work, but it was the only key he hadn't tried. Talking, explaining himself.

It had to unlock this mental block. Didn't it?

"I don't know if I can," he continued. "Maybe I'll push you away again, but I want to try. Whatever it is you'd want to do, what you'd normally do if I wasn't…you know."

"Do you want to have sex with me, Wes?"

"That's not even a real question, Cara. Of course I do. I just don't know if I can."

"But you want to try?"

"If you do."

"This is getting circular."

"Tell me what to do. I'm good with orders. I can follow orders." He nodded like that had to be it. The secret to solving all his problems. And, who knew, maybe it was.

"Ooh, I get to be in the driver's seat? Well, hey, there's *my* first."

He smiled. A Wes smile, kind of a quirk rather than wide and toothy. But a smile nonetheless.

"Well, maybe some other time I can tell you what to do." His smile died. "I—I mean, um, if—"

She pulled his head down to hers and kissed him. Talking about other times freaked her out, and there was only one freaker-outer allowed in the bedroom, and Wes had already won that title.

So she kissed him, letting her fingers trail over the muscles defined in his arms, his shoulders. "Touch me, Wes," she said against his mouth.

He hesitated, both kissing and touching, but after a moment a hand rested on her hip. Just rested there. Like when they'd kissed in the bathroom yesterday. That wasn't going to work for her.

"Sit up," she ordered. He did so without asking questions.

She crawled on to his lap, still wearing her panties. She rubbed against him until he groaned. Mmm, she liked that groan.

"Now, touch me. Really." She took his wrists and placed his hands on her rib cage, palm first. And then with gentle pressure, she tugged them upward until they were cupping her breasts.

She could hear his swallow in the quiet of the room, and then she rubbed against him again. His eyes fluttered closed.

"Keep your eyes open, honey." She smiled when he did. "Watch." Because she wanted him to see—not just to experience, but so he would know and understand what *he* could do.

She took the index finger of his hand and moved it across her nipple, sighing at the current of pleasure that waved through her. With very little guidance, he did the same with the other hand. Back and forth until she dropped her hands to his shoulders, arching so he'd do more. Touch more.

"Mmm. Fast learner."

"I do get the gist of the whole sex thing," he said hoarsely.

She did her best to arch an eyebrow, to make a challenge with her expression before she bent her head and trailed her tongue around his nipple. When she pulled her head back up, he was staring at her openmouthed. She wanted to hug him. For a minute or two. And then proceed. But sometimes he so needed a hug.

So, she indulged, wrapping her arms around his neck and giving him a little squeeze. When she loosened her hold, he kissed her shoulder, then the top of her breast, then right above her nipple. She whimpered, desperate for more and then—*Oh*—he did what she'd demonstrated, and her head fell back as she moved against him. His hands roamed down her sides, then back up again, fingers brushing over her nipples, watching his own hands quite intently.

He explored and she let him, because he needed it, because *she* needed it. Sex had always been easy, a light thing, but this wasn't light. Every touch of his fingers, or his mouth, was like a heavy weight. Somehow exhilarating and terrifying and meaningful.

Wes was in no hurry, and she wished she could be patient for him. She wished she could be exactly what he needed, and maybe if she didn't feel that weight, that fear that this was so much more than easy, she could be that.

But, nope, she needed action. She needed to get out of this place where each gentle caress, each increasingly confident kiss stroked more than just her skin. She felt it all deeper, and she wanted nothing to do with that.

"Condom," she said resolutely. Because moving things forward would solve everything.

"I—I d-don't have—"

She hopped out of bed. "No, I do. In my purse. Give me a second, and whatever you do, do not change your mind."

She scrambled into the kitchen where she'd dropped her bag and grabbed the required items. She scampered back to the room, determined to make this *easy*. It was going to be fine. They were going to be fine. She could walk him through this. He just needed a little guidance.

Who would trust you with guiding?

She pushed the nasty voice in her head away and forced a bounce into her step and a smile on her face as she reentered the room.

Wes was sitting on the bed, completely naked. Scowly resting face and all. *Hummina, hummina.* He really was a work of art.

"Got it," she said with a grin, sauntering over to the bed. He watched her so intently, she was kind of sure, even if this was a disappointment, it wouldn't feel that way. Wes might be nervous and new, but there was an attention he paid her. None of the guys she'd slept with had ever looked at her like that.

It might get kind of addictive.

Don't be stupid, Pruitt.

CHAPTER SIXTEEN

WES HAD A beautiful naked woman on his bed. Wanting to have sex with him.

Maybe he'd died. Or maybe, for once in his life, the good-luck stick was pointing his way. Whatever it was, however he'd gotten here, he wasn't going to miss the chance.

If he could figure out where to look. He wanted to look everywhere. Memorize every inch of her tanned skin, swaths of pale skin that never saw the light. Freckles. How did he…?

"Wes." She took his face between her hands. "You can talk, you know. Ask things. Ask for things. Everything is okay. This is an okay zone."

"I wasn't sure where to look." Christ, he sounded ridiculous. It wasn't like he'd *never* seen a naked woman before. He just couldn't quite get over the little voice in the back of his mind.

"Look wherever you want." She flipped her hair over her shoulder. "I'm kind of fabulous."

He shook his head. "Not kind of."

She smiled, not the sexy, seductive little grin, but a pleased smile. As if his compliment meant something. Then she crawled on to his legs, ripping open the condom packet. "Just for that, Mr. Stone, you are going to get yourself some."

She pulled the condom out of the packet and rolled it on him.

She grabbed his chin, forcing him to look at her. He blinked, trying to focus, trying to think. But all he could feel was Cara's other hand still around him.

"If something is wrong, if you don't like something, speak up," she instructed, and the firm way she said it helped center the moment. Yes, he was good at taking orders. He'd excelled at that. "And if you do something I don't like, I'll tell you, and it won't be a big thing. So don't worry about messing up. You won't. You *can't*."

Somehow those words mattered. A lot. They eased the tension that had been curling in his gut. The bad tension. So all that was left was uncertainty, but he could deal with uncertainty. He could deal with anything with Cara. Which might have been a scarier thought if he'd had any more room in his brain.

"Why are you doing this for me?" It felt like some kind of gift, only he didn't know what he'd ever done to deserve it.

"Oh, honey, it's not just for you." She grasped him and slowly enveloped him in soft heat, an amazing sensation.

He hissed out a breath, some mumble of sounds that didn't sound like words to his own ears.

He had to press his forehead to her shoulder to keep himself from shaking or saying something stupid. Like, *you're amazing and perfect.*

"If you get a little nervous, just do whatever I'm doing to you." She kissed his neck, his shoulder. She ran her hands over his arms, and then after a few seconds she began to move.

She felt good. Everything about her. Every inch of skin. There was only good.

His hands roamed her body, the same way her hands roamed his. Wherever, sometimes lingering, sometimes brushing over. He dragged his palms down the smooth curve of her back.

"Mmm, calluses."

She leaned her chest closer to his face, and this was *happening.* And he wasn't losing it. No, he was enjoying it. So he ignored the nerves.

Her pace quickened. Her breathing got more rapid, and she leaned in, her mouth to his. He was doing something right, so he kept doing it, palms sliding down her sides to her hips.

"Keep. Doing. That." She nibbled on the top of his ear. It sent a shot of electricity right through him.

"That's it." She increased the pace, faster and faster until she was saying "there, there, there" over and over in his ear.

He couldn't concentrate anymore. He wanted to be in control. He wanted this to be something she *couldn't* laugh at, even though she never would.

He gritted his teeth, holding her hips tighter as she groaned. "Oh, Wes." She collapsed against him. She sighed, running her fingers through his hair from the base of his scalp upward.

Then she kissed him, fisting her hands in his hair. He was starting to think he was seeing stars. Everything seemed so unreal because she had...

A few more thrusts and he was done, because he'd made her orgasm first. He'd really managed it. The climax washed over him, and Cara wrapped her arms around his neck as he tried to catch his breath. He'd had sex. He was no longer the pathetic thirty-one-year-old virgin.

It was every bit as amazing as he'd ever dreamed, because Cara was amazing. She'd done that. Somehow fixed him.

Which was silly. She hadn't. The truth had. He'd never told any woman that stuff. Telling her had made this possible, but so had her reaction. The way she'd led him through it as if it wasn't completely stupid he needed leading.

She breathed heavily against him, arms wrapped around his neck, his cheek pressed against the center of her chest.

But she wasn't letting go of him, so he didn't let go of her, either.

CARA LAY PERFECTLY STILL. In Wes's bed. In Wes's arms. For a while, it had been nice. Dozing off with him, all tangled up together. For a while, she'd felt like a freaking queen. She'd given Wes something no one else had.

Dinner forgotten, they'd fallen asleep. Something about the stress and probably lack of sleep the night before had apparently given them both a reason to nod off.

But hours later, she'd woken up with a start when the door to the bedroom creaked. In the dark she could just barely make out the shadow of a dog, probably Phantom.

Then she didn't feel so great. Because Wes was still a guy who had a therapy dog. A guy with injuries she'd all but forgotten when she'd ridden him into oblivion.

Oh, God, she was terrible. There should have been more talking. More preparing. Talking about what it meant. Did he think she was going to be his girlfriend now? She'd been so focused on sex she hadn't thought about the *other* side of sex. Intimacy. Emotion. All those things that got her burned if she ever tried to enter them into the equation.

Life was so much easier when you dated assholes. You never had to worry about hurting their feelings. They were the ones sneaking out at four in the morning. They were the ones purposefully getting caught by their supposed ex-girlfriends.

Ugh. She was not letting herself think about the Kevin fiasco right now. She had to think about how to fix what she'd done to Wes. If he expected things from her now, she'd be powerless to say no. Because she didn't want to hurt him. Because he was hot and cute rolled into one grumpy, flannelly package.

Then he'd have to dump her when she couldn't deal with all his baggage, and she'd feel even worse than she already did for not knowing how to be the good, comforting girlfriend.

Get the hell out. Get the hell out.

Carefully, hoping not to wake him, she wriggled out of Wes's grasp. He rolled over but was back to even, heavy breathing in a second flat.

She had to get up in a few hours and work for the guy. Know what to say. How to act. She had to get out of here. Maybe it was stupid. Maybe it was panic, but she could not wake up with him. She could not wake up and see signs of expectation on his face.

Ugh. She crawled out of bed, doing her best to quietly find her clothes. She could feel Phantom's eyes on her. Judging her.

He's a dog. He's not judging you.

The clock read 4:45 in bright red letters. She could feasibly tell Wes she'd left to take a shower and get ready for work. She could feasibly pretend like nothing had ever happened. Maybe that's what *he* wanted? She'd never know, because she'd been too stupid to ask.

She inched through the crack in Wes's bedroom door, then leaned against the hallway wall and squeezed her eyes shut. She was the girl version of the kind of guy who took a girl's virginity and ran.

But how could she just *face* him? Even if he didn't expect anything, there was an intimacy here. She'd given him something no one ever had. No one. She was it.

Everything in her revolted against the idea that she could possibly be special enough to deserve that.

Such a coward. If only she could be a forward-thinking coward who wouldn't put herself in this position by seducing the poor guy. Who hadn't *forced* the issue. Why hadn't she thought about this part? The part where you laid down the ground rules. Now she was going to sneak out and reject him?

"I suck." She needed a glass of water and to clear her head. Maybe get her bag and shoes and bolt. *No.* She couldn't do that. Not to Wes. She had to be brave and…talk it out.

Oh, God, run.

When she got to the kitchen, all she could see

was the front door. Outside the window was the teeniest tiniest hint of light over the hill to the east.

"Just a breath of fresh air," she muttered to herself, slipping on her shoes. She didn't even grab her bag, so she wasn't bolting.

Yet. *No, Cara, you are not going to be a coward. Not* now.

She shook her head and opened the door, and then screamed and fell backward at the not-dog animal standing *right there*.

Of course from her position on the floor, she could make out that it was a sheep. A damn sheep.

"I thought you couldn't walk very well, you little—"

"Cara." Wes stumbled into the kitchen, looking bleary-eyed and mussed and cute and wonderful, and oh, she was terrible.

He knelt next to her. "Are you okay?"

She nodded, then pointed at Shrimp. "That a-hole scared me."

He glanced at Shrimp, then back at her, specifically at her shoes. "You were going?"

"No. No. I was just getting…air."

He made one of his Wes smiles, but she didn't count it as a smile. It looked sad. No. No. No sad Wes. "Sure."

"Really! Look, I don't even have my purse!"

He got to his feet. "It's okay, Cara. You can leave if you want. It won't hurt my feelings."

"But I wasn't."

"Thinking about it, though." He pulled a glass down from his cabinet, filled it with tap water. He leaned his good hip against the counter, and because of the shadowy dark she couldn't make out his face.

"Don't let me keep you."

"I wasn't going." He had to believe that. He had to know…this was her. Like when he'd rejected her and said it was him. His issues. Well, he could buck up and realize she had issues of her own.

"It's fine."

She realized she was still sitting on the ground where she'd fallen and pushed to her feet. "It is not fine because I was not leaving." She wouldn't let him accuse her of something she hadn't been actually going to do—just had considered.

He drank his water in silence.

"I wasn't! I was thinking."

"About leaving," he supplied.

"Damn it, Wes. You know what?" She was going to be honest, because he couldn't judge her for that. Because they had built this little…thing between them on saying uncomfortable truths. On being honest. On freaking out, out loud, instead of buried down so low no one could even guess you were a mess. "I was freaking out a little. Because I would so have sex with you a million times over, but the relationship stuff is not my forte."

"Were you expecting a marriage proposal?"

She didn't like the edge to his voice. Not even a little. "No. I just—"

"Then, go. Feel free to go. Did you think it would scar me for life? I'll survive. You successfully cured me. I owe you one."

She stared at him openmouthed. So sex *could* turn all guys into jerks. What had she been thinking? She'd cured him, maybe, in a way of speaking, but of course she'd failed at everything else.

Typical Cara.

You will not cry. Not over this. Not in front of him. But there was a lump in her throat and burning in her eyes, and oh, *shit*. She had to get it together. "You know, I have my issues, too. Just because yours are bigger, it doesn't mean mine don't exist."

He put the glass down on the counter. No slam. No thud. But then he took a few slow, measured steps toward her, and she almost wished he had slammed it. This was a lot more intimidating.

"I didn't ask you for anything, Cara. *You* pushed. *You* demanded. You…"

Oh, God, how was she getting turned on right now? She was mad at him. But he said her name, and he was all growly. Mmm.

Not allowed! They were having an argument. "I wanted to help, and I did. But I didn't consider the implications. And maybe I didn't consider myself, okay? I don't have the best reputation. I doubt sleeping with my boss is going to help. I wasn't thinking about me."

He took a few more steps toward her, and she felt the need to back away. She could kind of make out his intense expression now. Zoomed right in on her.

Hot.

"What do you care about your reputation? It's a dumb small town with a lot of people who'd do better caring about their own lives rather than obsessing about other people's."

"Right. Well. My parents and sisters and soon-to-be brother-in-law all live in that town, and they don't need Liz Fetter telling them I'm the town slut."

Finally there was nowhere for her to go. She was trapped against the wall, and he was standing way too close. But he softened at the mention of Liz.

"She'd be wrong."

"It doesn't have to be right to hurt."

"Yeah." He let out a long breath. "Yeah, I get that."

Cara couldn't look at him, because if she did she'd want to jump him. Or cry into his shoulder. So, she stared out the window, watching the sky lighten.

"You said if I did something you didn't like, you'd tell me," he said, and when she forced herself to look at him, his eyebrows were drawn together in concentration. "And I couldn't be wrong, because you'd say no, and it wouldn't be a big deal. Right?"

"Well, yeah, I—"

And then he kissed her. Grabbed her face like last night, and oh, she did like grabby, but it was sweet this time. Like kissing a scrape.

What was that weird fluttering in her chest? Not nerves. But he pulled his mouth away before she could analyze it.

"I can't even imagine being in a relationship," he said, his big hands still cupping her face. "If that's what you're worried about. Just because I finally did this doesn't mean I'm not a mess."

"You're wonderful." It slipped out before she could make it sound less pathetic, but oh, well, maybe Wes deserved some idiot girl being all pathetic over him.

"You must be delirious from taking my virginity."

She snorted, resisted leaning toward him by sheer force of will. He *was* wonderful. It didn't erase his issues, and it really didn't erase hers but he was.

"I'd get grumpy with any romantic gesture, and I'd never remember an important date. So, maybe it's just sex, and we're both okay with that?"

Cara bit her lip, trying to ignore the little sliver of disappointment. She *wasn't* disappointed. Not even a little bit. Because she was bad at all that stuff, too. Expectation and hope and *future*. Nope, she was not that girl.

"So, like, we could *keep* having sex and not be in any kind of relationship?"

"Yeah. Although, if you want to sleep with someone else, I'd kind of want to know first. But other than that, yeah. What was that word you used? No expectation. No hope. And we're both fine."

"Except for the part where we're emotionally stunted and afraid of relationships?"

"I can only handle one big overcoming-the-odds thing at a time. And I definitely choose sex over fixing my emotional stuntedness."

"Me. Too." This would be fine. Better than fine. It would be *great*.

CHAPTER SEVENTEEN

WES SAT AGAINST his headboard, watching Cara scurry around his bedroom finding her clothes and, sadly, putting them back on.

He had things to do, too. Though he'd already made his barn rounds when he'd had to put Shrimp back into his pen. There was still his normal routine. Exercise. Shower. There was the everyday work of dog treat making and packaging to be done.

But Cara was pulling on her skinny jeans, then hopping as she pulled on socks. A curtain of light brown hair fell over her face, and the slope of her shoulder with a smattering of freckles was damn near mesmerizing. All the while she mumbled on and on under her breath about being late.

In his room. After sex. He sat and he watched, and he figured if that wasn't what he was supposed to do, she'd tell him.

He felt lighter than he had in years, even with his hip kind of aching. What was a little hip pain when he had sex with this woman under his belt?

"I may be back here a little late for work."

Right. She worked for him. She worked for him *because* he'd thought that would somehow put her in the employee zone. Instead, he'd slept with her.

It was strange, but the normal self-flagellation and irritation didn't come. He was too damn smug.

Cara took one last look around the room before glancing at him. Then she grinned. "Look at you all smiley."

She stepped over to the bed and kissed him on the cheek. "I was supposed to meet Mia at my place in five minutes to talk wedding stuff. I should be back by nine, tops."

She headed for the door, but he said her name before he could think it through.

She stopped and turned, cocking her head with a smile. Her hair was a mess, and her makeup was all worn off and *how* had he gotten this lucky?

"Listen, um, thanks for everything."

She stalked back over to the bed. "You thank me again, you're in big trouble, mister. Not fun bedroom trouble, either. We both had a good time. No thank-yous necessary."

"Yes, ma'am."

"One of these days you're going to be giving me some orders, and I'm going to be the one saying 'yes, sir.'" She gave him a quick peck, then was sashaying out the door before he even had the wherewithal to respond.

"I'll be back," she called, followed by the front door slamming shut and reverberating all the way to his room.

Phantom whined from his spot on the floor.

"Oh, get up here."

The dog hopped onto the bed and rested his head imploringly on Wes's chest. Wes scratched him behind the ears. "You're a good dog, aren't you? Don't go getting all worried. This is just a temporary thing."

Sex. Nothing else to make it any more complicated. Besides, eventually Cara would get her life together and get a job doing pies or something she loved, and this would all fade away.

But for now, he'd get what he could out of it.

CARA PULLED HER car into a spot in front of the apartment complex. Mia's truck was already there. Oh, she was going to get lectured.

She could try to hide the signs she'd spent the night elsewhere. Apply some lipstick, run her fingers through her hair, put a sweater on over her shirt, but Mia had lived with her too long to be fooled.

Cara squared her shoulders and prepared herself for a disappointed-Mia stare and sigh. That was one of the few things she did not miss about sharing a place with her sister.

Not that Mia had ever said anything, but Cara

could always sense the disapproval. And, she wasn't sure she could bear the weight of disapproval right now. Everything was so shaky. Even with Wes's determination that he was fine and not looking for everything, her heart felt shaky. Fragile.

And what was her heart doing anywhere *near* this equation?

Cara opened the door and mustered her best bright smile. "You're here! So, do you have the magazines?"

Mia pursed her lips. "Yes."

Cara clapped her hands together and moved for the kitchen table. "Great, let's get started. I have to be at work by—"

"You're fifteen minutes late."

Cara stiffened, looking at the stack of bridal magazines instead of Mia. "So?"

"Wearing no makeup and what I assume are yesterday's clothes."

Cara sighed. "Just spit it out, Mia. You're no longer the dewy-eyed virgin."

"And now you're being mean." Mia touched a hand to Cara's shoulder. "What's wrong?"

Oh, she hated sympathy even more than disapproval. Poor, dumb Cara, always doing the wrong thing, failing the test, dating the wrong guy. "Nothing is wrong." She was totally fine. Everything was normal and fine and great.

Mia slid into a seat, looking at her imploringly. "I didn't plan this meet-up so we could look through magazines."

That brought Cara out of her inner freak out. "Huh?"

"You haven't been yourself lately. We're worried."

"Who's we?"

"Everyone. Mom and Dad and Anna. Mackenzie sent me a Facebook message yesterday saying you'd had a fight with her. You're not happy, and it isn't something recent. It's been happening for, like, a year."

"I seriously don't know what you're talking about, hon. I'm no different than I usually am. And the fight with Mackenzie..." Cara frowned. "You don't even like Mackenzie."

"No, I don't, but, my God, if *that girl* notices something is wrong, something is terribly, terribly wrong."

"She's just mad I called her on her BS."

Mia bit her lip. "If that's true, I applaud you, because she is drowning in it, but..."

"But what?"

"I've been a little preoccupied, what with Dell and the merger and now the engagement, and maybe I thought you'd figure it out on your—"

"There's nothing to figure out," Cara said through gritted teeth.

"You helped me out so much when we started the market stand. I don't just mean with business stuff. With me stuff and getting past all my social weirdness. You were there kicking my butt, and I want to do the same for you."

"Mia. God. Look, I'm fine. Besides, you did all that on your own. All I did was suggest a decent haircut."

Silence followed, and Cara refused to look at her sister. She was too thin-skinned to do this right now. She needed armor she didn't have to fight this off, to not break down in front of Mia.

"I used to think it was sweet you wouldn't take credit for anything. Now…"

"Now what?"

"Don't be mad, but it's kind of stupid. You should take credit for the good you do, not just the mistakes you make. It's the easy way out of failure."

What? The good she did? The random good she did was lame. A haircut. Some sex. Who cared?

The idea she only focused on her mistakes was…

Right on the money.

No. No way. She wasn't that screwy. Her mistakes just happened to outweigh her not-mistakes. Something Mia wouldn't know, because being socially awkward was basically her worst crime and she'd overcome that. "Is this going some-where? I have a job to get to. If this isn't about wedding stuff—"

"Where were you last night?"

Cara shrugged. "When did you ever care about my many conquests?"

"Cara, the only guy I've seen you eye recently is that Wes guy. Your *boss*. You didn't sleep with him, did you?"

"I don't know what that has to do with—"

"It isn't like you. You quit your job at the salon, and you're working for that guy out in the woods, and from what little I know of him, he is so not your type and we're worried, Cara. We love you, and we want you to be happy. How could a guy with the kind of problems he has make you happy?"

The kind of problems he has. Meaning the kind of problems she had no business dealing with.

Again, right on the money, and it hurt. But if she let Mia see that…she'd have to deal with the fallout. She'd have to act like it mattered that she was the royal screwup of the family, and then she would be well and truly pathetic.

She couldn't live like that. "I'm fine. And Wes is fine. Great, actually, and okay it sounds bad to sleep with your boss and maybe it is, but there are extenuating circumstances."

"I said I wanted you to be happy, not fine. How

great for you is a guy who lives by himself with a bunch of dogs and never talks to anybody?"

Yes, how great is he? Cara rubbed at the discomfort in her chest. It didn't matter. "Can't you be obsessed with your wedding and leave my little quarter-life crisis be?"

"Aha! You admit something is wrong."

"If I admit it, will you go away?" She didn't like talking about this. It made her want to defend Wes to Mia, and that made her think about her stupid disappointment over their just-sex arrangement and that made her feel like an even bigger idiot. "Please, go home."

"No. Why don't you tell me about Wes? He's great, you say. Like how?"

Cara marched over to the sink, not sure what for. "It's not a relationship."

"Oh."

"But he's not an asshole, either. Which might be a first."

"Possibly."

"I don't know. Things aren't bad. They're not. I like working for him, and I *wanted* to sleep with him. I'm not losing it or anything. I'm trying to change directions. Or something. But I'm okay. Really." Maybe if she said it enough times, it'd be true.

"I know you don't want me big-sistering you, but, well, you were always poking at me and telling me what to do. So, it's my turn. You need to find something you want. Something to work for. That's what helped me, and I know it's different but it's kind of the same. I had to find a way to be comfortable with me. You have to find a way to find you. That's normal twenty-something stuff we all have to go through."

Cara had wanted the pie-baking thing, but she hadn't been able to get it. Except she had promised Wes, hadn't she? Their pact. "So, why does it feel so hard?"

A scary question because it spoke to some fears she normally didn't let anyone see, not even Mia. Maybe not even herself.

"Because we're wimps."

Cara laughed, glaring over at Mia. "Yeah, you're real wimpy with your smoking hot fiancé." Cara glanced at the magazines with wedding dresses on them, desperate to change the subject from her. "What about Grandma's dress?"

Mia fidgeted. "I didn't think… I mean, it seems more fitting for you to have it."

"I don't think I'm the marriage-and-babies type."

"You're whatever type you want to be."

"Ha."

"What? I changed. Look at me. Mia, Queen of the Geeks, marrying the smoking hot Naked

Farmer. Because he is head over heels for me. Retainer and all."

"Oh, God, you let him see you in that?"

"Focus on the point, Cara."

"The point. People can change." Perfect people, maybe. Smart, driven people. Not everyone could change, or there wouldn't be so many miserable people in the world.

"All you have to do is believe you can."

Ha. Well, there was the problem, then. "Yeah, right, and look. I'm not unhappy." At Mia's pursed-lip look, Cara rolled her eyes. "I'm not! I'm working on figuring stuff out. That's not unhappy, it's just, you know. It just is."

"Okay. I'll give you that. As long as you promise you're actually figuring stuff out and not..."

Cara frowned, not having the slightest clue what Mia was going to say. "Not what?"

"Hiding away in the new job in the middle of nowhere, in a new guy who isn't the one for you. Don't hide or pretend. Don't sit around reliving all your mistakes and being down on yourself."

"I don't do that."

"Remember when I caught you playing Barbies when you were like six or seven, and the Cara Barbie was getting a lecture on all the things she'd done wrong, which, coincidentally, was everything you'd gotten in trouble for that week?"

"I was *seven*. It was dolls."

"You never stopped doing it. Mom's worrying doesn't help. I thought moving out and working at the salon had really helped you, but I think you only got better at hiding it. Pretending you weren't so hard on yourself."

"I have to get to work."

"Right, well." Mia pushed out of the chair and skirted the table. "If the Wes thing ever becomes more of a thing, maybe we can double date or something. I'd like to get to know him."

"To make sure he's not a serial killer."

"If you say he's great, I believe it."

"Yeah. Sure." Why would Mia have any cause to believe it? Cara had never made the right choice in guys before, and Wes's recluse reputation didn't exactly do him any favors.

It didn't even matter, because they'd both agreed anything more than sex was way beyond their abilities.

Mia wrapped her arms around Cara's shoulders and squeezed. "See the good in yourself. Please."

"Look, Dr. Phil, I have to get ready for work."

"Remember, if not for you, I'd still have a perm and clunky glasses. Oh, and those mom jeans."

Cara snorted. "I am a miracle worker." Okay, so she'd helped Mia with superficial stuff. But the whole point of changing the way Mia dressed and all that was so she'd feel confident enough to overcome some of her social anxiety.

And she had.

Then there was Wes. She'd helped him do something he'd been struggling with since high school. That was a pretty big deal, even if she was kind of out of her league when it came to dealing with his issues.

"I'll let you get ready, but lunch at Moonrise Friday?"

"Yeah. I'll flag the bridesmaid dresses I like in here."

Mia finally released her and went to the door. "If you need anything or want to talk, just because I'm not here or I'm with Dell doesn't mean you can't call."

"I know." And she did, but she'd also been holding herself back. Not wanting to intrude on Mia's happy found-her-one-true-love time. Because Mia deserved happiness, but Cara didn't know where she fit in it.

"Good." Mia stepped outside, and Cara started walking to the hallway but Mia's words and the pact she'd made with Wes kept playing over and over in her head.

All you have to do is believe you can. Wes slapping the pad of paper down on the table, demanding she write out what she needed to say. So certain she could do this when he'd been so certain *he* couldn't do his things.

But he had. He had. The guy with real problems. She was just a girl with a bad case of the folds-under-pressures.

She stood contemplating for who knew how long, but finally she pulled out her cell phone and brought up Sam's number. Really, if she could help socialize her sister *and* devirginize a guy, surely she could convince another guy to let her bake him some pies.

CHAPTER EIGHTEEN

WES GLANCED AT the clock, then immediately berated himself since he'd only looked two minutes ago.

But where was she? She said she'd be late, but not eleven-o'clock late. It'd be time for his lunch break by the time she got here.

If she ever did. Maybe this morning had been a hoax, or a lie, or... *You know what? No.* Maybe she'd decided not to come back for whatever reason, but it hadn't been this morning, and it hadn't been last night.

You sure about that?

"Yes." Oh, man, now he was talking *out loud* to himself. Time to get a grip. He'd spent five years in this cabin never waiting for someone to return. Or come at all.

Cara had whirlwinded into his life a few weeks ago, and suddenly everything was so quiet. And he wasn't a virgin. And he was behind on his work.

It scared the crap out of him, but balancing out

that fear was a weird buzz of anticipation. That had to be the sex, but it was there nonetheless.

He wanted her to come back. He wanted to hear her voice. And kiss her shoulder freckles.

A few weeks and he was already thinking freckle kissing? No wonder she'd been trying to escape this morning. Next thing he knew he'd be writing poems and picking flowers for her.

With an irritated grunt he yanked the bowl of batter out of the mixer and began pouring it into the molds.

He shouldn't be irritated. He should go back to being satisfied. Proud of himself. Sex master of the world. *Got a ways to go to be any kind of master, buddy.*

But there was this feeling in his chest. Wanting her back. He had nothing to offer her. Everything he'd said when she'd "not been leaving" early this morning had been honest. He would never be any good at a relationship. Besides, she had no interest.

So, why did he keep thinking about that? That moment when she said she didn't want one and he said he didn't want one, and they'd both meant it.

Why play it over and over and over and feel this weird longing? The same kind of longing he got when he couldn't help an animal that was sick or hurt.

That was a good comparison. Because he'd

never be a vet, and he'd sure as hell never be Cara's boyfriend.

Luckily, he didn't have to keep convincing himself of that because Cara's little car finally popped into his view from the kitchen window.

Some of that longing eased. *Or you're an idiot.* Both, maybe?

The front door burst open in a blur of color. A pink-and-blue dress, some flowy knit sweater thing that couldn't actually keep anyone warm. Red lips. Bright red lips.

"Hi," she said breathlessly. "I'm so sorry. I'm never late for work, but, oh, wow, it has been a morning."

He blinked away from staring at her mouth. "Everything okay?"

"Better than." She grinned and gave him a quick squeeze. So quick he stood there and took it like an immobile moron.

"I called Sam. And I told him about making the pies beforehand. In fact, I kind of spitballed this whole idea about supplying pies rather than working *for* him in the restaurant, you know? More like an independent contractor type thing."

"He said yes."

"He'd been so busy he hadn't been able to look for anyone else. So, he told me to bring a pie over. I took him two of my frozen pies, and he called me when I was halfway here. I sat on the side of the road at Levelly Junction talking details. It's only temporary or probationary or whatever it's called. To see if it works. And then if it does, it *could* become permanent. Just weekends to start, but if that did well it could be every day. *Every day.*"

She looked so happy and excited he thought he'd grab her and kiss her, but he had dog treat batter all over his hands. By the time he'd washed them off and turned to her, some of her excitement and exuberance had diminished.

"I mean, it's possible nothing could come of it. But I don't know. My pie in a restaurant? That's kind of cool. Even if it's only once or twice."

"*Kind of* cool?"

"Don't go pumping my tires, Wes. It's temporary." She nudged him with her elbow, wearing a smile that somehow wasn't as joyful as the smile she'd walked in with.

"Probationary. That's different." And it was. Really different. He wanted to see that initial joy on her face again, not this hopeless look she suddenly had going on.

"Well, whatever. Let's not get all… I don't want to psych myself out. It's a lot of work, so many different ways to mess it up. So, let's change the subject." She wrapped her arms around him and pressed a kiss to his mouth, her whole body leaning against his, which pretty much caused an immediate erection.

"You're all cute looking like you're baking, even if the food is for dogs."

He cleared his clogged throat. "Um. Thank you. But, uh, we should probably have rules or guidelines or something. For work. And this."

She wrinkled her nose. "I'm not very good with rules."

"Why are you always telling me you're not good with stuff that you seem pretty okay at?"

Any cheerfulness in her expression completely faded, and she dropped her arms and stepped away. "Man, is it pick-on-Cara day?" She dropped her bag on the table right outside the kitchen. "I've got work to do."

"Who else is picking on you? Not that I was. I was making an observation." It had been a long time since he'd felt protective of someone who wasn't four legged and covered in fur. He'd made a conscious choice to shut himself away from anyone who might need him.

Cara didn't need him. No matter what kind of mess she thought she was. She could fight her own battles. He shouldn't feel the need to take up any for her.

He followed her into the office, where she stared at his desk, hands fisted on her hips. "We need to talk new business cards. And the bag designs."

She tsked, she moved stacks, she didn't look at him once. And she didn't appear to be doing any actual work. Just moving things around, trying to look busy.

Finally he was driven by that instinct to protect that had come from somewhere long ago, growing up the only boy in a house with a mother who always seemed to need protecting. From emotionally abusive boyfriends, from herself, from him screwing it all up.

"Who was bothering you?" he demanded, probably too roughly.

She lifted her chin and crossed her arms over her chest. "Did you make an appointment for your surgery?"

"Wha-What?"

"You want to butt into my business, I get to butt into yours. Turnabout is fair play." Then she stepped toward him and poked him in the chest. Hard. He grabbed her hand to stop her from doing it again.

"Do not poke me."

"Why the hell not? I have had my fill of being psychoanalyzed today. By people who actually know me. People who do not hide from humanity in a damn shack in the woods. *I* am fine. I did the pie thing, didn't I? Didn't I?"

"And belittled it. Played it down."

"So what?"

"Be proud. I may hide away from humanity, but I am proud of what I do and what I built."

"I'm not you."

"You're better than me, and you should act like it."

"Or maybe *you* should be better. *Try harder*, Wes. Remember that little sliver of advice?"

He opened his mouth to say something back, but what was there to say? She was right. Completely right. That time by the creek he'd told her to try harder, and he was here telling her not to belittle her successes when he'd been belittling and downplaying the success he'd had with her just last night.

She cocked her head. "Gotcha there, didn't I?" She sauntered past him. "I have to go to the bathroom."

Wes watched her go but didn't make a move to go after her. It wasn't his place. Cara's issues weren't his issues, and it wasn't his job to make her see herself for what she really was. It certainly wasn't his job to feel protective of her.

But it seemed like such a *waste*. She was… She was amazing. Certainly no one else had swept into his life and made it a little better, not even his own mother. She should see that.

But who was he to make her see? Who was

he to do much of anything? Maybe he needed to keep his mouth shut and let this whole thing fade away.

That stupid longing feeling centered itself in his chest once again, but he wasn't about to dwell on it. He had actual work to do. Work that, thank everything holy, didn't have anything to do with people and trying to figure them out.

CARA FELT LIKE an ass. She *was* an ass. It was just that she'd done the thing she was supposed to do, and apparently that still wasn't good enough? Because she wasn't being optimistic about it? God, didn't Wes get it? Optimism was her recipe for disaster. She'd come here all giddy and excited, and then he had to echo things Mia had said. Him! That was ludicrous and hypocritical, and, oh, she'd been a big jerk to him. And he'd shut himself away for the rest of the afternoon.

She deserved the cold shoulder. The fact he cared was kind of sweet. Somehow in a very short period of time, they'd twined their issues around each other, and there was something nice about it because they'd both moved forward.

How it had happened, she had *no* idea. But it had, and she shouldn't be a jerk to the guy. Which meant she needed to apologize before she left for the day. Maybe with sex?

"Oh, be a grown-up for once, Pruitt," she muttered, brushing her hands over the front of her skirt and walking with purpose to the kitchen, where Wes had been working for hours without a peep.

He stood at the counter, his packaging supplies lined up in assembly order. Though he must have heard her enter, he didn't stop his meticulous process. This was where she saw the soldier in him the most. Mind focused on a task, plan clear and easy.

It made her think of last night. How unsure he'd been. Scared, almost. To think he'd been carrying all that baggage around.

Her throat got tight because she shouldn't be here. Wes needed so much more than anything she could offer. The fact she even wanted to offer, after a few weeks of barely friendship and one night of sex was just...

She had to go home before she did something stupid. Maybe make it clear that all that should be between them was work. "Hey, um, I know I owe you a few hours. I can make them up tomorrow."

He didn't look away from the treats he was packaging. "That'll work."

In twenty-four hours she'd managed to sleep with him, make him think she was running out this morning, sleep with him again then be a jerk.

This is the kind of thing that happens to girls

who don't follow the rules, Cara Pruitt. Cara had to close her eyes against Mom's voice in her head.

You're not very supportive. This is hard, and you've kind of made it worse. James. That one had stung for a long time.

For the second time in the same day, she knew she had to get out of this house. "Well, I'll see you tomorrow, then."

"Sure thing."

She grabbed Sweetness's leash and her bag and stepped outside. Sweetness came racing up to the porch, and Cara bent down to pet her.

Cara had escaped. She was out of Wes's house and was pretty sure whatever arrangement they had was a thing of the past.

So, good. They could go back to being coworkers, and she could stay far away from his heartbreaking issues because she didn't belong there.

She didn't feel relief as she walked with Sweetness to her car. She felt like crying. Or running back. Apologizing and leaning into him. Needing him.

Maybe Mia was right. Maybe even with the pie thing sorted, she was still a complete and utter mess. Which, well, wasn't surprising. What was surprising was that she wanted to fix the mess.

Especially the mess she was leaving behind. But she didn't have a clue as to how.

Mia said she had to believe she could, but she

had no skills for this. For him. For… Sweetness yipped, hopping into the backseat and jumping up to look out the back window. Yipping at Wes's slowly disappearing cabin.

Cara blew out a shaky breath. Something had to change. She had to figure out some way to *make* things change.

You have to believe you can.

Yeah, that was going to take some work.

CHAPTER NINETEEN

WES ALMOST DIDN'T expect Cara to show up. And, the way things had ended, it made a whole lot of sense for her to never come back.

Apparently, Cara's response to awkward wasn't to hide away, though, because there her Camry was, bumping up the drive as he finished up his chores.

Keeping his morning the same day after day as his own basic training was probably strange, but he liked the routine of it, the feeling of being in control of his own life, even if sometimes his limbs didn't cooperate.

He'd overworked his arm yesterday and this morning, and now that Cara had arrived, he wasn't in the mood. Not for people. Not for her perfume and the awkwardness she made him feel.

Yup. Not a virgin anymore, but still an awkward moron.

Cara made her way to him, her bag looking bulkier than usual. She had one of those determined looks on her face. As if he was wrong and she was going to prove it to him.

Except she didn't need to prove it. Whatever it was, he was wrong. Always. Wrong and stupid and—

He needed to get a handle on this.

She stopped in front of him, her chin tilted upward. "I have a peace offering."

"Did you need one?"

She smiled, but not one of those dazzling so-sure-of-herself ones. This one made him feel as though he wasn't the only one feeling any discomfort.

Her eyes followed Sweetness up the stairs of the porch. "Things got weird yesterday. I wanted to put that behind us. Come on." She marched toward the house in that easy, take-charge way she had, making him feel even less like dealing with all of this.

Why couldn't they ignore it? That method served him so well. He trudged after her up the porch stairs and inside. She didn't stop until she was at his desk. Then she pointed to the chair. "Sit."

"I'm not a dog, Cara."

She lifted an eyebrow, and, okay, he wasn't that far removed from a dog, so he sat. Path of least resistance and all that.

She dug around in her bag, her hair falling in front of her face, reminding him of yesterday morning when she'd been getting dressed. After they'd had sex. Twice.

How could he get back there? There was nice. Awesome. There had been things he didn't feel very often. Normal. Satisfied. Maybe even a little proud of himself.

Yeah, he couldn't remember feeling that too often.

Cara interrupted his thoughts by shoving a piece of paper in his face. He frowned at the drawing that looked like Phantom. On the collar of the dog it read Stone Organic Dog Treats. It was all in black and white, but looked like a logo or something.

"I don't…"

"My sister Anna, she's good at this stuff. She makes most of Mia's signs and decorations. Your booth is so plain in the middle of all the color at the market, and I mean, bright and glittery isn't you. But I thought a little illustration might, you know, help. We can put it on the labels with the treat names, the bags…everything."

Wes could only stare at the drawing, his brain not kick-starting enough to give him the appropriate response to this.

"Not that you *need* help. I know it's pretty ludicrous, me giving you any advice about running your own business, but it's not even my advice.

I've seen what Mia's had success with and..." She made a waving motion toward the sign.

Finally he worked it through his head to look at her. She was staring at the drawing, too, eyebrows scrunched together and lips pursed. He didn't understand that expression. This. Anything. "Why?"

She let out a gusty sigh and looked around the room. When she didn't find what she was looking for, she plopped onto the floor cross-legged. It made his hip hurt just looking at her.

"So, yesterday got weird, and I wanted a gesture to show you that this part doesn't have to be. I mean, me working for you doesn't have anything to do with..." She picked at a spot on the carpet, then shook her head. "This is so awkward. I have never in my life felt uncomfortable talking about sex, but I just..."

"Maybe when we had sex it was, like, one of those mind-switching things."

She snorted out a laugh, her eyes meeting his for the first time all morning. "Are you feeling like a flighty twenty-five-year-old?"

"No, I pretty much feel like a messed-up thirty-one-year-old."

Her shoulders slumped. "I want you to know—all the weird yesterday? My fault. I'm not good with people when it's serious stuff. Just some fun? I'm your girl, but life stuff?" She shrugged. "I have a bad track record with that."

He opened his mouth to argue with her, but remembered in time that opening his big mouth was what had ruined yesterday. She might want to take the blame, but if he hadn't felt the need to champion her *to* her, it never would have blown up.

"Maybe we could go back to the way things were?" Pretend the whole thing never happened. That had worked pretty well with, oh, his entire life. At least, on the outside you could pretend, and then the only person you ever had to deal with was yourself.

Of course, Cara, being Cara, didn't jump up and down in agreement. She cocked her head, gave him a hint of that sly, sexy smile. "When *before*, exactly?"

"Um."

"You know, before I came back yesterday? Or before yesterday morning? Or before we slept together? Before the haircut? Because the hair's already been cut, so to speak."

"Um." He cleared his throat. What exactly did he say to that? "Well, I guess that depends on what you want. I'm pretty flexible."

"I'm *very* flexible." She smiled up at him, all pretty and easy. She made him feel like that ease was possible. Made him like it and hate it and not know which way was up all at the same time.

He had to focus. Find a way to deal with this and her, because she wasn't going away on her own. She wasn't pretending, not really. The only way for him to be able to pretend would be to get rid of her.

He didn't want to do that. He really didn't. Firsts were flying at him right and left. "So, maybe, just to yesterday morning. Before you left." Because he didn't know much about this whole having-sex-repeatedly-with-a-person thing, but he did know an offer when he heard one.

"I was hoping you'd say that. *That* I can very much deal with." She unfolded herself into a standing position and slid easily onto his desk, the side of her thigh brushing his arm and the arm of the chair.

She leaned toward him, angling her mouth toward his ear. "But you're going to have to get out of my chair, because it's work hours and I have a job to do." Then she leaned back, grinning.

"Right. Work."

"For now, anyway."

"Right." He got up from the chair. Gingerly, because a simple brush on the arm from Cara and now he was hard as a rock.

She slid into the seat he'd vacated, apparently none the wiser, then picked up the paper with the illustration. "So, um, did you like it? She drew a few others, but this was my favorite. I have the others—"

"It's perfect." And it was. Nothing flashy or overly colorful like most of the other booths. Like things that never would have fit him. A simple black-and-white drawing. Phantom. A name for his business.

"So, you'll use it?"

"Well, sure. Yeah, I mean if it's okay with her."

"Yeah. She loves doing stuff like that. Just keep her name at the bottom. I can order you a new sign and business cards, if you want. Obviously you don't have to—"

"Yes." For some reason her nervous energy made him want to calm her. Especially since she had nothing to be nervous about. Not when she was helping him out in this amazing way.

She didn't see that. And he couldn't tell her she didn't see it because that's how they'd gotten things tangled yesterday. But maybe there could be some way he could show her. Maybe...

A random pain shot down his arm, so unexpected he sucked in a breath and winced, trying to clench and unclench his forearm muscle to ride it out.

"Is your arm okay?" She brushed her fingertips from his shoulder to his elbow, but before she could get all the way down to his hand, he jerked away from her touch.

"Fine." He knew he snapped at her, but it was a knee-jerk response. The last things he ever wanted to talk about were how his injuries nagged him and how that one place he'd finally belonged got blasted away along with his vet dreams.

He could make a million firsts, a million forward steps, and that would always be there. The things he was good at got blasted away from him. The things he wanted were always out of reach. Irrevocably.

Maybe she could revoke the virgin stuff, but even Cara's magic didn't extend to his injuries and his life.

When he finally forced himself to look at her, she didn't look at him pityingly or as if he'd hurt her. She just looked sad. Kind of like she had yesterday when they'd fought.

"I can't possibly ever be the person you'd need in your life. Just to put that out there," she said quietly, meekly almost. Cara being meek. It didn't compute.

"I don't want anyone in my life, so I guess we're good." Which was true. It was. It had always been true, and yet it felt wrong to say to Cara. There was a stabbing feeling in his gut, as if it was a lie.

"I should get some work done."

"Yeah. Yeah. I'll do that, too." He nodded and left. No clearer about where they stood than he'd been this morning.

CARA FOCUSED ON Stone Organic Dog Treats all day. She even canceled her lunch date with Mia. She worked on incorporating Anna's logo into Wes's business, got all the treat names lined up, ordered labels. He wouldn't be all ready for the new and improved Stone at market tomorrow, but it felt like real work. Something she could do and not screw up.

It had put them back on even ground. Sort of. The part where his arm had obviously hurt, and he'd snapped at her hadn't been nice but it was back to normal.

Even if it prompted all sorts of uncomfortable feelings. Feelings she didn't know what to do with.

She wanted to help him, soothe him, force him to tell her what was wrong, and as strong as all that want was, the bottom line was once he told her, she'd inevitably fail to do any of it.

She was the girl who got dumped by the guy whose best friend had committed suicide. And it had been because she couldn't handle the emotion and made him uncomfortable. The girl who hadn't visited Grandma in the hospital because she would have cracked in two.

When it came to emotion, the kind that hurt and broke, she vanished. Because otherwise she'd fall apart.

She'd dealt with all that by surrounding herself with people who'd never need more from her than a laugh and a drink.

Even worse than that knowledge was the bone-deep desire *to* help. A kind of deep ache that was only overshadowed by the blinding fear that followed it.

When there'd been a goal—to get the guy out of Virgin City—it had seemed easy enough. But what was she doing now besides getting wrapped up in him? She didn't need to teach him how to seduce a woman. He'd learned all he needed to know from her.

What more did he need from her? Not a damn thing.

Cara leaned her forehead against her palms. God, this was too much thinking. Way too much feeling.

Then a dog nosed her thigh. Phantom. The tears almost immediately followed, because he was a *therapy* dog for a guy who'd been in *war* and she was just some idiot girl who couldn't seem to figure out what to do about much of anything. And every forward step almost immediately felt like a shove in the opposite direction.

"Cara? It's past four thirty, you can—" Wes

stopped abruptly, presumably because he recognized her almost-breakdown stance by now. She kept having them around him. It must be all his fault, really.

"You okay?"

She nodded, swallowing at the lump in her throat. For some reason, all this bad feeling made her think of yesterday with Mia. Mia saying she only ever focused on her mistakes. But they were so big. How could she not?

"You don't seem okay."

"I'm having a bit of a…" She cleared her throat, trying to smile or laugh or make light of it all in some way. "Quarter-life crisis. I'm basically a John Mayer song. Just wishing gravity would stay the hell away from me and all that."

"I have no idea what to say to that."

"Yeah, listen, I'm going to take off." Get out of this bizarro place where she thought about all the pain and emotions and bad stuff. She didn't dwell on that. She focused on the happy, and if she couldn't, she drank or sexed it away.

Briefly, she considered propositioning him because that had been the plan. But she was beginning to think it couldn't be *just* sex with Wes. She hadn't analyzed all these feelings or even felt some of them before she met him, so he had to be the reason. He had to be to blame.

She had to get out of here. "I'll see you next week." She abruptly stood, almost knocking the chair sideways, which reminded her of Wes the night he'd told her he was a virgin.

Was she turning *into* him?

"Tomorrow."

"Tomorrow? Why—oh, the market." She met his gaze for a second, enough to recognize concern etched across his face.

She felt sick to her stomach and grabbed her bag. *He* could not be concerned about *her*. "Yup. Saturday. B-bye." And stuttering, perfect. She scurried out the door, trying to ignore him and Phantom following her. She whistled for Sweetness, who bounded from her curled-up spot under the dining room table.

Cara tugged the leash out of her purse, causing a few papers to spill out. She struggled to pick them up and leash Sweetness at the same time.

"Are you sure everything is all—"

"Just peachy." She popped up even though the clip of the leash hadn't fastened. She knew she wasn't fooling him for a second, because she was panicking inwardly *and* outwardly.

But she couldn't stop herself. She was going to break down. She'd been barely avoiding it for weeks now, but she couldn't stem the tide anymore. Everything in her life wasn't just ill-fitting now, it was topsy-turvy. Well and truly unrecognizable.

So, she hurried to her car where she would be alone and safe and tried to ignore the tears building.

When she glanced back at his house, Wes was standing on the porch. Watching her go. That push of want, the pull of ensured failure coiled around her lungs. For the second day in a row, she was running away from him.

A little voice in her head told her to believe she could face this. To believe she could learn how to navigate Wes's issues and hers, but the little voice held no weight.

She got in the car, because it was better to bolt and panic than it was to try and fail. Everything was better than disappointing people, letting them down.

So running away had to be better, and it was time she stopped fighting it.

CHAPTER TWENTY

WES STOOD BEHIND his booth, trying not to be too obvious about the fact he was trying to catch a glimpse of Cara over at her sister's booth. Unfortunately, the Pruitt Morning Sun Farms table was one row over and partially hidden behind the person across from him, so he wasn't even sure she was over there.

He tried to talk himself out of caring, but, well, he wasn't having any luck. Fact of the matter was, Cara had smashed into his life, and he was kind of reticent to turn back the clock.

Which was so weird he didn't even know how to fight it. But watching her run away yesterday had given him an unfamiliar feeling. For the first time in his life, it felt as if *he* was the one flipping the domino. Where Liz and bombs had been the things to sweep in and change his plans, he was the one changing them now.

He was the one deciding that, despite everything wrong with him, despite everything that would probably end up destroyed, he didn't want to go back to the person he'd been. He'd found someone who felt as though she belonged in his life, and he wanted to see where that could go.

He didn't have much hope it'd go anywhere fantastic, but it certainly couldn't be worse than an explosion or public ridicule.

He hoped.

When Cara finally appeared, she was walking toward him with something tucked under her arm. But even though she was coming for him, she didn't look up from her shoes, didn't meet his gaze.

So unlike her. "Hey," he offered when she was close enough to hear.

"Hi." She tucked a strand of hair behind her ear, and he got the distinct impression she was nervous. That shouldn't have surprised him after the way she'd bolted yesterday. Whatever was going on with her suddenly made her act differently around him.

There'd been a few times where he'd started to wonder if *he* was the problem, if he was the one making her that way, but despite that knee-jerk reaction, he talked himself out of it every time.

He wasn't causing whatever was up with her. It was a strange relief, one that gave him a confidence he'd never felt around anyone else before.

"So, I picked up the labels I had made for you." She pulled out a few sheets of heavy paper. "Um,

I charged it to your business account and everything, and I'll file the receipt Monday."

"That looks great."

She awkwardly moved toward the bins on his table, still not meeting his gaze. "Yeah, I thought so. I haven't seen too many stop by your booth today. Maybe this will help."

"Maybe." He tried to catch her eye, but she was having none of it.

She started peeling stickers and carefully placing them on the bins. He read the names, and they weren't outrageously cheesy. Sweet Pup-tatoes, like she'd suggested earlier. Peagles. A little punny, but not ridiculous.

"You know these are amazing, right?" His booth was suddenly transformed into something that fit in with the rest of the crowd. He'd never thought about wanting to do that, but now he could see the difference. How the sparseness might have kept some people from approaching him.

She shrugged and took a deep breath. "I hope it helps."

He did something he couldn't have imagined doing forty-eight hours ago. He reached out and gave her shoulder a squeeze. Quick. Platonic. Mostly. He was pleased with himself for how normal that was, despite how she was acting.

He almost liked this guy. He was reminding

himself of who he used to be in the army. Once he'd gotten past basic training and understood the general structure of everything. He'd been comfortable. He might not have known if a bomb was going to go off when he walked into a situation, but he had known what was expected of him.

Now he didn't know what Cara expected of him, but he was starting to understand what he expected from himself, and that was very, very new. *Flick that domino.*

He nodded. "Thanks for getting this together. Bringing me stuff seems to be your new habit."

She smiled at that. "Well, I do work for you, and this is business."

Business. Right. That's what he couldn't get a handle on the past few days. What exactly Cara wanted from him, or was offering of herself. Where her issues were coming from. "Um, I know I'm kind of new to this whole flirtation dynamic thing, but you're confusing the hell out of me."

Her friendly smile fell. "Ugh. I'm sorry, Wes. Really. I'm in a weird place right now. Trying to figure out me, I guess. It doesn't have anything to do with you."

"You know…" He couldn't believe he was about to say this, but she brought it out in him. That long-buried need to help people, not just animals. He'd never helped any person; that's why he'd buried the instinct.

But, every once in a while, she made him believe he could do something for her. Even if he was totally delusional, it was a feeling he couldn't fight. Because she'd given him something he'd given up on so many times.

She deserved some piece of himself in return. Some *attempt* at a piece of himself, anyway.

"I know what it's like to not have any direction. Coming back from Afghanistan, I didn't know what I was going to do, and being in the army was the only time I'd ever felt like, I don't know, myself. I had a purpose, and I didn't feel like an outcast. It was a good place for me, and I didn't have that anymore, and I didn't have my vet dream anymore and I didn't know anything."

"I can't believe you're even comparing the two, Wes. I'm some idiot who's never had anything really bad happen to her and you—"

"Are a pathetic mess of bad things?"

"Are so sweet it hurts." She shook her head. "Thanks for saying all that. Really. The last thing I want to do is drag you into my crap."

"I find myself oddly not minding. The thing is, regardless of if the circumstances are easy or tragic, figuring out who you are sucks. But it happens. It'll happen for you."

She stared up at him, like how she did when

he'd suggested baking her pies at home instead of the restaurant. All wonder and amazement.

Which was both amazing and uncomfortable at the same time. He had to look away, clear his throat.

"I do not know what to do about you, Wes Stone," she said, shaking her head.

"If it helps, I feel that way a *lot*."

She laughed as he'd hoped, but then she looked a little sad again. He hated seeing that. Hated that she felt as though she couldn't get a handle on herself when she had done so much for him.

"Listen, um, do you want to..." He couldn't believe he was about to do this. But he had to. For himself. Regardless of the outcome, he owed it to himself to try. "Have dinner with me?"

"Like a date?"

"Yes. I am asking you out on a date." He'd throw up over that later. That and the fact she was staring up at him, wide-eyed, as if he'd asked her to jump into no-man's-land.

"Oh. Well." She let out a long breath. "Remember yesterday when I said I wouldn't be any good for your stuff?"

"Yeah, and I don't think I'd be any good for yours, but maybe we should do it anyway. I haven't wanted to try anything hard in a long time. And now I do? I guess. I don't know. Things are weird. You kind of pushed me into the weird."

"Ditto, honey."

He chuckled. "So, what do you say? Try this out. If we fail spectacularly, we do it together." He tried not to squirm or fall back into those nerves.

Because all the stuff he'd just said to her was true. He'd had to find himself again after the army and losing the vet chances, and he hadn't realized it in the past few years but he actually had. He'd built this business and himself in the process.

He understood—what she was going through, where she was coming from. The way uncertainty and failure clawed at you until you felt like some weird shell of yourself. So, if they had amazing sex and almost kind of understood each other, why shouldn't they try?

He wasn't scared of her—or life. Maybe he hadn't figured out his family issues, but he had figured out what he needed and he went about giving himself that. It hadn't been easy, but here he was. Successful business, *not* a virgin and asking someone out.

"I don't think failing spectacularly is an *if*, more of a *when*."

He shrugged and held out his hand. "So be it?"

CARA STARED AT Wes's outstretched hand. Who was this guy? Not a stutter or blush or anything. He was giving her life advice and asking her out with barely an "um." How had things gotten all topsy-turvy?

She couldn't believe she was even contemplating it. An actual date. With a guy who was life skilling and experiencing her out of the water.

And she was scared. She felt things for Wes, and the two times she'd gone into a date with feelings or hope, as with Kevin and James, Kevin had tricked her and she'd failed James.

But Wes was standing there looking so hopeful. The fact of the matter was, she *did* want to go on a date with him. Maybe if she went in knowing it wouldn't go anywhere—because one of them was bound to ruin it—then the ending wouldn't have to be that painful, even if she went in with feelings.

"You can say no, Cara. I won't be scarred into not asking a woman out for another thirty-one years, really."

He seemed to mean it, but she was reminded how little experience Wes had. There was no way she was the right woman to handle his baggage, but maybe she could be the right woman to give him a quick, fun relationship that would lead him on to less quick, more fun, deeper relationships.

She ignored the little pinch in her heart at the thought of other women and smiled. "I'm not going to say no." She took his still-outstretched hand and shook it. "The race to see who screws this up first is on."

"Your optimism warms my heart," he said dryly.

She couldn't comment on that, because a family approached the booth, and they seemed to bc regulars because Wes greeted them with news about some new size of treat he'd made for smaller dogs.

Cara offered a little wave before heading back to Mia's booth. Maybe the idea of an actual date was intimidating, but with a mission—give Wes a fun dating experience—everything would be fine. And he figured they'd fail, so there was no expectation. No one would be hurt when they weren't right for each other.

A few minutes later, her phone chimed. Pick you up at seven?

She looked back at Wes's booth and offered a smile and a nod. Everything would be fine, and they would both have fun and it'd be great.

If the little pool of dread in her stomach didn't dissipate, she'd make sure it did before seven.

CHAPTER TWENTY-ONE

WES STOOD AT his truck, fighting the urge to pull out his cell phone and text a "sorry, can't make it" to Cara.

Why on earth had he thought this was a good idea? Something he needed to do? Something he wanted to do? A frigging date. A date. At a restaurant. With people.

With Cara.

Screw the dominoes. He'd kick them all over and throw them away and go home and…

No. He yanked open the truck door and climbed in. He was better than this. He was. He could be. If he tried. Because he cared, and he couldn't cut that out or ignore it away, so this was his only choice.

Pulling triggers right and left. That's what they were doing. Which was insane and probably why it was working for him.

He drove to town, maybe clutching the steering wheel a little tight. Maybe having some second thoughts, but he didn't stop and he didn't turn around. He was making progress. Damn it.

He pulled the truck into the spot behind her car in front of her little apartment complex. Some old building that could use a face-lift for sure.

The nerves returned, but he ignored them. Because, at the end of the day, he'd already slept with her. Had asked her out. He'd hurdled all these issues with her and she kept saying yes. Kept agreeing to work with him and sleep with him and go on a date with him.

So, what was the worst that could happen? They ran out of things to talk about? She changed her mind? Big deal. He had a pocket full of things he'd done once, which meant he could do them again. Even if it was with someone else.

He flexed his hand, ignoring the little zing of pain from clutching the steering wheel too tight. It'd go away. So would the dull headache. It would all fade, and he would be fine.

Maybe he'd even move on enough to believe that he could be fine long-term.

Sex has broken your brain.

But what a way to go. When he got to Cara's, he knocked on the door, and it was flung open after a few seconds. She was wearing a dress that was all swirly blues and purples and greens. It dipped low at the top and came to a stop considerably above her knees. Her hair was all piled on top of her head, and her lips were pink, her eyes all sparkly.

Any doubts he'd had vanished for the time being. "Hi."

"Howdy," she offered with a grin as Sweetness sniffed at his shoes.

"Did you get your pies done?"

Her face softened, which always made his chest feel tight. "You remembered."

"Well, it's a big deal. Your first pie weekend. Right?"

She swallowed and nodded. "It *is* a big deal. And, yes, pies were made and delivered. And I don't want to think about that for the rest of the night."

"Oh." That kind of ruined the date he had planned.

"What?"

"I don't know. I thought we could go there. And you could order your own pie. You know. To see. But—"

"Wes."

He'd never understand how that sweet, mystified way she said his name could make him feel both like king of the world and terrified at the same time.

"That is…" She shook her head, eyes looking a little shiny.

He wanted to back away, but he didn't have anywhere to go. "We don't have to. I can think of something else and—"

She cut him off with a kiss, a squeeze—that easy, exuberant way she had with people that he could never begin to match. The way that had been missing the past few days. Now it was back.

"You are the sweetest thing." She released him and grabbed a sparkly black purse off the table, then slipped into some really high-looking heels that somehow managed to make her legs look even longer. "Let's go."

"But you said—"

"I was wrong. Time to emphasize the success and forget the mistakes."

"Wow, you can do that?"

"I'm sure as hell going to try."

He followed her out the door. If she was going to try, so was he.

CARA HAD NEVER felt so nervous and out of place on a date in her life. She didn't do tiny little niche restaurants with food on the menu she'd never even heard of. She was lucky if a guy took her out to Applebee's instead of the local bar.

This date felt so much more real and adult and important on its own than any other crap date she'd been on prior, she didn't need the added out-of-her-realm ambiance. She might be sick.

Luckily, Wes didn't look any more comfortable. Totally adorable in his khaki pants and flannel shirt all buttoned up and clean and crisp. He even looked as if he'd trimmed his beard a bit.

What she needed was a drink, but the locally brewed beer had been exorbitantly expensive. So, she'd ordered water. And a weird salad with locally grown dried peaches.

She pushed the greens around on her plate, then leaned forward when she noticed Wes was poking at the beet thing he'd ordered.

"I am *so* out of place here," she whispered.

"You? That guy over there is wearing skinny jeans and has a handlebar mustache."

She had to cover her mouth to keep from laughing too loud. Yeah, they were sticking out like two sore thumbs, but something about doing it with Wes was kind of fun. Awkward fun. That had to be a Wes specialty.

The waitress appeared with their slices of pie. *Her* pie. She'd made this morning with her own two hands. She glanced at Wes, who was grinning at her. A real grin.

Gah, he was the sweetest. *And not for you.* She pushed that thought away. She was celebrating her successes, like Mia had told her to do. All her gooey unacceptable feelings for Wes would have to take a backseat.

"This is our locally made and baked pie," the waitress explained. "Made by a baker from a nearby small farming community. They were a real hit last night and going fast tonight. If you enjoy, make sure to come back next weekend, when we'll be serving them again."

Cara had to bite her lip to keep from giggling as the waitress disappeared. *She* was a baker from a small farming community. She was being served to all these strangers. A real hit.

"Okay, this is kind of dumb, but, um—" she dug her phone out of her purse "—take a picture of me with the pie?"

"Not dumb," he said, taking the phone from her and snapping a picture before handing it back. "Now you."

"No. No, I am not photogenic."

"Oh, come on, you're adorable."

"Great. Adorable. That's manly." But he smiled uncomfortably, holding up a forkful of pie.

She hit the button then giggled because his eyes were half closed, and his smile was more of a grimace. Yeah, not exactly photogenic.

"You put that on your refrigerator, I'll kill you."

She grinned at him. "It gets a special place of honor. A magnetic frame right at eye level on the freezer." She looked around the restaurant real quick, then pulled her chair over to Wes's side. "Here. Selfie time."

She held out the phone until she got both of their faces in the frame, then clicked the button. "Hey, that's not half-bad!" And it wasn't. His eyes were open with a kind of kill-me-now almost smile on his face.

"You must be magic."

She laughed, but then she kissed him on the cheek because it was so wonderful and scary that he could make her *feel* like magic. *Easy, girl.*

Her phone chimed, and she looked at the text from her friend Mackenzie. Come out tonight. Please, please, please, please.

"Everything okay?"

Belatedly, she realized she was frowning, so she focused on smiling and moving her chair back to her side of the table.

"Oh, my friends, they usually go to Juniors on Saturday nights. A friend of mine was asking me to come." Cara waved it off, not wanting to explain how much she didn't want to go, how much she didn't want to *pretend* things were fine when they weren't. Which was the only thing Mackenzie would want from her tonight. "I'll get there next time."

He fidgeted, clearing his throat like he did when he was nervous. "We could go. If you wanted to."

She didn't. At all, but... "You want to meet my friends?"

He shrugged, scooping up his last bite of pie. "If that's what you want to do."

Cara had to blink at him for a second. She

couldn't imagine him fitting in at the bar. It was loud and crazy and her "friends" would have something to say about her and Wes. He wasn't exactly the kind of guy she routinely dated. He wasn't exactly the kind of guy any of them hung out with, like, ever.

But she was trying to be the fun date. Maybe that's what Wes needed. Some normalcy. A bar on a Saturday night with a group of people. Maybe she could help him loosen up and make some friends.

And maybe a little selfishly she could rub Wes in Kevin's face. Prove to her friends that their brand of friendship no longer needed to encompass her Saturday nights.

So, she grinned. "Okay. That sounds fun."

IT WASN'T HIS first mistake of the night, but agreeing to meet Cara's friends at a bar was definitely the biggest.

It was smoky and loud. His hand was numb, his head throbbed, and he felt even more out of place than he had at the restaurant.

There was drinking. Lots of drinking. Lots of laughter, but the part that kept his shoulders tense and his fists clenched was the way these people all talked to each other. It was worse than the army, worse than high school. The constant ragging on each other, arguing, slapping—arms, butts. And it wasn't just her friends. Cara was part of it. Ridiculing and pushing and acting like it was *fun*.

He wanted to go home. Badly. But most of the time Cara was plastered to his side. Once she'd even sat on his lap for a few minutes. So, maybe he could endure for a little while longer.

"Wes. Darts, man?" The guy he liked the least thus far held out a few darts, but Wes shook his head.

"I'll, uh, have to pass."

"What kind of pussy did you bring us, Car?"

"Oh, my God, Kevin," one of the girls, he'd lost track of their names, said, slapping the table. She was definitely the drunkest of the four, though, and, he thought, possibly engaged to Kevin and definitely giving Cara many an evil eye. "He was, like, hurt in the war! Don't you pay attention to anything?"

Kevin shrugged. Cara squeezed his arm. "Ignore them," she said into his ear.

He'd love to ignore them. In the comfort of his cabin.

"You know, I've never known Cara to go for the uptight military type." Kevin tossed the darts onto the table, all but sneering. "Usually it's more of the fun, rebel type."

Which earned him a death glare from his drunk fiancée, and if Wes didn't feel so awful, he'd laugh at this moron thinking himself some kind of rebel.

"I could have been in the army. Look, no offense," another guy—C.J.?—said, leaning back in his chair and folding his arms behind his head. "But it doesn't take brains or anything."

"Yeah, and you're so well known for your brains. Someone needs to cut you off." Cara nudged his half-drunk fifth or sixth beer away from his reach.

"Oh, don't be such a sensitive bitch," he snapped back, giving her arm a push.

Wes shoved away from the table and ignored the driving need to take a swing at the guy. "Okay, I've had enough. Let's go."

She blinked up at him from her seat all surprised. "Oh. Okay." She grabbed her purse and said something to the table, but Wes was already walking away.

"I'm sorry you're upset, but it's fine," she said, grabbing for his arm. "Really. This is our norm. It's fun."

He stopped in his tracks. Was she serious right now? "Fun? This is how you treat friends? How you let them treat you? I know I don't have friends, but that is not friendship."

"Well, we're joking around. Look, it's fine. I'll tell them to lay off the army stuff and we can go ba—"

"He called you names and pushed your arm. I go back there, I'm going to clock the guy."

"He doesn't mean anything by it. These are my friends. We've been friends forever."

"Your friends suck. And they're bullies. And you're kind of one, too, when you're with them. I'm not going to stick around and be a part of that anymore. So, I'll see you later." He didn't want to be angry with her, not when her friends were so awful.

But they *were* her friends. And she was defending them. He couldn't deal with that. So, he stalked out of the bar. Outside he could breathe again, though the thumping of the music still reverberated through his head.

He needed a few minutes of quiet, then he'd go back in and apologize and ask if she needed a ride home. But he was not going to go hang out with those people again. Not for another painful minute.

At the sound of crunching gravel, Wes looked back. Cara was stomping toward him, eyes blazing.

"I am not a bully."

"Could have fooled me," he muttered.

"They…they have been being jerks to me for… months. So, maybe I dished it right back out tonight. But…that has nothing to do with you."

"Then I will get home and get out of your way.

Because you know what, Cara? My idea of a good time isn't being jerks to people who are jerks to me. There are plenty of jerks in the world."

"Yes, and you prefer to hide from them instead of build relationships with them."

"At the risk of sounding like the girl with her tongue down the other guy's throat 75 percent of the time, *duh*."

"And that's somehow better? Ignoring the people who've known you forever. Who are supposed to be you friends. Who are supposed to care."

"They. Don't."

She looked as if she'd been slapped, and he didn't know what to do about that. How could she not see that her friends did not give a crap about her?

"What do you know about caring?"

That grated, and if he wasn't so angry with her and them it might have hurt, but with the haze of anger boiling in his blood, he didn't have to dwell on that. "Oh, I don't know, maybe I care about you. And not one person in there treated you with an ounce of respect."

"Maybe you're projecting your issues onto my friends."

She was right. Kind of. This group reminded him all too much of Mom's old boyfriend. The guy had been an asshole, and Mom had taken the insults like some kind of due.

Which wasn't any different than what he'd done with Liz. Or any of the guys in the army who'd ragged on him, although that had never been as bad as high school or Rick the Dick.

"You know what? If you're going to snipe at me when I don't do exactly what you think I should, I don't want to date you. Or sleep with you. I know I'm not perfect, but I get enough of that kind of judgment from my mother, thank you very much."

"You're not perfect, but I'm not going to… I'm not going to try for something that scares me with someone who refuses to see herself." How could she see how wonderful she was and let those people treat her like dirt?

"I don't know who the heck myself is, how can I see it? We keep having this same fight, and I don't want to anymore. I want to have fun, and that is *not* going to be us. So, go home."

She started stalking past him toward the road.

"Let me drive you." He didn't want to spend time in a car with her, because she was right. He wasn't fun, and this was a failure. But at least it was an honest failure, not Liz basically setting him up to fail and be a laughingstock. This was just something not working.

"Go to hell."

Really not working. "Cara, this wasn't how it was supposed to go." Why couldn't he ever keep his mouth shut around her? For five years his best skill had been pretty much not saying anything that wasn't completely necessary. To Mom. To customers. To doctors. He'd kept it all in.

Why did it leak out around her?

"No shit. I thought we'd have some fun. Not you getting all self-righteous on me."

He was not going to say anything to that. He was learning his lesson. No more telling her she deserved better, because she didn't want to believe it. "Please, let me drive you home," he forced through gritted teeth.

"Fine," she grumbled. "But only because I'm wearing these stupid heels."

In silence they walked to his truck. In silence he drove to her apartment. In silence she opened her door and hopped out. He started to do the same.

"You don't have to walk me to my door. It's, like, ten feet." She slammed the door behind her.

She was right. He got the rest of the way out anyway. He didn't want to leave things like this. He didn't know how to fix it, but he didn't want to leave it, either.

What had he been thinking?

She jammed her key into her door, muttering to herself about the old lock, and he stood at the bottom of the stairs, watching her like some kind of creeper.

"Cara."

"What? Want to tell me my door opening technique is wrong? Or… Or…" She kicked the door.

Yeah, he couldn't leave it like this because as much as parts of it were about him, obviously some of it was about *her.* She wanted to blame him, but that wasn't really it.

He climbed the stairs while she jiggled her key, finally getting the door open.

"I just don't like most people," he started, having no idea where he was going. But he kept saying dumb things without thinking, so why not keep at it? "I haven't felt compelled to *be* with anyone, even just hang out with anyone, in years. So, you're different and you're special, and listening to people treat you like crap, it really bugs me."

It came out of nowhere. No forward thought. No planning or prep. He tipped his head down and kissed her. He kissed her all the way into her apartment.

"What are you doing?" she asked, wide-eyed. She was clutching his shoulders, holding on, not pushing him away.

It was that that kept him going. "I have literally no idea." But his mouth was on hers again, and she was kissing him back so, well, that's what he was going to do.

CHAPTER TWENTY-TWO

THIS WAS CRAZY. She was mad at him. He was annoying and judgmental and right. And so freaking hot she could barely stand it. She pulled at the buttons of his shirt.

His hands were in her hair, ruining the time she'd spent making it look casual and touchable. Who cared, when he was kissing her with a kind of bold, completely not stuttery desperation that made her think about being pushed against the wall and dirty, dirty things.

Anything was better than the heart-clenching feeling of him thinking she deserved to be treated better. Coming to that conclusion herself was one thing, having someone who'd known her a matter of weeks confirming it was something so huge and encompassing she didn't know *how* to act.

So, she'd do this instead. She finally got all his buttons undone and tugged at the shirt until it fell off. Without her even having to ask or do it herself or dare him into it, he reached behind him and pulled the T-shirt over his head.

"Take me to your bedroom."

"Are you giving me orders?"

"Y-yes." Then he scowled, presumably at himself. "Yes," he repeated, not stuttering this time.

Hot. She kicked off her shoes, then took his hand and led him down the hall to her bedroom. He stepped inside, but instead of tossing her onto the bed like she'd hoped, he stood in the doorway.

"You should…" He swallowed, then crossed his arms over his chest. Determined. Determined to be Mr. In Charge. Yeah. It was hard to remember why she'd been mad. "Take off your dress."

She reached behind her and undid the button at the back of her neck, then grabbed the hem of her dress, lifting it slowly up and over.

"Wow."

Man, one minute he was tearing her ego down, the next—*zoom.* Through the roof. He looked at her was as if she was the most amazing thing he'd ever seen, and that was addictive.

Then he propelled her back to the bed, covered her, kissed her, touched her. No hesitation. No second thoughts.

Apparently, tonight had really flipped his switches.

"You have condoms?"

She nodded to her nightstand. "In the drawer."

"Good."

"Do I ruin the moment and ask how we went from arguing and being mad to this?"

"Do you want to?"

She took in the long, lean torso. Muscles and a *very* happy trail and oh, they could fight and be done later. She began unbuckling his belt. "Nope."

"Good."

His gaze stayed glued to her hands. Unbuckling, unbuttoning, unzipping and then she tucked her hand into his boxers and found the long, hard length of him.

Oh, hello again.

She stroked, watching the muscles of his left arm flex as he held himself above her. He gently took her wrist and pulled her hand out of his underwear, then crawled off the bed. She was about to protest, but he tugged off his boots and opened the nightstand, then pulled a condom out of the box she kept there.

He handed the packet to her, standing at the edge of the bed.

She rolled the condom on him slowly, watching the muscles in his legs tense. She ran her palms over the coarse hair covering his thighs. "Now what?"

"Lie down."

She scooted back on the bed until her head was on the pillow. He followed her slowly and gently settled himself between her legs.

"You'll stop me if I do something you don't like, and it won't be a big deal."

She was pretty sure he said it more for his own benefit than for hers, but she nodded. "Yup. FYI, Bossy Wes works for me."

"All right, well, Bossy Wes says you're the most beautiful woman he's ever been with."

"Not funny."

"It's true. There is no comparison."

She ran her fingers down his back, all the way down to his butt, then pinched.

"Bossy Wes does not approve."

"Mmm, Bossy Wes can feel free to punish me."

"Hmm." He trailed fingers up the side of her calf slowly. Like ridiculously slowly. Then he kissed her knee, her thigh and her hip bone right above the edge of her panties.

It was all slow and attentive and not at all what she'd imagined when he'd grabbed her and kissed her in the doorway. But he kept kissing. Her belly button, her side, between her breasts.

Even with all the Bossy Wes jokes, it was unbearably sweet. Meaningful. How was this happening, when they'd been yelling at each other in a bar parking lot fifteen minutes ago? When meaningful was the last thing she wanted?

He kissed her collarbone from one side all the way to the other. "Wes…what…" She didn't even know what she was trying to say. This was too much. It made her feel all vulnerable and emotional and—oh, damn him.

"I am not willing to walk away from this yet." He positioned himself at her entrance, flexing his right hand before shifting to his forearms.

"Does your hand—" He thrust deep, and anything she would have asked about him being okay turned into a groan.

Any hesitation or timidity or pauses that had happened the first few times they'd had sex were gone. Wes set the speed. His hands roamed. He kissed her mouth, her neck, her shoulder. It was all very purposeful and certain.

You did that. Oh, such a weird thought. It made her stomach flip and the excitement in her belly tighten and sharpen.

He increased the pace, his hand clamping on to her hip, finding the right spot that had her arching her back, crying out and spiraling into orgasm.

He wasn't far behind, pushing deep on a low moan, his left hand still gripping her hip tight as he leaned all his weight on to his right forearm.

She wanted to cozy in, hold him, not let go, but he pulled his head back, looking directly at her. It made her uncomfortable.

"Wes."

His hand slid from her hip, up her side, shoulder and neck, to cup her face, his eyes never breaking their gaze on hers. "You're beautiful and amazing. You are." He was so earnest, and he kept holding her face so she couldn't look away. Not from the truth in his gorgeous blue eyes. "I'm bad at all of this, but never doubt that."

"You know, if I can't be down on myself, and my friends can't make fun of each other, then you have to stop saying how bad you are at things."

"I don't—" He rolled off her, though he kept her close. He blew out a breath. "Okay, I'll work on it." She handed him some tissues so he could get rid of the condom. He was quiet for a long time after that, his fingers trailing back and forth over her shoulder.

"You were somewhat right," he said quietly. "There was some projecting. Hiding is my coping thing. You can't get hurt or watch other people get hurt if you're alone. People can't hurt you as much, but I guess it doesn't change that it happens."

"I've known my friends since we were, like, babies. I keep telling myself they…don't mean anything by it."

"Okay, maybe that's true, but why be with people who say nasty things about you, even if they don't mean it? Do your sisters do that to you?"

"Well, no, but they're different."

"But—" he scrubbed a hand over his face "—one of the things we talked about in therapy was surrounding yourself with things that make you happy. That make you feel right. It's like with the pie thing and doing it in a non-stressful environment. You undermine the triggers when you can."

"Did you sex me into a puddle so you could therapize me?"

"I like you."

"Aw, honey, I like you, too." She let out a gusty sigh. "But I don't want to keep having the same fight with you." And she didn't want to feel as if this was real, even though that's what it felt like right this minute. He had a point about…choosing how she spent her time and with whom. About undermining the triggers.

The fact of the matter was, her friends made her feel like less. Like a failure. And she already felt that way enough on her own. She'd actually been oddly happier without them the past few weeks, even *with* all the stuff with Wes.

"Do you think we're having the same fight, or is it evolving?"

She shook her head. Sometimes she couldn't believe what came out of his mouth. "You know, when the cute guy with the shaggy hair helped me up after my vicious dog attack—"

He snorted, so she gave him a little push. "I never thought I'd be having conversations about evolving and triggers and… You're kind of amazing yourself. I just hate that you're right all the time."

He grinned, but then she felt him shift and he flexed his hand again. "Your hand is bothering you."

He shrugged. "That's what it does."

"When's your surgery?"

He shrugged again. "Not sure yet."

"Is there anything I can do to help? Ice? A heating pad?"

"It's fine." He sat up, grabbing his pants from the edge of the bed. "I should get going."

His injuries were a sore spot. She imagined the hand bothered him the most since that's what had kept him from becoming a vet. Even though she was a little disappointed there wasn't something she could do to help, she didn't have any right to push.

So, she worked up a smile and patted her bed. "You could stay."

He tugged on the jeans, covering up most of the fun. "I'd like to, really, but I have to get back to the dogs."

"Oh."

He grabbed his boots, then paused. "You could come with."

"You sure? I use up a lot of hot water in the morning."

"I'm sure. In fact, if you come, maybe Bossy Wes will make another appearance."

"Jokes and bossy sex. Man, I really am good for you."

He got that thoughtful look on his face, then leaned down and kissed her forehead. "You really are."

Melted. Dead. That was her. It made her want to decline the offer, back out. But she didn't want to be the girl who kept giving him mixed signals. They *were* dating. She had to remind herself from time to time that Wes was someone she was helping have some fun.

Definitely not someone she was falling for.

THE PAIN WAS UNBEARABLE. Sharp. Burning. Everywhere. A dream mixed up with reality.

When he finally managed to get his eyes open and sit up, Phantom was at the edge of the bed, pressing his nose to Wes's side.

Wes sat perfectly still for a few seconds, but Cara didn't stir. He slid out of bed and did his best to tiptoe out of the room, Phantom padding after him.

He flexed his hand, then rested it on top of Phantom's head. It didn't help the pain, but it helped him remember to breathe.

He was lucky enough not to suffer from dreams of the explosion too often. Just every once in a while, when the pain was particularly bad. It was less of a dream and more snatches of memory.

The blast. The heat. The pain.

Phantom whimpered, leaning against Wes's legs. Yeah, he needed to let it go. Doing his best to be quiet, he eased the front door open and stepped out onto the porch. Late spring evening was cool without being cold. It was a clear night, all stars and moon. The sound of frogs and insects buzzing worked together to form the low hum of the woods at night.

He took a deep breath and let it out, trying to push the memories and the pain out with it. It didn't make them disappear, but the dream faded even if the pain didn't.

He needed to make the appointment for surgery. Or get a second opinion. Or something. He needed to act.

But the sad fact was, he'd rather ignore it. Put it off for another day. He could live with a little pain. He'd lived with it so far. Not like it was going to cause any more damage. The damage had been caused.

Tension crept into his shoulders even as he knelt down to pet Phantom. He didn't want to be thinking about any of this. He just wanted it to go away.

The door creaked. "Wes?"

He stood and turned to Cara, who he could

barely make out in the dark. "Sorry, thought I heard Shrimp. Must have been opossums or raccoons." He wasn't sure why the lie popped out. Why he wasn't straight with her about the pain. He was straight with her about everything else.

But he didn't want to worry her. He didn't want that at all between them.

He'd rather pretend it didn't exist. He might be able to change some pieces of himself, some beliefs, some ways he handled the world, but his injuries were there. Always. Irrevocable. Talking or worrying about them would be completely pointless.

She leaned against his back. "Mmm. So pretty out here."

He looked up at the sky, littered with stars and the Milky Way and a near-full moon. "Yeah." He shifted, hopefully subtly, so that he could put his left arm around her shoulders.

"You okay? You're all tense."

"Just hoping it's not an opossum. They're disgusting."

"The dogs don't chase them off?"

Didn't think that lie through, did he? "Lazy."

She laughed at that, then took his face in her hands. "Come back to bed, honey." She pulled him toward the door, then looked at Phantom on his heels.

"Phantom. Stay."

Wes watched as Phantom sat, head cocked. He didn't always take orders from others, but apparently Cara was an exception.

Yeah, that seemed about right.

"He listened to me," she said, clearly pleased with herself. "You better watch out. He's going to want to come live with me and Sweetness, too."

"I wouldn't blame him a bit."

She tugged his right arm, and he fought against the outward reaction to the sharp pain. Since she kept tugging, she obviously didn't notice. And he'd take a lot of pain to keep it that way.

CHAPTER TWENTY-THREE

"AT SOME POINT, someone is going to see us and call the cops."

Cara disentangled herself from Wes. "I don't think it's illegal to make out in a car."

"It might be in a farmers' market full of people."

She peered out the window. "Please, there's barely anyone here. Besides, it's nothing I haven't caught Mia and Dell doing." Of course, that had been the morning they got engaged.

The lung-squeezing feeling that was becoming practically second nature coiled in her chest. She was in some sort of vortex. One she wanted to get out of, but it kept sucking her deeper.

Deeper into *feelings* with Wes. Lots of sex and making out in cars and just wanting to be with him.

Stop it. "Well, let's get to work, then." She popped out of Wes's truck, already trying to come up with an excuse to have Mia drive her home. Maybe if she managed to get some distance from him and his damn wonderfulness, she could figure out how to extricate herself from this mess where she was in an actual relationship and enjoying it.

She was seriously warped.

She helped Wes set up his table while the dogs found their spots in the early morning sun. Cara put out the new signs she'd had made for his different treats. Made sure he'd replaced his old business cards with the new logoed ones.

"You know, you've made a real difference here."

"Huh?"

He pointed to the table. "The labels, the sign, the cards, everything looks so much more professional. I never would have thought of those little touches."

"It's nothing."

He cocked his head, his eyebrows drawn together. "It's something. An important something."

There was that vortex again. Pleasure at the compliment sucking her under even as a little voice in her head told her it was all wrong. This didn't matter. The weekend pies didn't matter. Nothing mattered for a girl like her.

And that wasn't the least bit fun. There had been a week or two where she'd started to feel happy. Like this new life she'd built was a good fit for her, smooth as could be. Everything seemed to be going *right*. The pies, Wes.

But they'd started talking about Mia's wedding

so much, and Cara had caught herself...thinking. Which scared the crap out of her. She'd been dating Wes for a few weeks. She couldn't...think like that. She'd never been that girl. She couldn't be that girl.

She'd dreamed of a wedding. And it wasn't Mia's. Worse, morning sex and making out in his truck had done nothing to alleviate that image in her head.

"Well, I'm going to head over to Mia's booth." She forced a smile, walked over and kissed him on the cheek. "Sell lots, honey."

She could feel him watching her as she walked away, and he probably saw right through her.

She needed to get out of this and fast. When Cara made her way over to Mia's booth, her sisters were waiting with goofy smiles.

Anna let out a high-pitched "ooh" followed by ridiculous kissing noises.

"Oh, be nice," Mia admonished, grinning like an idiot. "I think it's sweet. I've never seen Cara all mushy before."

"I am not mushy." She was crazy. And in big trouble. "We're dating. Having fun."

"Oh, where have I heard that before?" Mia tapped her chin, a comically thoughtful look on her face. "Oh, yes, my *fiancé* said that once," she said, pointing to where Dell and his brother were unloading the truck. "When we were dating and 'having fun until it wasn't.' Whoops."

"You're gonna marry the shaggy hermit!" Anna hopped and clapped, and Cara glared at her.

"I have literally been dating the guy for two weeks. Take back the *M* word this instant." A few weeks. A few *weeks*. You didn't just become someone else in a few weeks. There was still work to do. The pie thing wasn't permanent, and Wes still hadn't scheduled his surgery.

Why would anyone be thinking about anything more than dating—let alone *her*?

"You never know. I mean, isn't that the point of dating at your age? To find someone to spend forever with?"

"At my age? Listen here—"

Mia put a hand over Cara's pointed finger, her head cocked in that concerned big sister way. Ew.

"Why are you freaking out? We're teasing."

"Yeah, well, it's not funny."

"Ah."

"Don't do that." Cara wrangled her finger free and pointed it in Mia's face. "Do not 'ah' me."

"You've been a lot happier the past few weeks."

"No."

"It wouldn't be the end of the world."

"Yes, it would!"

Mia and Anna exchanged a glance. Not a how-can-we-needle-her-more glance, a what's-wrong-with-her glance.

They'd never understand. Mia was marrying the first guy to ever freaking kiss her, and Anna... Anna was eighteen and sure of everything.

She had to fix this. Fight out of the vortex, right now, before it sank her any deeper or brought any more people into thinking that she and Wes were anything more than her teaching him how to have a good time with a girl.

Because those moments of thinking they could be more were some of the scariest moments of her life.

She glanced over at Wes's booth. She could only make out his shoulder and Phantom's missing-a-chunk tail. Her heart clutched, but she had to do this. For all of them.

"HEY, HONEY."

Wes tensed. He'd maybe only known Cara a little while, but especially the past few weeks of dating, he'd been paying attention. Kind of like the way he did with a new dog, which was probably insulting, but so be it. You watched, observed and figured out what made them skittish, and either plied them with treats or avoided the trigger.

He'd done that with himself, too.

He hadn't figured out all Cara's triggers, but he

knew when she used that syrupy-sweet "honey," she was not in a good place. And so far, he'd been able to distract her from that not good place, but he was beginning to think their time was running out.

Things had been good. Dating and sex and having fun, but it hadn't escaped his notice that there was this little sliver of something that didn't click quite right. He hadn't figured it out yet, but her *honey* made him wonder if he'd even get the chance.

"You ready to go?"

She smiled, but there was absolutely no warmth behind it. "You know, I'm actually going to go home with Mia."

"Ah."

Her smile tightened, though he didn't know why his one-word answer caused that. "Anyway, I think I'm going to cancel tonight. I should probably hang out with my friends. That's our tradition. Saturday nights."

He had to clench his jaw on that one. Her *friends*. The ones she admitted hadn't treated her well. The ones she'd stopped hanging out with because they made her feel bad about herself.

He could argue with her, but obviously Cara had made up her mind to dump him. Hey, getting dumped was on his list of to-be-experienced things. Lucky him.

But, it was the *why* he didn't understand. Had he done something wrong?

"Anyway, I'll see you Monday."

Her cavalier wave and complete lack of acting as if anything mattered grated along every last nerve. "If you're breaking up with me, I'd appreciate you being a little bit more direct."

She stopped in her tracks and shook her hair back, failing to achieve the careless air she seemed to be aiming for. "Okay, well, we've had our fun, and you got to date and sleep with somebody for a bit. You know, I'm the type who gets bored after a while. And you, you should totally sleep with…lots of girls before you get serious about someone."

She pretended to look at him, but her gaze was more on his nose or forehead than his eyes. So, he took a step toward her, unable to swallow down the irritation simmering in his gut. "You're bored, huh?"

For a second, her sad attempt at casual ease slipped. "Well, you know. You're a bit of a homebody. That's great for you, but I like bars and hanging out with my friends. So. It's time."

"Yeah, guess so."

Her eyes flicked to his for the briefest of seconds, then she shrugged and fake smiled. "Glad you agree."

But he couldn't just let it go or keep it in. Not

when he saw so clearly that this was *not* about him or being a homebody. This was so not his fault. He thought they'd walked over this hurdle, but now he realized they'd just sidestepped it.

He wouldn't let her do that. She could walk away, but he was going to give her something she'd given to him. Honesty. "Just so you know, I see through what you're doing here, Cara."

She blinked at him, took a step away. "I don't know what you mean."

"And I can deal with a lot of your crap, but lying to me is stupid."

"I'm not—"

"You want to go? Go. But be honest—that this is about you having no faith or belief in yourself. And having no good reason for that."

For the first time, anger snuck into her expression. "You don't know me, Wes."

"The hell I don't. You think I don't recognize someone hiding away from everything? Been there, done that, sweetheart. I had a way better reason for it."

She fisted her hands on her hips. "Oh, so we're back to 'try harder' and 'your baggage is bigger than mine.'"

"No, we're back to 'you don't want to see beyond the little fiction you've created for yourself because it's safe.'"

"Go to hell, Wes." She turned on a heel and left.

He didn't even feel bad. Angry? Yes. Livid, actually, because he'd finally worked for something real with someone, and she couldn't see past her own stupidity or fear and damn it if he didn't feel sorry for her because he knew how hard that was.

It didn't matter what little hard stuff she'd gone through in comparison to him, because something had made her not see herself.

But he didn't know what he could possibly do about that. Except maybe hope she figured it out.

CHAPTER TWENTY-FOUR

"Earth to Cara."

"Huh?" Cara looked over at Anna, who was curled up on the couch. They'd been waiting for Mia to show up for more wedding planning, and reruns of *Full House,* and Anna had been yapping about how much she couldn't wait to move into her college dorm in the fall.

Cara had been zoning out. Throwing herself a pity party. Because she couldn't get Wes's anger yesterday out of her mind. She wasn't sure what she'd expected when she'd delivered the brush-off, but anger and calling her out had not been it.

It had stuck with her. Curled up in her gut, making her feel sick during her all-night drinking session at Juniors with awful people, which was followed the next day by a hangover and self-pity.

"What is *up* with you? You are being so weird lately."

"What's up with you and Mia being all in my business lately?"

"Uh, we're your sisters, duh."

"Anna Catherine Pruitt!" Mom yelled from somewhere else in the house.

"Uh-oh," Anna muttered. "I'm about to get the 'penises are evil' lecture. Save yourself."

"You are out of your God-given mind if you think for one second I am letting you live in a coed dorm." Mom appeared in the TV room, hands fisted on her hips, cheeks red with outrage.

Which was Mom's look about 75 percent of the time.

"Well, it's too late, because that's what I signed up for."

"Those coed dorms are nothing but cesspools of bad behavior. Do you know what kind of trouble you're asking for by living in one?" Mom walked between them and the TV.

"Oh, here I thought I was being a normal human being who knows how to handle herself."

Mom wagged a finger at Anna, and even though she wasn't the one in trouble, Cara had been on the end of that finger wag enough times to feel that familiar folding in on herself.

"Bad choices lead to terrible consequences." Mom said it the same way she'd been saying it since...since as long as Cara could remember.

"Mom, just because you don't agree with it, doesn't mean it's a bad decision. And just because I live around boys doesn't mean I have to make bad decisions."

"You will not defy me on this, young lady. If you live around boys, who knows what kind of things you'll get roped into."

"Or, I'll say no to those things and be fine. Or I'll even make a not-so-great decision and still be fine."

Anna hadn't taken her eyes off the TV, no matter how Mom tried to get in the way. Anna acted as if this was nothing. While Cara had acted as if Mom's crazy worry was, well, just that—crazy— she'd still felt Mom's words each time she'd made a mistake.

So, it struck her—Anna's calm, rolly-eyed dismissal of Mom's paranoia. Maybe because of everything with Wes or what Mia had said a few weeks ago, but for the first time in her life she saw where that self-defeat came from. Clearly. As if she'd been suddenly cured of blindness.

While she'd spent her life flaunting her bad decisions in the face of Mom's admonitions and anxiety, when it came down to it, she believed all the bad that befell her was because of that. Of not doing everything right. Because she wasn't like Mia and Anna, getting things right had never been easy for her.

She'd always been led by her heart, which tended to get her into trouble. The older she got, the more she realized her heart was so amazingly fallible she'd had to ignore it or hide from it.

If something might cause heartbreak, she ran because…how could she not? How was she supposed to face her dying grandmother in the hospital bed? You couldn't beg someone who was sick and in pain and *wanting* to die to stay alive. You couldn't sob and tell them you'd never be able to survive without them.

And those would have been the only things she could have done. Same with James and his friend. She didn't know how to listen, how to soothe, because then she would have had to relive all the horrible pain of losing Grandma. She would have cried, and you didn't cry about your own hurt when someone else was hurting.

She'd viewed those times as failures, but maybe they…weren't. Maybe they weren't the inevitable *Cara* way of doing something. Maybe it was simply that bad things happened, and sometimes you didn't know how to deal. So you dealt the best way you knew how.

Sometimes it was wrong, but she…could be right. She'd helped Wes. She'd found a way to break off from her friends and build the chance at a career. She wasn't a *failure*. She was just stumbling along trying to avoid…

She was so much like Wes, and she'd never even realized it. He hid in his cabin; she'd hidden behind a carefree party girl persona. When things got hard, he'd pushed her away. When things had been hard for her, she ran.

But each time they'd come back to each other, determined to do better, be better—for each other.

She kept running away from a man who had actual issues, but he treated her with compassion and forgiveness—repeatedly—in ways her life-long friends had not. And he was always there, ready to try again.

Her chest ached. That she could be so blind. That he could be so good.

After running out on Wes, she felt terrible. Even delivering pies and getting a compliment from Sam yesterday hadn't cheered her up. It had made her feel worse, because Wes had been part of the reason she'd even gone after that job after she'd screwed up the interview.

"Tell her, Cara."

She stared at Anna, then at Mom. She didn't know what direction the conversation had taken, but she did know one thing. "I think Anna is one of the smartest, strongest people I know. You should trust her, Mom."

Anna and Mom both blinked at her. It hadn't been a typical "Cara" thing to say, but she meant it. From the bottom of her heart.

Maybe it was time to trust her heart again and pray it would do a little better leading her than her head had.

WES COULDN'T WORK through the frustration dogging him. Everywhere in his house there were little reminders of Cara. She'd forgotten the stupid sparkly leash she'd brought for Sweetness. Anytime he saw the Stone logo, he thought of her having it made for him.

Then there was his bed, and he didn't want to think about that at all.

So, he paced. Phantom watched uneasily from the door.

This was stupid. He finally wanted to be with someone, and she had to be just as screwy as he was. Didn't that figure.

He should rewind the time in his head. Forget that this whole weird spring had ever happened. At least until she showed up for work Monday. If she still would.

And that really pissed him off, because she'd done so much for his business. Not just organizing everything, but the logo, the labels and naming the treats. And he knew she'd smoothed a few clients' feathers on the phone without telling him as much.

Stupid. Stupid. Stupid.

But he wasn't required to sit here fuming. There weren't any rules for the right thing to do in this situation. Which meant he could do anything.

That used to be terrifying, but honestly, when it came to Cara, it was kind of a relief.

Because he could go talk to her. Demand an explanation. Tell her that her devaluing herself was stupid and useless, and she needed to get over it. She needed to *try harder*, and if she didn't like it, she could shut the door in his face.

It couldn't be worse than sitting around here muttering to himself.

"I'M FINE WITH the green, Mia. Really." Cara switched the phone from one ear to the other so she could snuggle into the couch with Sweetness.

"I want you to like it."

"Why? It's *your* wedding."

"But—" A loud banging on Cara's door muffled whatever Mia said.

"Look, we talked about this ad nauseam over dinner. I'm done, Bridezilla. And someone is at the door." She forced herself off the couch. Maybe it was Mackenzie, ready to ply her with more liquor. God knew she needed a little liquid courage to figure out how to deal with the Wes situation, and maybe there was some way to redeem her friendship with Mackenzie. Maybe they could grow up together.

"I'm not being a Bridezilla, am I?"

At the hurt note in Mia's voice, Cara felt about two inches tall. Which, hey, seemed to be the way things were going lately. "No, honey, I'm—"

Someone pounded at the door again. "I gotta get that. Talk tomorrow." Cara clicked End. She was not fit for human contact today.

When she looked out the peephole, it was full of beard, and her heart stopped. She flung open the door, Sweetness yipping at her feet.

"Wes. What are you doing here?" What could he possibly be doing here? She was going to have to face him tomorrow, but she hadn't found the words to apologize. To, well, put into words whatever her epiphany had meant, tell him what it meant for them.

And now here he was, looking angry.

"I want Sweetness back."

"What?" she screeched.

"She's my dog, and I'd like her back."

She stared, openmouthed, in shocked silence. After a few moments, she managed to get her mouth to work again. "But you gave her to me."

"So? She's just a dog. Give her back." He knelt down toward Sweetness, but Cara moved fast enough to stop him.

She couldn't believe this. Sweetness was hers. "You can't have her. I lo—" At the little smirk on his face, she realized she was being played. So well it hurt.

"You care about her? Developed a bond with her? Want to keep spending time with her?"

"Don't think I don't know what you're doing. And comparing yourself to a dog is insulting."

"To who?"

"Wes."

"Let me in."

"I know I said I liked Bossy Wes, but—"

"Let me in, Cara. We need to talk."

"Are you going to steal my dog?"

"Not now that I know you care."

She swallowed. How could he have thought she didn't care? She cared so much she didn't know what to do with it all without making an idiot of herself.

Oh, wait, all this running away from him meant she was already making an idiot of herself.

She moved out of the way so he could step inside, trying to remember what her epiphany had been. That maybe she wasn't destined to have bad things happen to her just because she made bad choices.

Could Wes maybe, just maybe, not be a bad choice? He was so much nicer than all the other guys she'd dated. He saw and cared that she wasn't always her own biggest fan. Had anyone besides her sisters and grandmother ever picked up on that?

"So, what do you want to talk about?" She tried

to find a casual way to stand, to look at him, but everything was awkward and wrong.

"Us. Because I think there should be an us, and I think you breaking up with me was not because I did anything wrong or because we weren't a good fit, but because you were doubting yourself. I know I'm a mess, and you don't think *you* can handle it but you have been. Admirably, until yesterday."

"I don't want to hurt you. And that's kind of what I do."

"You haven't hurt me yet."

"B-but I will!"

"How do you know?"

She turned away from him. She was all jumbled up. She needed time to think, to figure things out. Not be forced into having this conversation with him. Not yet.

She would hurt him, like she'd hurt other people who'd needed her, expected some kind of care or comfort from her.

Or it'll be fine. You'll try and you'll succeed or you'll try and you'll fail, but no one will die because of it, and you'll be fine and so will he.

She rubbed a hand over her face. Everything felt so raw and scary. She wanted to run away, but she had nowhere to go, and maybe that was the theme of this crisis she'd been dealing with.

So, maybe she had to face it.

But how?

"Cara, the bottom line is, I can't think of the last person I ever missed being around. My solitude gives me everything I need. Or it did, until you."

Oh. *Oh.* It was by far the sweetest thing anyone had ever said to her. Ever. And it made everything seem even more possible.

"I don't think you were bored with me. I think you were scared. I recognize scared. If you really are bored by my solitude or my aversion to going out with your friends, tell me. But don't lie to me because you're afraid. Please."

She blinked back the tears in her eyes and swallowed the lump in her throat. He had to go be all perceptive and right. Geez. But here was her moment. She could run away with a lie like he was begging her not to, or she could try to be brave. Try for something hard.

She'd done it with the pies. Fixed her first interview mistake. She could do it here. And if she didn't, well, she'd still be okay.

She turned around, forced herself to look him in the eye. "It was a lie."

"Thank Christ." Then his mouth was on hers and his hands were on her face, and, okay, yeah, this was kind of worth the trying thing.

His hands smoothed down her back, but then

he stopped kissing her. He rested his forehead against hers, looked straight into her eyes.

Whoa, was this the same blushing, stuttering guy? He seemed to have cured himself pretty quickly. Now she was the floundering one, and that didn't seem fair.

"I don't know how to be a boyfriend or whatever. I don't even know how to be a friend or a normal human being half the time, but you'll tell me when I'm wrong. I'll tell you when you are. Like you said before when we were, you know. Making a mistake does not have to be the end of the world."

She pressed a hand to her heart, because what he'd said was so close to what she'd been knocked over with earlier. All the things she'd done, or not done, or failed at... In her head they'd been the end of the world, but in reality she'd just had to keep going and they hadn't been the end of anything.

She rested her other hand over his heart, then let her fingers brush down the front of his T-shirt. "You, sir, are absolutely right." She swallowed at the emotion clogging her throat and smiled up at him. "I panicked a little." At his raised eyebrows she blew out a breath. "Okay, a lot. I can't promise it won't happen again, but I do think this is a turning point. Like, personally, and then maybe that means it can be a turning point for us."

"For the record, I also reserve the right to panic at some point in the future."

"Duly noted," she replied. "Now, I think it is time for the talking portion of the evening to cease."

"Ah, I can be okay with that."

"And Bossy Wes is welcome now."

"That a fact?"

"Very, *very* welcome."

His mouth covered hers again, never leaving it while he propelled her back through the hallway.

Jittery anticipation settled in her stomach. Like before a roller-coaster dip. When it felt as if there'd be nothing to catch her in the end, but the thrill might be worth it.

She wanted to be naked before they got to the bottom of that hill, though. She pulled his shirt up until he leaned forward enough for her to pull it off. She tossed his shirt on the floor, then quickly made work of hers. "What do you want to do tonight? Tell me. In great detail." She tugged at the button of his jeans, but he stilled.

"I…" He cleared his throat. "I don't like it when you want me to talk about everything."

She blinked in surprise, trying to make sense of that. "What?"

He didn't let go of her, but he pulled away, eyes intent on hers. "I don't like to feel like I have to narrate or whatever. I can't… I get in my head, and then I'm not thinking about you. About us."

"Oh. Oh, well, okay. That's okay. You don't have to like everything."

"Good." He nodded, his eyes all but boring holes into hers. "Is there anything I do that you don't like?"

"Like keeping your pants on?"

"I'm serious. I want to be clear and honest. I want…" He trailed off, gaze still blazing into hers. It reminded her of that night after the Liz run-in when he'd been all fierce and determined. But this wasn't about Liz. It was about her.

It was about them.

And she was in the vortex again, sinking under all the amazing things he was, but this time she wanted to fight the panic instead of what she might feel for him.

"No. Nothing yet. I'd tell you."

"Good. Good." And then he kissed her, softly. Unbearably sweet.

"Are you sure we can do this?" She wanted to be sure, but how, when she'd never done it before?

"I'm sure we should try. Really try. You?"

She nodded, slowly at first, then more emphatically. "Yes," she said on little more than a whisper. Yes, she wanted to try. A real relationship. And believe she wouldn't ruin everything, that she might make mistakes, but it would be okay. It would be fine.

Because that's how life worked.

"I want to try."

CHAPTER TWENTY-FIVE

"I'M TIRED OF SUMMER," Cara whined, collapsing onto her couch. She was sweaty and sticky, thanks to the air conditioner at her apartment breaking down in the middle of pie baking today.

"I thought summer was your favorite season."

She draped her arm over her forehead. "Just looking at your beard makes me sweaty."

"I don't know what my beard making you all hot and bothered has anything to do with summer."

Cara grinned. Four months of dating Wes—her longest relationship by far—and it still amazed her when he made jokes like that. He amazed her in a lot of ways. He made her think about the *L* word, which made her feel itchy and uncomfortable.

But she wasn't going to panic. She'd take the *L* word business one day at a time.

He rocked back on his heels and frowned at the air-conditioning unit. "You're going to have to call the landlord."

"Ugh. Ugh. Ugh. I still have four pies to bake."

On a Tuesday, because with the summer fruits available, Sam had asked her to add two week-days to her supply schedule. Even hot, sweaty and achy from bending over the counter to perfect a lattice, she'd had to grin at that.

Sam was talking about doing pie service every night. Damn if things weren't going perfectly. All she'd had to do was believe they could. All she had to do was believe that things would be okay, regardless. Imagine that.

"You could bake them at my place. And spend the night."

"Oh, gee, as if I don't do that enough."

He grinned, nudging her over so he had a sliver of cushion to sit on. "You're welcome to stay here and sweat to death."

She sat up and tugged on his beard. "Shave. Feel the cool air on your face."

"What happened to your pro-beard agenda?"

"It's too hot to be pro-beard. Besides, I think the beard loses some effectiveness without the flannel." She could already imagine Wes's cool, dark, private cabin. Funny how it had become her favorite place. Exactly what she wanted.

Then she remembered it was Tuesday. "Oh, crud, I promised I'd have dinner at home tonight. You could come, and then we could head out to your place after."

He stiffened like he always did. She tried not

to care like she always did. That was relationships, right? Nothing was perfect, but you ignored it. Didn't panic or get upset. Just dealt. Or something.

"The dogs. I have that conference call at six."

"I still don't understand how you can have a weekly conference call about dog treats. That's, like, overkill, isn't it?" She wasn't cranky that he was circumnavigating going to her parents' house again. She didn't care. Nope. It was good this way. Who knew what Mom would think of him? Mom had barely warmed up to Dell, and he was charming, personable and clean shaven.

"It's not about the treats. It's about profits and supplies and stuff."

"Right." She rolled her shoulders because she was not tense or irritated by all that vague stuff. She was possibly, maybe in the *L* word with him, and she was not going to mess that up by being needy.

Not when he was so sweet. A good guy. She was with a good guy who did nice things like try to fix her air-conditioning and offer his kitchen for pie making and take in every stray that walked in his path.

So what if he wouldn't eat dinner with her crazy family? One flaw. She was not going to make a deal out of it.

"Well, I guess if the landlord can't get some-

one to fix it today, I'll come out after dinner. If
that's okay?"

"That is always okay." He pushed to his feet.
"You know what? I'll go buy you a fan. It'll at
least get the air circulating." He glanced at his
watch. "I have to be gone by four. Plenty of time."

"You don't have to—"

But he cut her off with a quick kiss. "I'll be
back in a bit." He strode out the door, leaving
her feeling...

She didn't know. She felt unsatisfied and irritated at herself for the feeling, since he was going
to buy her a fan; but no matter how much she
tried to talk herself out of it, the dissatisfaction
remained.

WES TRIED TO concentrate on Mom's words about
some company she saw as his competition. Considering the company was in Wisconsin, he was
having trouble seeing the point.

More, it was hard to concentrate on that stuff
when he'd lied to Cara. Again. For a while there
he'd been able to justify it to himself. The first
month or two. He and Mom mostly talked business, so it *was* a conference call of sorts.

But he'd seen the way her face fell when he'd
said no to dinner at her parents' again, and he
hated being that guy. He hated the way it had
become a pattern, one he didn't know how to

break. Because he also hated the idea of having to make small talk with anyone, especially people he would be trying to impress.

He liked what they'd created. Their relationship, and the dog treat sales had increased just by incorporating Anna's logo.

He didn't want to risk that for anything, and he had a bad feeling that getting in a five-foot radius of anyone she cared about would do just that.

"Wes? Are you listening?"

"Yes. Yeah. Right." He forced himself to look at the screen and Mom's overly hopeful face. The usual headache began drumming harder. He needed this to be over.

"So, you'll be home? The twenty-third. Three o'clock?"

"What? Yeah. Sure." Wait, was that Cara's car outside? She was way early. Shit.

"Wes?"

"Mom, I have to go." He stood, ready to snap the laptop shut.

"We have to talk about the buyout offer, Wes. They want an answer by tomorrow."

"I'm not selling, Mom." Cara stepped out of her car. "I have to go."

"Let me explain why it's such a great opportunity. Please." The imploring note in her voice, the *please*. He couldn't hang up on her, but Cara was walking up to the cabin, Sweetness prancing at her feet.

"Give me a second."

He hurried to the front door, a panic he didn't understand working through him. This wasn't a big deal. He could explain everything to Cara. It didn't have to be this cover-up he couldn't seem to help himself from enacting.

When he flung the door open, Cara was already on the porch.

She smiled. "Hey, that's quite a greeting."

He tried to smile back but knew he failed. "Um, I'm still finishing up. Do you think you could head out to the barn?"

Her whole face changed—just like that the smile and the happiness melted away. "Excuse me?"

"Put Monster on the runner. Get Shrimp some more water. Um, you know, to help me out."

She didn't move. Instead, she folded her arms over her chest, swallowing before she spoke. "It'd be that terrible if I, someone you happen to employ, as well as sleep with, overheard your business talk?"

"No, I'd be distracted and, um—" he gestured uselessly at the cabin "—there's some talk of mergers and buyouts, and I need to concentrate."

Her brows drew together, and she looked at the

cabin, then over at the barn. "All right," she said quietly. "Come on, Sweet."

He squeezed his eyes shut. Why was he doing this? He should come clean.

But the reality of that made his gut tighten and head pound even harder.

He'd gotten over his initial insecurity when it came to Cara. He was a decent guy, and she'd helped him through a lot of stuff and he'd helped her, too, which was some kind of miracle. But they'd made each other better, and he hadn't worried he wasn't good enough for her for a while.

Except when it came to this. Why would she want to be with a guy who hadn't worked out all his issues with his mother? Or worse, what if Cara wanted him to accept the way Mom treated him, as if he were broken?

He had to keep the things separate. He had to. Things would be all jumbled otherwise, and he liked things as they were. Things were perfect the way they were, aside from his hand.

He trudged back into the house and his office. Mom was still on the screen, but she was smiling at someone off to the side.

"Bring her to dinner," she said to the person off screen.

"You sure?"

Wes didn't recognize the voice, but he had a pretty good idea it was one of his stepbrothers, whom he'd only ever awkwardly talked to via video call.

"Mom."

Mom returned her attention to him, all smiles. "There you are. Everything okay?"

"Yeah, someone trying to sell something."

Mom cocked her head. "You know, you've been so much more relaxed lately. I thought maybe you'd made some friends. Maybe a lady friend. Your brother was telling me about his new girlfriend."

Not my brother, Wes wanted to say.

"Back to selling. I don't want to. I know you think it'd set me up nicely and help pay for the surgery, but that's what insurance and VA stuff is for. I like having this to work on. To do."

"Well, I know, but you're always complaining about the organizing and whatnot, I thought maybe someone could take over the business end and—"

"I don't want that," he snapped, more irritated than soothed when Phantom rested a head on his knee.

"Okay. I'll tell them no, then." She offered a small smile. "And I'll let you go. Just don't forget about the twenty-third?"

Twenty-third? He didn't remember what she'd said. "Sure. Yeah."

"All right. I love you, baby. Talk next week."

"Yeah, you, too. Bye." He slapped the laptop shut.

He had trouble saying I love you to his own mother and couldn't escape the jealousy he had for her new life, even when he had things going well in his own. What was he doing, trying to…?

He took a deep breath. He wasn't letting himself go down that road. Right or wrong, four months with Cara in his life—he wasn't giving that up.

All he had to do was keep the bad stuff he didn't want to handle separate. And things would keep being fine.

He stood and went out to the barn to find her. To make it right. He was good at that when it came to her.

She stood in the setting sun, throwing a ratty rope bone to Monster. The other dogs, except Phantom, who was standing at his side, were yipping, running and playing. Everything glowed in the summer evening, and everything he wanted was right here and he wished he had an idea how to make that permanent. Maybe he needed more time. More practice. And if or when Cara told him she loved him, maybe he could say the words.

She shaded her eyes against the sun, looking at him and then back at the dogs. He couldn't make out her expression until he got closer.

Sad. Damn it.

"Done with your important business?" She was trying to ask nicely but couldn't resist a little snip in her tone.

He deserved every bit of it. "Yeah, I told them I'm happy with the way things are. No merger. No buyout."

"Great."

Yeah, he didn't think so. "I'm sorry. It was an important discussion, and I needed to concentrate." Not a lie. Not a lie.

Liar.

She poked at a tuft of grass with her toe. Nails painted bright turquoise, flip-flops covered in colorful jewel things.

"I guess I get it."

"So, you're not upset? Because you are important to Stone. You've done so much to help me. I don't want you to feel as though you're..."

She looked up at him with pursed lips. "I dated this guy once. I really liked him," she suddenly said. He didn't know what this had to do with him. He didn't particularly care to hear about the other guys she'd been with.

"It was kind of a thing when he asked me out because he was older, and I'd had a crush on him since high school. Anyway, he asked me out, he hadn't broken up with this mutual friend of ours like he said he had, and I was basically a prop to enact some revenge on her. The point is—"

she looked up, her gaze zeroing in on him, all serious and determined and hurt "—I don't like being shut out. Or lied to. It's a shit feeling to be tricked, and even if that's not what you're doing, it's what it feels like."

"I would never. Even if I could, Cara—"

"I know. That's what I'm saying. I know you're not doing anything nasty. This does hurt, though. To be kept separate." Her gaze dropped. "Even if that's needy or whatever, it does hurt. I want to be honest about that. I don't like it."

"I'm sorry."

Her mouth kind of quirked at that. "You're a very good apologizer, you know that? I always believe you."

"I always mean it." He took a few steps closer. "There are a few things I'm still getting used to sharing."

She glanced at Phantom pressed against his legs. "Head, hand or hip?"

He opened his mouth to say something, but she crossed to him and touched his forehead. "You get this line right here when it's your head." She smoothed her thumb over a crease in his forehead, and then she sighed. "Look, it's okay. Really. Maybe try to open up a little bit more."

"I will."

She stared up at him in silence for a while,

eyebrows drawn together as if she were trying to figure him out.

Good luck there.

"You're going to come to the wedding, right?" Her voice was soft. Uncertain. So unlike Cara. "Mia and Dell's wedding? I know I haven't officially asked, but you will, won't you? It's only a month away, and Mia wanted a head count. So, you'll come, right? Be my date?"

Suits and people and a wedding. Jesus, he didn't want to have to deal with that. Especially since Cara was in the wedding, so he'd be the weirdo in the corner. Making her look bad.

But while he might not be the brightest when it came to relationships, he wasn't stupid enough to think *no* would be an okay answer.

"I put it in your calendar, and I know you don't have anything else that day and I need to know you'll do this for me." Her voice broke, and he stepped forward, wrapped his arms around her.

"It's important," she squeaked. "Even if it seems dumb to you."

"Hey, I'll come." He cupped her face, making sure to look her in the eye. "I'm coming. It's in my calendar. I'm there."

She nodded, chewing on her lip. "You promise?"

"Yeah, I promise." He'd regret that. Hell, he regretted it already, but he'd regret her walking away a lot more.

CHAPTER TWENTY-SIX

CARA WALKED INTO the back door of Edibles with a stack of pies. Sam had supplied her with boxes. Adorable boxes that said *Edibles Restaurant. All local, all the time. Pies by Cara.*

That's how he displayed them, too. At least until they ran out for the night, which they did more nights than not.

She had never known how flipping awesome success could be, especially success at something she loved. It made everything else feel good, too, her shiny little gold star. Even Mom was impressed, and that was like impressing the pope.

"Hey, Cara." Sam greeted her with a wave while he stirred something with the other hand. "Drop those off with Curt, then I want to talk to you if you have a sec."

"Um, sure." Not at all scary or intimidating. Her mind certainly didn't jump to him firing her. Nope. She was way too secure for that.

Maybe he didn't like the idea of her freezing pies next week for the weekend of Mia's wedding. Maybe he was going to demand she work that weekend. Maybe…

Oh, get a grip.

She returned to Sam, determined to be cool, poised, professional and adult.

Man, that was a lot of things to be. "So, things are good?" she asked, hoping it didn't come out as squeaky as it sounded to her own ears.

"Great, actually. Summer has been awesome. Your pies have been a hit."

"Well, that's good to hear."

"The apple crop is starting out great this year, too. Can't ask for things to be going much better."

"Great. You, um, wanted to talk to me about something?"

"Yeah, you know, I'd like to keep offering pies through winter. Pie is such a comfort food, and local winter cuisine definitely won't be our biggest seller. I'd like to see you supplying for us year-round. All dinner services."

Cara could have hugged him. But she was cool. Poised. Whatever. "I'd be very interested in that."

Look at you, sounding all business.

"Let's set up a meeting, then, go over the details. I have some addenda to our previous agreement, and we'll need to discuss numbers and contracts. I know you're busy with Mia's wedding, but a little bit after that, maybe? Last week of October? Monday morning?"

"Yeah, sure, that sounds good."

"All right. We can talk times later. I wanted to give you a heads-up, so you can start planning."

"Yeah, thanks, this is great. Really. I'll, uh, see you tomorrow."

He nodded, his eyes and concentration back on his cooking. She walked out of the restaurant holding her breath, afraid if she made a wrong move it would all crumble underneath her.

She'd done it. Full-time pie making for an actual restaurant. Her own business. Contracts. Thank God for Mia's and Wes's help and advice and experience, or she'd be lost, but regardless…

She'd *done* it. Sitting in the driver's seat of her little car, she did a full-on bootie dance. She was queen of the damn world.

She pulled out her phone to call Mia, then thought maybe she'd tell her tomorrow. A happy announcement on the last day of the market. Something to celebrate along with another successful season.

Yeah, that's what she'd do. Tonight she'd head out to Wes's and *really* celebrate. She flipped on the radio and sang the entire way home to pick up Sweetness and change into sexier underwear. Then she sang herself hoarse all the way to Wes's.

She couldn't believe the thought popped into her head and didn't cause more than a tiny bubble of panic, but she realized she wouldn't mind living here. The pretty, peaceful solitude that didn't translate to lonely because of Wes, the dogs, even the asshole sheep.

Crazy. Crazy to think this thing with Wes, this *relationship*, this *long-term* relationship, could be even more long-term. Even more serious. Even crazier that she wasn't totally averse to the idea. In fact, she liked it. She wanted it.

She was ready for something more. For a future. To believe in the possibility of not screwing it up or screwing it up only enough that they could always fix it.

When she rounded the last curve and the entire space came into view, her giddy excitement died.

There was a car sitting next to Wes's truck. Her stomach rolled. She'd never seen another car parked there. Ever. Who could be visiting him?

Sweetness whined and pawed at the window until Cara crawled out of the car.

There was a possibility this wasn't an innocuous visitor, given how rarely Wes had any. She walked up the porch stairs. She'd gotten in the habit of bursting in unannounced, but she felt hesitant now.

She knocked.

Wes pulled the door open, such a range of expressions on his face it would take her a few minutes to decipher them all.

But when he stepped out onto the porch, clos-ing the door behind him, she didn't want to know what any of them were.

"What's going on?" she demanded.

He scratched a hand through his hair. "It's my mother. She dropped by."

It wasn't that she didn't believe him, it was just… Why was he being so weird about it? "She 'dropped by' all the way from California? And you're not going to introduce me?"

"Um, no. I'm not."

She swallowed the lump in her throat. It hadn't escaped her notice that the few things she knew about Wes's childhood were not happy. He almost never mentioned his mother, so maybe they had a terrible relationship that he didn't want to drag her into. She should accept that and leave. Give him space.

But she couldn't. She was tired of accepting these nonanswers from him, and she didn't want to keep hoping for more and coming up short or convincing herself it didn't matter. Because it did. It so did. That sparkly possible future she'd been so sure of minutes ago faded.

So, she didn't leave. Instead, she fisted her hands on her hips. He'd pushed her once. Well, now it was her turn to push him. "Why the hell not?" If he wasn't going to introduce her, the least he could do was explain why.

WES COULD ONLY blink at Cara. He'd known she wouldn't be happy the minute he'd opened the door, but he hadn't expected a challenge. Demands. He'd expected sadness and hurt. That aching pain in his chest when he saw those things on her face. But he had not expected her anger.

And he was still wrapping his mind around Mom showing up out of the blue. Three o'clock on the twenty-third, because apparently she'd told him she was going to.

He had a headache. "It's complicated."

"Not an answer."

Why was she pushing this? Why couldn't she go home and let him deal with one thing at a time? "She surprised me. I need some time to—"

"To push me away. Pretend this part of your life doesn't exist. Pretend—" she shook her head "—I can't keep pretending with you, Wes."

"I don't know what you mean."

She took a deep breath. One of those scary deep breaths where you knew the person doing the deep breathing was considering punching your lights out. Or irrevocably breaking your heart. "Think really hard about lying to me."

"I'm not lying to you."

"You don't pretend with me, ever? Pretend your arm doesn't hurt or your conference call is so important I can't even be in the same house.

Tell me you don't pretend business, so you don't have to ever meet my family."

"All of those are legitimate reasons I have for—"

Without warning, she pushed past him, flinging the door open and storming inside. What was she doing? He scrambled after her, but she'd already found Mom standing wide-eyed in the living room.

"Hi, Wes's Mom. I'm Cara."

At Mom's confused look, Cara's eyes went wide; her nostrils might have even flared. "Seriously?" she demanded of him. "You couldn't even mention my name?"

"Cara—"

"Oh, so you are capable of uttering those two syllables. Great." She turned back to his mother. "Hi. Like I said, I'm Cara. Your son's assistant and his girlfriend for a little while there, but I think both are coming to a close, actually." She squared her shoulders. He'd never seen her angry like this. Full guns blazing. No self-defeat or frustration, just *anger*.

Threatening to break up with him.

"I want to tell you that he needs surgery. He's been ignoring it, but the nerve damage in his arm has been hurting him more and more and I haven't wanted to push because—" her shoulders slumped a little "—I don't know. A lot of reasons.

You know when you care about someone and you don't want to hurt them and you swallow down these things? But then that hurts you? Anyway, that's what I've been doing, and I'm done. So, please, make sure he schedules it. He needs it."

Then, without sparing him a glance, she turned on a heel and stalked out. She *was* breaking up with him.

Well, we knew that was going to happen. The defeatist voice in his head only served to piss him off. He *didn't* know that. He had been making plans. Kind of. Fuzzy maybe-plans, but still plans.

Cara could not break up with him just because he wanted a few things ignored or pretended or whatever.

"Cara." He jogged after her, catching up with her on the porch. "Please, understand."

She whirled on him. "You know what? I do understand. A lot, actually. There are some things you want to keep me separate from. Keep yourself separate from."

Relief washed over him. For as angry as she was acting, she understood. "Yes! Exactly. So—"

"I can't do this. I can't keep pretending. Pretending I don't want more. Pretending it doesn't hurt. I thought I was pretending because I didn't want to cause you pain, but I was pretending, I think, because I knew if I pushed, you wouldn't give."

"There's nothing to push. The things… The things I don't talk about with you are separate. Like you said."

"Separate from what?"

He tried to make sense of her question. He opened his mouth, but nothing came out.

"Exactly. The thing is, if there's an *us*, if there's ever going to be love and whatever involved, there's no separate. I mean, yeah, you don't have to share every detail of your childhood, and I don't need to recount every guy I ever slept with, but I should get a say in your surgery and be able to ask you to actually interact with my family."

"But those are such small things. Not imp—"

"They're important to me." She fisted her hand over her heart. "You pushed this all those months ago. I panicked and ran out and you *pushed*. Do you remember that?"

"Of course, I—"

"If you still want what you wanted then, you have to let me into everything."

He didn't even open his mouth this time. What was there to say? She wanted everything, and he didn't want to give it. Even now, he didn't want to fold her into the body stuff, the Mom stuff, and he didn't want to be folded into her family stuff.

He wanted what they had now. It was good enough for him. Better than good enough. It was great. Why did she want to change it?

"I'm going to go. I'd offer to help find my replacement, but—"

"You can't quit," he said weakly.

"Your business will survive without me."

"But you've done so much, made it better. You shouldn't quit over us."

The weariness on her face morphed back into anger so fast he blinked, not even understanding how he was setting her off now.

"Oh, shouldn't I?" She poked him in the chest, exactly the way he hated. "Sam offered me a full-time supplier contract. I don't need your part-time job anymore, and, yeah, I'd probably keep working it if you weren't so dang clueless, but I can't come here every day..." She trailed off, tears filling her eyes. "I can't come here three days a week *loving* you and knowing you can't do it back."

He reached for her arm. "But I do, I do."

She shook her head, tears spilling over. "You don't have a clue. You can't say it. You can't let me in. You can't... Screw your job, Wes. And this stupid cabin and that ridiculous beard and your dogs—no, I love them. But the rest. Screw you and the rest."

She stomped down the stairs, but he didn't know how to go after her this time. She said she loved him. *Loved* him. And he'd said he loved her, too, kind of. But she was still walking away. Still driving away. Still gone.

How did that make any sense?

There was a hard lump in his throat, a constricting band around his lungs.

Mom stepped out. Phantom slunk from the door to sit behind Wes.

"Things didn't go well, I take it?"

"No."

"She's pretty."

"She's…" *Everything.* "Gone."

"Well, I'm sure you can work it out. You need some time. Both of you. Cool off. Have a calm, rational discussion. Dustin and I—"

"Don't." He turned away, gripping the railing of the porch. He could not listen to his mother's relationship advice. Could not listen to her talk about her one true love of a husband.

He wanted nothing to do with that.

"Is what she said true? You need another surgery?"

"Don't worry about it. I've got it handled." If he chose to handle it by pretending, so be it. He'd been broken by a damn bomb fighting for his country. *He* got to pick how he dealt with that. Not some woman.

Whom you love.

"She made it sound as though, maybe—"

"I said I've got it handled. I do. I have since the beginning, haven't I?"

"Yes, of course." She was quiet for a long while,

and he stood there, gripping the railing. Maybe if he squeezed hard enough and the pain dug deep enough, he'd be able to find some way of fixing things.

I can't come here three days a week loving you and knowing you can't do it back.

But he did love her. How could she not see that? Why did she have to want the parts of him he could only deal with alone? Closed off. Safe. Where no one would have to see how badly he failed.

This wasn't the same as when she'd panicked, because he wasn't walking away from her. He was asking her to stay out of certain things. That wasn't the same at all.

"I could be here when you have it done. I could help."

"I wouldn't want to take you away from your family." He winced at the disgust in his own voice. Not exactly the way to pretend it didn't matter.

I can't keep pretending I don't want more. Why would she want more from him? He gave her all the best parts of himself.

"You're my son. I'll always be available when you need me."

He tried to keep his mouth shut. Will it away. The anger, the pain and the hurt that lie caused, but the day had been too much, and he didn't have any reserves left. He whirled around to face her. "*You* left me! You abandoned me for a whole new family. Don't pretend I'm more important than they are."

Her face crumpled, tears slipping down her cheeks. "You wouldn't let me anywhere near you when you got back. You didn't want to come to California. What was I supposed to—"

"Push! Be here! Make me come anyway. Not throw money at me and hope I disappeared."

She turned away from him, stepping toward the door. "We shouldn't be yelling. I didn't come all this way to argue with you. Let's just—"

"Forget it. Ignore it. Pretend it doesn't exist. Yup. Sounds good." Exactly what Cara accused him of. Well, at least he came by it honestly.

She turned, her hands clasped in front of her. "You are my son," she said in her calm, let's-keep-the-peace voice. "I did everything I could to provide for you, and I know it wasn't enough. I know everything that's happened is my fault." Her voice broke. "Don't think I don't know that."

He slammed his good fist against the railing. "It's nobody's fault! It's just bad luck, damn it."

"I was supposed to be able to care for you. Give you the things I never had. I failed. That isn't luck—"

"What were you supposed to do with a kid and

not even a high school diploma? You did everything you could, and I never resented it. Never."

"Don't tell me you didn't resent me when you signed up for the army. Don't tell me—"

"Resent you? I wanted you to be proud of me. That I wouldn't screw anything up. I wanted to show you I could be better."

Mom sank onto the little bench next to the door, her hand covering her mouth, tears streaming down her cheeks. "I've only ever wanted you to be happy," she managed to croak out.

He was making everyone cry? Screwing everything up. *Typical Wes.*

CHAPTER TWENTY-SEVEN

IT WAS NO use trying to pretend she hadn't cried the entire way back into town. She was a blotchy, red-eyed mess. She could try to makeup it away, but even if she fooled Mia, she'd probably break down the minute she got the words out of her mouth.

The worst part, the part that kept her crying, was the little voice inside her head telling her she'd messed this up. She should have handled everything differently.

Was it so wrong to need more from him? To be let in, to hear that stupid *L* word instead of "I do, too." Oh, blech, that made her mad all over again.

She pulled her car up to Mia and Dell's place on the edge of Dell's family property. The Wainwright farm wasn't much different than the Pruitt farm. In the early fall, it was a beautiful maze of just-turning leaves and green hills and the last fruiting plants of the season.

But it made her think about Wes's place and what an idiot she'd been to think she could live there at some point And have what Mia and Dell had.

No, she was not the idiot. *He* was. They could have kept working toward something like this, but, *nooo*, he had to be *him*.

She forced herself out of the car, Sweetness following and sniffing every little blade of grass.

Maybe she should have gone home and wallowed alone. Mia was two weeks away from wedded bliss. Did it make Cara a crap sister to want a little comfort now?

Probably. But Anna wouldn't be back home for another week, and talking to Mom was so not an option.

Oh, damn him for changing her. Things were so much simpler when she didn't care about anything.

Yeah, but you weren't happy.

Screw happy. She wasn't happy now. Why couldn't he have let her walk away when it wouldn't have hurt nearly this bad?

She knocked lightly on Mia's door. She heard voices. Laughter. She closed her eyes. Oh, why had she thought coming here would help?

Mia opened the door, a smile on her face, her clothes and hair looking a little rumpled.

"Cara, hey." Her smile immediately died. "Oh, what's wrong?"

Cara could see Dell shirtless in the background. She backed away from the door. "You guys are busy. Ignore me."

"You're crying." Mia grabbed her arm so she couldn't bolt.

She tried to pry herself away. "I'm interrupting."

"You are not."

"He's shirtless."

Mia glanced back at Dell and rolled her eyes. "He's always shirtless. Come on inside." Mia pulled, surprisingly forcefully for all five foot barely anything of her. Or maybe Cara just really wanted to be led.

"Sorry," she offered to Dell.

He shrugged, an easy smile on his face. "Nothing to be sorry about."

Mia propelled her toward the kitchen. "What happened? What's wrong?"

"I just…" Cara cleared her throat and tried to get the words out without crying or squeaking. "Broke up with Wes." And failed on both counts.

Mia's arms wrapped around her. "Oh, I'm sorry. What'd the jerk do?"

Cara leaned onto Mia's shoulder. "Just jerk stuff."

"Need me to beat him up for you?"

She lifted her head from Mia's shoulder and offered Dell a smile. That was nice. No one had ever threatened to beat someone up for her. Except Wes. Which made Dell's offer momentarily tempting. "No. Thanks."

"All right. Well, I'll make myself scarce, then."

"You don't have to—" But he was already gone. "He doesn't have to go. This is his house. I—"

"Go sit on the porch. Make yourself comfortable. I'll get us something to drink."

She was too exhausted and heartachey to argue, so she went to the porch and settled herself on the stairs. All around her were trees and farmland and...home.

Except this wasn't her home, and home wasn't her home, and Wes's wasn't her home. She was metaphorically homeless and heartbroken.

Mia returned with a bottle of wine.

"Aw, you're the best."

Mia settled herself next to Cara on the porch stair. "I learned from you." She handed off the wine.

Cara tried to find some kind of good feeling in that. "Unfortunately, I don't think Wes will be coming after me with declarations of love like Dell did for you." She took a big gulp. Maybe Mia'd let her drink the whole thing.

"You never know. You've been happy. I guess I don't know much about him, but I've never seen you all relationshippy."

Cara shook her head. No, he was too...whatever. Together they'd both changed, made each other better, but maybe they'd come to the end of that. They'd each done what they could, but it wasn't enough for more.

"I wanted him to let me all the way in. And he won't. Or can't. Or something. He wouldn't even introduce me to his mom."

"What?"

"That's wrong, right? I'm not being too hard on him? I mean, if it was love or whatever, he'd let me in. Tell me what's going on. Want to be a part of my life. He'd *want* that, right? He'd try."

"I think so."

Cara took another drink and then handed the bottle to Mia. They sat in silence for a while, passing the wine bottle back and forth. The sun was beginning to set, the air getting slightly cooler as the minutes ticked on.

"The thing is, I do love the idiot. Is it gross and unfeminist to say he helped me change for the better?"

"No. Look, lots of people come into our lives. Friends, boyfriends, sisters." Mia slung an arm around her shoulder. "And, the good ones help us change for the better. Or make us better or make us want to be better. That's not wrong. I mean, you helped him change, too, right?"

"I think so. Parts, anyway. But not all the parts I needed."

Mia squeezed. "Well, there you have it. Just because he helped you find some change in your life doesn't mean you have to stay with him. Not if he can't give you what you need from a relationship."

"You, oh wise one, who have had one relationship."

"I am getting married in two weeks. I am an insufferably happy expert."

Cara leaned her head on Mia's shoulder. "I don't want it to be over."

"I know. But you deserve someone who'll give you the relationship you need. The relationship you want. If it's not Wes, it'll be somebody else."

Which only made the lump in her throat get harder to swallow around. Impossible, really. "Sam wants to do a full-time supplier contract for the pies," she blurted, hoping to avoid another round of sobbing. Today had not been a total bust. There were good things to celebrate.

Mia squealed. "Cara! That's amazing. Amazing. Look at you, little sister. You are kicking ass and taking names. I am so, so proud of you."

"Why do I feel like shit?"

"Adulthood kind of sucks?"

"I'll drink to that." She took a long swig, wishing she could drink faster, dull the pain faster. But it kept aching in her chest like some kind of deep, festering wound. "Thanks. For this."

"That's what sisters are for."

"I've been keeping my distance a bit since the whole Dell thing happened."

Mia looked at her hands. "Yeah, I've noticed. But you always said I was big-sistering you and—"

"It's not your fault. Really. I've been so happy to see you happy. I guess I felt left out. Then I finally got happy, and we've both been busy. Now I'm unhappy and back at your doorstep."

"My doorstep is always, *always* open. Happy, unhappy and everything in between."

Cara nodded. "Mine is, too."

"Good."

It did feel good. It felt good to have someone who was there through thick and thin. And Cara would always be there for Mia, too.

As for Wes. "You think I did the right thing?"

"I know you did. And if you want, we can go egg his truck. Just don't get me thrown in jail for my wedding."

Cara snorted. She watched a bird glide through the air and land on a tree. "I love you." Some love could be enough. The love of a sister, anyway.

"I love you, too." Mia wrapped her other arm around Cara so it was a full-on hug. "And it'll be okay. It really will."

"Yeah. It will." Broken hearts mended all the time, right?

Wes lay in bed, staring at his ceiling. The migraine that had been assaulting him for the past two days had been nasty, but he usually worked through that kind of pain.

With Mom staying with him—indefinitely, she said—he lay in bed and let work pile up. Let the phone calls and emails pile up. He supposed Mom was handling it, and if not?

He hadn't worked up the energy to care.

Phantom's snout nudged his side, but he ignored him. Just wallowed. In the pain—both his head and the unfamiliar constricting pain in his chest that even an idiot like him knew had nothing to do with his body's limitations and everything to do with missing Cara.

"Knock, knock." Mom swept in, cell phone in one hand, plate of food in the other.

"I'm not hungry."

"Oh, well, that works out then, because this isn't for you until you make a phone call." She plopped the phone onto his bed, then pulled a piece of paper out of her pocket and dropped that next to the phone.

He looked at the paper, saw the name of the hospital and immediately slumped back down. "Not interested in that, either."

"Too bad."

He looked at his mother in shock. Even when

he'd been a kid, she'd never been very firm. "What are you doing?"

"I'm pushing. You gave me permission to, re-member?"

"No, I—"

"Too late. What's said is said." She pushed the phone at him. "Make the appointment. Or your mommy will do it for you."

Wes could only stare.

"Make the call, Wesley Stone. You have five minutes."

She looked around the room, then placed the plate on his dresser before going to the other side of the bed where Phantom lay. She began scratching the dog's head.

He wanted to argue, but what would be the point? Mom had gotten it into her head she needed to be a hard-ass? Fine. After all, he could always cancel the appointment. Unless she knocked him out and dropped him off at the hospital, she couldn't make him get the surgery.

So, he made the call. Got a slot next month and called it a day.

"Now, that wasn't so hard, was it?" She shoved the plate at him. "Eat. You've barely eaten for two days, and while I understand heartache does that to a person, you need to eat. Your migraine medication said so."

"I didn't take any."

She popped up and disappeared before returning with a pill and a glass of water. "Take it."

"Mom. This is…"

"What I should have been doing all along."

He rubbed at his chest because it ached even harder. He didn't know what to do with her taking care of him. Didn't know how to combat something he'd… God, he'd wanted this, and as much as he wanted to blame her for moving to California while he was deployed and not coming back when he was discharged, it was his own fault.

He hadn't wanted to try to fit in to her new family, so he'd purposefully kept himself apart. Pushed her away. He'd always known she wouldn't push back, even though he'd wanted her to, somewhere deep down.

He was a mess.

But he took the pill and ate the sandwich she'd made him. "You don't have to watch me eat."

"We need to talk."

"About what?"

"That young lady who burst in here the other day." Mom eased onto the edge of his bed. "She seems nice."

"The five minutes you saw her were not nice."

"No, but she clearly loves you, which *is* nice."

Why didn't she stab him in the chest while she was at it? "Well, it's over. So…"

"Do you want it to be over?"

"Can't you pick one thing to poke at me about? I scheduled the damn surgery. Leave me alone."

"No, sir, you wanted me to push. I'm pushing. I'm making up for years upon years of not pushing. How can you make it up to her? Flowers? Groveling?"

"Impossible."

"Nonsense. Nonsense. She loves you. You obviously love her, or you wouldn't be moping about, ignoring work, ignoring that terrible sheep in your barn. I fed him, and I swear the thing stared at me with soulless demon eyes. And I love all creatures."

"Mom."

"She's quite lovely and good for you. I'd noticed you'd seemed lighter lately, but I thought you'd made friends. I didn't know you'd fallen in love."

"Had. Over. Forget it."

"It doesn't have to be, if you'd analyze where things went wrong and figure out—"

"No! It's over. It's over. There's no analyzing. No figuring. I don't want her to…"

"To?"

He pushed the plate off his lap and the blankets off his legs and got out of the bed because he couldn't sit there under Mom's steady gaze as if this was somehow normal. As if it was okay she'd dropped into his life with all her pushing.

Even if he *had* said that's what he wanted, that didn't mean she could do it.

"Cara doesn't need to get all wrapped up in my legion of issues, okay? I want to pretend they're not there, and she won't let me, so it's over. Over." That was that. She didn't like the way he needed to live. What other options were there? Changing even more? He'd already changed so much. "Is it so wrong to not want to deal with certain things? To avoid them? That's not wrong. It's healthy."

"Oh, sweetie, that's ridiculous."

He rested his forehead against the wall with a thunk. "Why are you here?"

"Because I wanted things to change. Because I was tired of what we are. I will always feel like I failed you, but—"

"I don't want you to feel that way."

"I know. But how would I know that if I hadn't come and argued with you and found that out?" Her hand rested on his shoulder. "You have no idea how glad I am I came. How glad I am that we had this talk. That you lost your temper. It opened up this space where we can change."

"I am tired of change."

"Well, I'm sorry life doesn't work that way. Even if you've gone through enough change to last a lifetime, even if you've had enough hurt and pain to last a lifetime, sometimes it keeps coming at you. And I understand. I do. Sometimes life is so hard, pretending is the only thing that gets us through."

She dropped her hand. "Those years of struggling. Trying to provide for us. I had to pretend everything was okay, or I wouldn't have been able to get up in the morning. I'm sorry if I set a bad example."

"Stop blaming yourself. You're the only one who does."

"Oh, Wes." Her voice wavered, but she took a loud, deep breath. "I will work on that. I really will."

"Great. Now can I—"

"We've come through so much and are on the other side now. Let's make something of it. You love this business. You love this place. You love that girl. Fight for them, honey. Fight for happiness, and, more, believe in it. You deserve it." She patted his shoulder. "Now I am going to go answer some messages and emails for you while you finish your sandwich. Then you're going to get up and do some work."

With that, she left him. Alone. Half-eaten sandwich sitting on his bed, migraine slicing through his skull as he rested against the wall, heart aching as if it was a frigging bone that could break.

You deserve it.

Fight for them.

CHAPTER TWENTY-EIGHT

"You look so handsome!"

Wes winced. "I feel like an idiot. This is stupid. Terrible idea. Why am I doing this?"

"Because you love that girl, and you want her in your life."

"But it's her sister's wedding. I shouldn't distract her from that. She's the maid of honor. She—"

"It's a symbol, remember? You are the one who came up with the idea." Mom straightened his tie, and it was like a creepy version of prom. For a thirty-one-year-old man and his mother fixing his tie.

"I should drop you off at the airport. I should—"

"Oh, stop with your excuses. I have a rental car, and I know I've outstayed my welcome. Besides, you'll want an empty house tonight."

"Unless she says no," Wes muttered, but Mom nudged him toward the door.

"How could she resist you? She probably won't even recognize you."

Wes ran a hand over his clean-shaven jaw. He'd

done it yesterday, and it still felt so weird and uncomfortable and *naked*. Which was pretty in keeping with how he'd felt since he'd hatched this idiotic plan.

He stared at the door. Why was he doing this stupid, stupid thing? Well, the answer to that was pretty straightforward. Cara.

He wanted her back. He'd reached the point where he'd do anything, *anything* to get that. Show up uninvited at her sister's wedding. Talk to her family. Ask her to be there for his surgery. He'd do anything. Anything.

Even if it all made him feel ill. "You sure you're okay getting to the airport on your—"

"I love you, sweetie. Now go get 'em. And call me tomorrow." She walked up behind him and gave him a push.

But Wes stood there and took a deep breath. If he was brave enough to face Cara at her sister's wedding, he had to be brave enough to do this. He turned back to Mom. "Thank you would never be enough. I don't mean for this visit. I mean forever."

She held her hands to her heart, then cleared her throat and managed a wobbly smile. "You have no idea how much that means to me, baby."

He walked stiffly over to her, feeling awkward, but he pushed through it. That was going to be the norm today. Force through awkward. He enveloped her in a hug. "I love you. I'll miss you."

She sniffled into his shoulder. "I'll miss you, too." She pulled away and patted his face. "Now go get your girl, and we'll visit again soon. Whether you want to or not."

He nodded and walked for the door. Phantom followed him out to the porch and whined when he gave the stay command. Wes bent down, trying to keep from getting too much dog hair on his suit.

"I'm okay, boy. Hopefully I'll be a lot more okay when I get back." He didn't want to think about if she said no or told him to go to hell. So, he wouldn't. Because he'd keep fighting, keep working to prove to her he wanted it all. That they deserved it all.

He got in his truck and drove into town, then through it toward the Pruitt farm. He ran a hand over his short hair a few times, frustrated that it wasn't long enough to scratch his fingers through.

There were hay bales and signs with arrows to the Pruitt-Wainwright wedding, and Wes followed them, wishing he could turn around and bolt.

But Cara was at the end of this particular obstacle, and for some reason, the possibility of her made everything necessary. Even with the sickness churning in his gut, he couldn't imagine running away.

He pulled his truck next to a line of cars and trucks on the side of a big red barn. It looked freshly painted; ribbons, lights and all kinds of decorations in white and green decorated the lawn and barn opening.

What do you think you're doing, man?

No damn clue, but he got out of the truck and walked, if a little stiffly, toward the bright white dress in the throng of people. He scanned the crowd for Cara.

Mia and Dell were talking and laughing with people, and Wes hung in the background, keeping a lookout for Cara.

When the group around Mia and Dell moved to enter the barn, Wes stepped forward, wincing before he even spoke. "Um, Mia, Dell."

They both looked at him, a little blankly at first. Then Mia's head cocked. "Wes?"

"Yeah, hi. I'm sorry. I know Cara probably took me off the guest list."

"Well, yeah."

"I just—" he took a deep breath and straightened his suit coat "—I need to talk to her. I don't want to interrupt anything, weddingwise. So, could I borrow her for about five or ten minutes now, or would it be better to wait until later?" He was going to fix this.

"Well, now is fine for me, but it's up to her i
she wants to talk to you," Mia said, arms crossed

"O-okay."

"She's inside by the photo booth."

"Great."

"She says no, you disappear. Got it?"

Wes kind of grimaced an attempt at a smile a
Dell. "Sure. Yeah." Maybe.

He wiped sweaty palms on his thighs and
stepped into the barn. There were lights hang
ing from rafters, more white and green. Hay
bales tied with ribbons. Music and laughter and
people.

He was going to be sick, he was pretty sure
But he still scanned the barn for the photo bootl
and Cara. He stopped midstride for a second
when he did see her. Her dress was the same
color green as the decorations. Her shoulders
were bare, her hair was all curly and down, and
he forgot about feeling sick or nervous. Because
he wanted to make things right. And he would
He'd do anything to make it right.

She was taking an older couple into the photo
booth when he finally got to her. She was giving
them instructions on how to use it, so he stoo
there like an idiot. Waiting.

When she was done, she turned to him al
smiles. "Did you want to get in li—" She stoppe

when her eyes met his, her smile melting into openmouthed shock. "Oh, my God, your beard is gone."

CARA REACHED OUT to touch his face and the long white scar along his jaw before she remembered. Oh, yeah, they were broken up. What the hell was he doing here looking all *gorgeous* with the short hair and the no beard and the suit, and, good God, who was he?

"What are you—"

"Um, I asked Mia first. If it was all right."

"If what was all right?" She finally remembered to snatch her hand back and then clasped her fingers behind her back so that she wouldn't touch him.

"If I could talk to you for a few minutes."

"I'm at my sister's wedding."

"I know. I need some… A minute. Five. Please. She said it was okay."

He seemed so perplexed, so wonderfully, perfectly Wes. If Mia had said it was okay…

"Oh, come on," she grumbled. She didn't want to do it but didn't see another way to get out of here effectively. She took his hand. Tried to ignore the way his fingers linked with hers, or how adorable it was that his palms were kind of sweaty.

If she was finding palm sweating adorable, sh
needed to get her sanity checked. She led him ou
a little side entrance of the barn. She was stil
amazed at everything Dad had done to make thi
a wedding venue. Once deemed unsuitable for th
cows, it had been his office, hardly resemblin
useful space.

Now it was gorgeous. And Mia was gorgeous
and the wedding had been perfect and everyon
was so happy.

And Wes was here, and she was holding hi
hand, leading him away from a crowd of peopl

*He can't give you what you want—remembe
that.*

Once they were safely tucked away behind
tree, she dropped his hand and crossed her arm
over her chest. She wasn't at all pleased with he
self when his gaze lingered there for a secon
or two.

Oh, so he was staring at her boobs?

"So? Five minutes. You better start now."

"I love you."

Her arms dropped to her sides. "What?"

"I love you." He said it slower this time, cleare
his eyes never leaving hers. All earnest, hone
Wes.

"Why are you…?" She shook her head, n
sure why her eyes were filling with tears. Tha
wasn't enough. An *I love you* wasn't enough, s

she should not want to throw herself at him and hold on for dear life. She should not want that at all.

"I scheduled my surgery for next month. Admittedly, my mom kind of made me because of what you said, and I was going to cancel, but I'm not going to now. I'm going to do it, and if you'll forgive me for needing some time to get here, I would very much appreciate your help."

"My help." She had to lean against the tree to keep herself upright. What was happening?

He cleared his throat, his eyes still steady on hers. "And, um, I want to come to dinner with your family the next time you do that. And I wanted to say how proud I am of you for getting the full-time pie deal, and if that means you don't have time to work for me, I understand. But your help is invaluable, and if you have time to do both, I would very much appreciate that. I like having you be a part of it."

"What is all this?"

"You were right. I wanted to pretend. Or ignore. Or whatever. I didn't want to deal with this stuff, and there's still a part of me that doesn't." He stepped forward and gingerly took her hand in his. "Cara, having you in my life is one of the best things that ever happened to me, and I would do anything to keep you there."

All she could do was stand there, her hand

limply in his, staring at him, because this had to
be a dream. It was all so perfect and lovely and
wonderful. Possibly a million other good adjec-
tives, too. She swallowed, trying to find her voice.
"I, um, are you sure that… I don't want you to
say that just because it's what I want? You should
be okay with all those things before you promise them."

"I am. I wasn't at first, but thinking you're
not in my life anymore is worse than facing the
things that are hard and awkward. And they are
things I should face. You've made me face a lot
of things, and it's always made everything better.
I went after you, called you out when you were
scared, and it all got better. So much a life I never
thought I'd have. So, why not? If it means loving you and having you, it'll always be worth it."

She went with what had been her first inclination when she'd seen him all clean shaven and
suited. She flung her arms around his neck and
squeezed as hard as she could. "You couldn't have
figured this out two weeks ago?"

He chuckled against her shoulder. "I'm slow
on the uptake sometimes."

"I'll say." But she didn't let him go. He was
here, wanting her back, wanting to give her whatever it took to make them okay. "You made me
face some things, too. I think that's why I was so

ingry. We're good for each other, and I knew we were, but I couldn't keep—"

"I know. I do. It might have taken me a few kicks in the butt from you and from my mom, which was weird, but I do know. That's why I'm here. I want us to keep being good for each other."

She blinked away a few tears. "And oh, you're ruining my makeup, too. You need to work on your timing."

"Let's work on not breaking up again."

She wasn't sure there was any piece of her heart left to melt, but if there was, that completely did her in. "Yes. That sounds like the perfect plan."

They should get back to the reception. Cake cutting would start soon, and she didn't want to miss Mia and Dell's first dance.

But this was so nice, too. Her own little moment. She held on for a little bit longer and then finally loosened her hold on him. "Will you grow the beard back?"

"Immediately. I hate this damn scar."

She pulled back enough that she could rub her thumb across it. Then she kissed it, and he smiled.

"Okay, it's growing on me."

She grinned. "I want you beardy and flannelly again. It is fall, after all."

"Consider your wish my command right now."

"Ooh, such power you give me. I wish you would stay for the rest of the reception, help with

cleanup, then take me home. Your place, I mean
because I miss your babies."

"Dogs. They are dogs."

"And I miss you."

"I miss you, too."

She didn't want to cry anymore, so she took his
hand and started pulling him back to the barn
"Oh! I also wish that you would dance with me
at the reception."

"If you don't mind me possibly breaking your
foot."

"You'll have to follow my lead."

He lifted her hand and kissed the back of it
stopping her in her tracks. "I will." He said i
very, very solemnly.

She grabbed his face and looked him right in
the eye. "I love you, you slow-on-the-uptake mess
of a man."

"And I love you, you beautiful, amazing
perf—"

She shut him up with a kiss, knowing there
would be a lot of kiss shutting up in her future
and looking forward to every second of it.

* * * * *

LARGER-PRINT BOOKS!
GET 2 FREE LARGER-PRINT NOVELS PLUS
2 FREE GIFTS!

⊕ HARLEQUIN®

Romance

From the Heart, For the Heart

YES! Please send me 2 FREE LARGER-PRINT Harlequin® Romance novels and my 2 FREE gifts (gifts are worth about $10). After receiving them, if I don't wish to receive any more books, I can return the shipping statement marked "cancel." If I don't cancel, I will receive 4 brand-new novels every month and be billed just $5.09 per book in the U.S. or $5.49 per book in Canada. That's a savings of at least 15% off the cover price! It's quite a bargain! Shipping and handling is just 50¢ per book in the U.S. and 75¢ per book in Canada.* I understand that accepting the 2 free books and gifts places me under no obligation to buy anything. I can always return a shipment and cancel at any time. Even if I never buy another book, the two free books and gifts are mine to keep forever.

119/319 HDN GHWC

Name	(PLEASE PRINT)	

Address		Apt. #

City	State/Prov.	Zip/Postal Code

Signature (if under 18, a parent or guardian must sign)

Mail to the Reader Service:
IN U.S.A.: P.O. Box 1867, Buffalo, NY 14240-1867
IN CANADA: P.O. Box 609, Fort Erie, Ontario L2A 5X3
Want to try two free books from another line?
Call 1-800-873-8635 or visit www.ReaderService.com.

* Terms and prices subject to change without notice. Prices do not include applicable taxes. Sales tax applicable in N.Y. Canadian residents will be charged applicable taxes. Offer not valid in Quebec. This offer is limited to one order per household. Not valid for current subscribers to Harlequin Romance Larger-Print books. All orders subject to credit approval. Credit or debit balances in a customer's account(s) may be offset by any other outstanding balance owed by or to the customer. Please allow 4 to 6 weeks for delivery. Offer available while quantities last.

Your Privacy—The Reader Service is committed to protecting your privacy. Our Privacy Policy is available online at www.ReaderService.com or upon request from the Reader Service.

We make a portion of our mailing list available to reputable third parties that offer products we believe may interest you. If you prefer that we not exchange your name with third parties, or if you wish to clarify or modify your communication preferences, please visit us at www.ReaderService.com/consumerschoice or write to us at Reader Service Preference Service, P.O. Box 9062, Buffalo, NY 14240-9062. Include your complete name and address.

HRLP15

LARGER-PRINT BOOKS!

HARLEQUIN

Presents

GET 2 FREE LARGER-PRINT NOVELS PLUS 2 FREE GIFTS!

YES! Please send me 2 FREE LARGER-PRINT Harlequin Presents® novels and my 2 FREE gifts (gifts are worth about $10). After receiving them, if I don't wish to receive any more books, I can return the shipping statement marked "cancel." If I don't cancel, I will receive 6 brand-new novels every month and be billed just $5.30 per book in the U.S. or $5.74 per book in Canada. That's a saving of at least 12% off the cover price! It's quite a bargain! Shipping and handling is just 50¢ per book in the U.S. and 75¢ per book in Canada.* I understand that accepting the 2 free books and gifts places me under no obligation to buy anything. I can always return a shipment and cancel at any time. Even if I never buy another book, the two free books and gifts are mine to keep forever.

176/376 HDN GHVY

Name	(PLEASE PRINT)	
Address		Apt. #
City	State/Prov.	Zip/Postal Code

Signature (if under 18, a parent or guardian must sign)

Mail to the **Reader Service:**
IN U.S.A.: P.O. Box 1867, Buffalo, NY 14240-1867
IN CANADA: P.O. Box 609, Fort Erie, Ontario L2A 5X3

Are you a subscriber to Harlequin Presents® books and want to receive the larger-print edition?
Call 1-800-873-8635 today or visit us at www.ReaderService.com.

* Terms and prices subject to change without notice. Prices do not include applicable taxes. Sales tax applicable in N.Y. Canadian residents will be charged applicable taxes. Offer not valid in Quebec. This offer is limited to one order per household. Not valid for current subscribers to Harlequin Presents Larger-Print books. All orders subject to credit approval. Credit or debit balances in a customer's account(s) may be offset by any other outstanding balance owed by or to the customer. Please allow 4 to 6 weeks for delivery. Offer available while quantities last.

Your Privacy—The Reader Service is committed to protecting your privacy. Our Privacy Policy is available online at www.ReaderService.com or upon request from the Reader Service.

We make a portion of our mailing list available to reputable third parties that offer products we believe may interest you. If you prefer that we not exchange your name with third parties, or if you wish to clarify or modify your communication preferences, please visit us at www.ReaderService.com/consumerchoice or write to us at Reader Service Preference Service, P.O. Box 9062, Buffalo, NY 14240-9062. Include your complete name and address.

HPLP

LARGER-PRINT BOOKS!
GET 2 FREE LARGER-PRINT NOVELS PLUS
2 FREE GIFTS!

⊕ HARLEQUIN®

INTRIGUE
BREATHTAKING ROMANTIC SUSPENSE

YES! Please send me 2 FREE LARGER-PRINT Harlequin® Intrigue novels and my 2 FREE gifts (gifts are worth about $10). After receiving them, if I don't wish to receive any more books, I can return the shipping statement marked "cancel." If I don't cancel, I will receive 6 brand-new novels every month and be billed just $5.49 per book in the U.S. or $6.24 per book in Canada. That's a saving of at least 11% off the cover price! It's quite a bargain! Shipping and handling is just 50¢ per book in the U.S. and 75¢ per book in Canada.* I understand that accepting the 2 free books and gifts places me under no obligation to buy anything. I can always return a shipment and cancel at any time. Even if I never buy another book, the two free books and gifts are mine to keep forever.

199/399 HDN GHWN

Name

(PLEASE PRINT)

Address

Apt. #

City

State/Prov.

Zip/Postal Code

Signature (if under 18, a parent or guardian must sign)

Mail to the **Reader Service:**
IN U.S.A.: P.O. Box 1867, Buffalo, NY 14240-1867
IN CANADA: P.O. Box 609, Fort Erie, Ontario L2A 5X3

Are you a subscriber to Harlequin® Intrigue books
and want to receive the larger-print edition?
Call 1-800-873-8635 today or visit www.ReaderService.com.

* Terms and prices subject to change without notice. Prices do not include applicable taxes. Sales tax applicable in N.Y. Canadian residents will be charged applicable taxes. Offer not valid in Quebec. This offer is limited to one order per household. Not valid for current subscribers to Harlequin Intrigue Larger-Print books. All orders subject to credit approval. Credit or debit balances in a customer's account(s) may be offset by any other outstanding balance owed by or to the customer. Please allow 4 to 6 weeks for delivery. Offer available while quantities last.

Your Privacy—The Reader Service is committed to protecting your privacy. Our Privacy Policy is available online at www.ReaderService.com or upon request from the Reader Service.

We make a portion of our mailing list available to reputable third parties that offer products we believe may interest you. If you prefer that we not exchange your name with third parties, or if you wish to clarify or modify your communication preferences, please visit us at www.ReaderService.com/consumerschoice or write to us at Reader Service Preference Service, P.O. Box 9062, Buffalo, NY 14240-9062. Include your complete name and address.

HILP15

READERSERVICE.COM

Manage your account online!

- Review your order history
- Manage your payments
- Update your address

---

*We've designed the
Reader Service website
just for you.*

Enjoy all the features!

- Discover new series available to you, and read excerpts from any series.
- Respond to mailings and special monthly offers.
- Connect with favorite authors at the blog.
- Browse the Bonus Bucks catalog and online-only exculsives.
- Share your feedback.

Visit us at:

ReaderService.com